Dear Little Black Dress Read

Thanks for picking up this Li ack Dress book, one of the great new titles from our series of fun, page-turning romance novels. Lucky you – you're about to have a fantastic romantic read that we know you won't be able to put down!

Why don't you make your Little Black Dress experience even better by logging on to

www.littleblackdressbooks.com

where you can:

- Enter our **monthly competitions** to win **gorgeous** prizes
- Get **hot-off-the-press** news about our latest titles
- Read **exclusive** preview chapters both from your **favourite** authors and from brilliant new writing talent
- Buy **up-and-coming** books online
- Sign up for an essential slice of romance via our **fortnightly email** newsletter

We love nothing more than to curl up and indulge in an addictive romance, and so we're delighted to welcome you into the Little Black Dress club!

With love from,

The *little black dress* team

Five interesting things about Nell Dixon:

1. I once crashed a Sinclair C5 into a tree. (Sinclair C5s were weird little concept cars that looked like go carts.)

2. I'm scared of heights and got stuck on a rope bridge on an assault course and had to be rescued by a very nice army man.

3. I used to be a midwife and have delivered over a hundred babies.

4. I sing to the music in supermarkets, loudly and tunelessly. Strangely, my family prefer me to shop alone.

5. I have dyscalculia which means I can't remember numbers and often read them back to front.

By Nell Dixon

Marrying Max
Blue Remembered Heels
Animal Instincts

Animal Instincts

Nell Dixon

First published in 2009
by LITTLE BLACK DRESS
An imprint of HEADLINE PUBLISHING GROUP

A LITTLE BLACK DRESS paperback

1

ISBN 978 0 7553 4520 5

Typeset in Transit511BT by Avon DataSet Ltd,
Bidford-on-Avon, Warwickshire

Printed and bound in Great Britain by
Clays Ltd, St Ives plc

HEADLINE PUBLISHING GROUP
An Hachette UK Company
338 Euston Road
London NW1 3BH

www.littleblackdressbooks.com
www.headline.co.uk
www.hachettelivre.co.uk

With admiration and respect to all the workers, volunteers and supporters of sanctuaries like Rainbow Ridge who do such wonderful work rescuing and re-homing animals.

This book is also especially dedicated to my husband, who has been suggesting for years that I should write a book about a parrot.

Acknowledgements

My grateful acknowledgements and thanks to all the animal experts who helped with my never-ending questions. To my brilliant critique partner Jessica Raymond for her unstinting support. A big thank you to everyone at Little Black Dress, especially Claire Baldwin and Sara Porter and also my lovely agent at Darley Anderson, Ella Andrews.

The light from the hall spilled out into the night, illuminating the two figures on my front doorstep.

'Surprise!' Immi wobbled on her heels and blinked owlishly at me. 'I've got a present for you.' She waved an unopened bottle of champagne in my face.

'That'll be sixty quid, miss.' The taxi driver supporting my sozzled stepsister propped her against the doorframe, a look of relief on his florid features. He must have driven her quite a distance to want sixty pounds, and it was typical of Immi not to have any money with her.

'Pay the man, Clo,' Immi ordered. She staggered sideways, flinging her arm round the driver's neck to steady herself.

'Whoops!' She giggled.

The only money I had in the house – the only cash I had at all – was hidden in the greedy pig cookie barrel in the kitchen. I left Immi and her new friend on the doorstep and scurried off to fetch the cash, mentally cursing her as I went.

As soon as the cabbie had been paid, I yanked her inside and closed the door.

She peered at me in the dim yellow light of the hallway. 'Wassup, Clo? Were you in bed?'

Well, duh, it was two o'clock in the morning and my pyjamas would be a big clue. I steered her into the kitchen and put the kettle on. One – or both of us – needed coffee.

Immi flopped on to one of the mismatched wooden chairs next to the Aga and plunked the champagne bottle down on the table. Her long blond hair was tousled and her usually immaculate make-up was smudged. She was dressed in a silvery minidress and matching cardi, as if she'd been out clubbing.

'God, I need a drink.' She leaned forward on to the table, scattering a pile of bills and final demands as she buried her head in her arms.

'I think you've had enough to drink.'

Having my half-cut stepsister turn up out of the blue at such an odd hour wasn't strange in itself. Normally, however, she would arrive with a full set of matching pink luggage, her mobile phone glued to her ear as she ranted on about whichever boyfriend of the moment had broken her heart. She would then stay for less than a day until the errant male in question arrived with his arms full of roses to beg her forgiveness.

She lifted her head. 'You don't understand, Clodagh. My life is over. Ruined.' The dramatic effect of her statement was slightly marred by the slurring. I wondered where she'd been to arrive on my doorstep at this hour of the night.

'I'm sure it can't be that bad.'

''S worse than bad.' She nodded her head drunkenly.

Her mood had changed from happy drunk to depths of despair during the short stagger from the hall to the kitchen. Oh, boy. At this rate I would be the one needing a drink; her current man trouble must be worse than usual. It had to be a boyfriend problem. Immi was the only person in the world with worse judgement than me when it came to men. I moved my book-keeping paper-work to one side and slid a mug of black coffee in front of her. 'Drink this.'

Immi fixed big, tear-filled blue eyes on me. 'I'm serious. I'm in big trouble.'

I wasn't unduly shocked by her declaration. My step-sister always thought her emotional crises were the end of the world. I'd been holding her hand and passing her tissues ever since she'd hit her teens. She always fell in love too hard and too fast.

I took the chair opposite hers. 'Who is it this time?' I'd been racking my brains while I'd made the coffee to try to recall the name of her current squeeze.

She sniffed and wiped away a tear with the side of her finger. 'It's not a man. It's a TV show.'

There was a roll of kitchen towel on the counter, so I passed it over. Career issues were also nothing new. Immi's an actress. Not A list, more like C list with aspirations. She's had some good supporting roles, is the face of Blitzclean mouthwash and has a part in a daytime soap. Her lifestyle is a million miles away from mine; hers is glamour and glitter, mine denim and doggy. I don't know much about Immi's world – I don't even own a TV any more.

'A TV show?' I remembered she'd sent me a confusing text a few weeks back about a live chat show. It had said BG BRK in capital letters a dozen times. I'd tried to call her but as usual had kept getting her voicemail instead.

Immi ripped off a sheet of kitchen towel and blew her nose. 'It was awful. I can never appear on TV again. My career's over. I'll be lucky to get a chorus job in a pantomime in the sticks after this.'

'What happened?' I yawned. I wanted to go back to my nice warm bed. I love Immi dearly but I love her better when she's in London. Her current problem didn't sound as if it was likely to be something I would be able to help her with and I'd had a long day.

She let out a wail. 'I was escorted off the set.'

Now that did sound bad. 'What did you do?'

'I'd had a few drinks in the green room. You know, just to relax a little before I went on. Honest to God, Clo, I only had a couple.' She broke off with a hiccup and dabbed at her eyes once more, leaving a streak of blue eyeliner along her cheek. Immi's drinking was a small bone of contention between us. Okay, a medium to large bone of contention.

'And?' My feet were freezing and I needed to get up at six to let the geese out into their field. I'm not normally unsympathetic but I was tired and she has a tendency to ramble, especially when she's had a few.

'You remember Kirk?'

Kirk had been one of the more memorable of Immi's men, another bit-part actor who'd recently hit the big time with a popular TV series. Now he was hot property and had recently landed a part in a big Hollywood movie – at least that was what the gossip magazines said.

'Uh-huh.' He and Immi had a truly spectacular break-up when Immi discovered that he'd installed secret video equipment inside her wardrobe. For a time she'd been concerned that she might have ended up doing a Paris Hilton all over the Internet. In revenge she'd burned his secret porn stash and rubbed white pepper along the seams of his underpants.

'He was there too. Mr Big Time, throwing his success in my face.' She scrubbed at her eyes again.

I could see where this was heading and it wasn't looking pretty. 'What did you do to get escorted off the show?'

'I was on first, the three-minute ice-break slot. Bottom of the bill always gets put on first – so unfair.'

'Immi!'

'He was on last, the fat-headed pimple on the face of humanity. He was so full of crap, going on about his show and his film deal and his new girlfriend and all the time having nasty little digs at me.' She scowled into her mug. 'Pretending to be nice, the patronising sleaze bucket!'

'Tell me what you did.' I knew my sister. She was as sweet and kind as the next person, but if anyone upset her then woe betide them. Kirk had been pretty horrid to her, though. I mean, I know she peppered his pants, but he broke the heels off all her designer shoes and bad-mouthed her to a big Hollywood director.

'He asked for it.' She pouted.

'What did you do?'

Immi was normally a happy drunk, but when she lost her temper she *really* lost it. It wouldn't be the first time she'd landed in hot water as a result. There had been an unfortunate incident a few years ago when she'd shoved a fellow Miss Teen Starlet into a fishpond on a photo shoot. Drink had been involved on that occasion too.

'Smacked him one. Right across his stupid, self-righteous, smug face.' She rubbed her knuckles in satisfaction at the memory.

'On live TV?'

A tear rolled down her cheek and landed with a fat blob on top of one of the outstanding vet bills. 'I called him as many names as I could think of and told everyone about all the awful things he'd done to me.'

'You mentioned the sex video?' I hoped she'd managed to ensure that every copy of that tape had been destroyed. There were probably a million hits on YouTube even now as people tried to track down a copy.

She wiped her eyes and continued with her tale of woe. 'Then his latest fling came rushing out of the green room – tarty little bitch with the most awful nose job – and we ended up brawling on the sofa.'

'Bloody hell.' I leaned back and pulled open the cutlery drawer. Now I did need a drink and I was sure there was a miniature of brandy in there, lurking under a pile of feed catalogues.

Immi grabbed the bottle from my hand as I unscrewed the cap and tipped a big slug into her coffee mug. I managed to snatch it back before she could drink the lot. I wanted a shot myself to help me think.

'What does Marty have to say about all this?' I was sure Immi's chain-smoking, ballsy agent would be out there firefighting on her behalf. After all, everyone knew a scandal was usually good for business, especially when that business was show business. I mean, Kate Moss and co. hadn't done so badly out of their headline-making antics.

'I don't know. I called and called her on my mobile all the way here until the battery died and she still wouldn't pick up. I must have left a zillion messages.'

That didn't sound good. 'Listen, I'll go and make up the spare bed. Perhaps Marty will ring in the morning once your phone's charged.'

Immi gave a doleful sniff. 'Suppose. Thanks, Clo.'

I left her nursing her mug of coffee and slipped upstairs to turf Clive, the cat, off the spare bed. Luckily there weren't too many hairs on the quilt. Immi gets quite funny about little things like that. Once the cat had been evicted and the electric blanket switched on to air the bed I called Marty on my own phone.

I left a message on her voicemail. 'It's Clodagh. Immi's here with me at the sanctuary. Call me.'

I'd barely had time to get across the landing to find Immi some nightclothes when my phone rang.

'Clodagh, Marty. God, all hell's broken loose here. Keep Imogen away from the press and out of the pub. I'll call tomorrow with an update.' I could hear another phone ringing in the background as she ended the call.

'Was that the phone?' Immi staggered into the hall on her high heels. 'If it was Marty I need to talk to her.'

'Wrong number.' It didn't seem like a great idea at this time in the morning to tell her what Marty had said.

'Oh.' Immi's face crumpled and she slid down the wall to sit crying on the bottom step.

'Come on, let's get you upstairs. Everything will seem better when you wake up.' At least, I hoped everything would seem better, otherwise Immi might be staying with me for a while and that would drive both of us mad.

I coaxed her up to her bedroom and hoped that the cat had enough sense to stay out of her way. Immi wasn't overly fond of pets, which was a snag as I ran an animal sanctuary. Whenever she stayed she complained about the cat, the geese, the general smell, and Dave, the parrot no one would take on because of his bad language.

With Immi safely tucked up under her duvet I checked the locks and headed back to bed. She might have troubles but I had problems enough of my own. Rainbow Ridge Animal Sanctuary was broke and if I didn't come up with some money soon it wasn't only the animals that would be homeless.

The alarm seemed to sound only seconds after I'd closed my eyes. I moved Clive, who had settled around my head like a feline fur hat, and tried to focus. Today was a big day. Once I'd seen to the animals, organised the volunteers, and poured more caffeine into Immi, I had an important afternoon appointment at the bank.

Not that I was hopeful about getting another loan from them. Mr Curzon, my not-so-friendly bank manager, had taken to avoiding seeing me in person.

Instead I kept receiving threatening letters via the post. Today I had actually managed to make an appointment, but unless I could come up with a fantabulous business plan by three o'clock I guessed I would be coming home empty-handed.

The volunteers who helped me run the sanctuary would be arriving soon so I scrambled into my jeans and sweater and headed downstairs. One of my aims had been to make enough money to employ staff instead of relying on goodwill. Since I barely made enough to cover a basic wage for myself my aim was rapidly becoming a distant dream.

'Cooee, Clodagh.' There was a sharp rap on the back door.

I opened the door for Susie. She's my longest-standing volunteer, not that she actually does very much – well, except make tea and talk a lot. She's very good at tea-making and talking. I'd kind of inherited her when I'd taken over the sanctuary.

'Ooh, it's a bit chilly this morning.' She wombled into the kitchen, unravelling a vast hand-knitted scarf from round her neck as she entered. I wondered how she would cope when it really did turn cold. We were only in September now and she was already muffled up in layers of wool.

Susie is a bit of an odd bod. She's in her late thirties and has never mentioned a family or a social life in all the time I've known her. I'm not even really sure how she can afford to spend most of her time at the sanctuary, since she doesn't have a job of any kind. She has a kind heart, though, and means well even if she can be a pain in the bottom sometimes.

'Tea?' I don't know why I bothered asking. Susie never turned down a cup of tea.

'Lovely.' She settled herself at the table and rubbed her hands together to warm them up.

I handed her a mug and grabbed my old wax jacket from the back of the pantry door. 'I'll go and let the geese out. Could you unveil Dave?'

Dave's cage was in the sitting room; I had to keep him well away from the public. His previous owner had owned a brothel and Dave had acquired a very colourful vocabulary from his time there. He also had a very vicious personality.

Susie's lips pursed and I waited for the excuse.

'I've got a bit of a sniffle at the moment, Clodagh; I wouldn't want to infect the animals. Perhaps I should tidy up for you. Jade could see to Dave when she gets here in a minute.' She produced a tissue from her pocket and blew her nose in an unconvincing fashion.

I guessed what she really wanted was an opportunity to snoop. She was incredibly nosy and on a couple of occasions I'd caught her reading private letters that I thought I'd put away in the cutlery drawer. I think she liked to feel she knew more about what was going on than the other volunteers. It was as if it made her feel important in some way.

'If you like.' I picked up the pile of books and invoices from the table. 'I'll pop these out of your way.' I carried them upstairs and dumped them on my bed; I didn't want her to know about the sanctuary's financial problems. Some things need to be kept private.

Immi's room was silent. I assumed she must still be sleeping off the events of the previous night and was glad of it. It would be better if she didn't run into Susie or any of the other volunteers. If Marty was to be believed, the press would be all over the sanctuary like a rash if they found out Immi was here. The last thing I needed was bad publicity and camera crews blocking the gates.

Susie was still at the table drinking her tea when I tiptoed back down to the kitchen.

'I'll be back in a few minutes.' I toed my feet into my wellies.

She glanced up from an old copy of *Pet Keepers Monthly*. 'Okay. Is it all right if I get a biscuit?'

'There are a few left in the tin.' I clumped off down the steps and left her to finish off the digestives. If I wasn't so short of helpers I might have been tempted to tell Susie to sling her hook ages ago. Perhaps that's a bit mean; she did have some good points when she wasn't being nosy and annoying. She was quite good at organising the rest of the volunteers and, to tell the truth, it was nice to have someone to talk to. Well, apart from Dave, that is.

I let the geese into their field and put out the feed. A pale mist hovered over the dewy grass, which sparkled in the early morning light. Mr Sheen, the goat, peered hopefully at me over his fence as I made my way back to the house to finish my morning cuppa. He always hoped more food would be headed his way. Goats don't have a reputation for being greedy for nothing.

Jade, the other volunteer, had arrived and was standing in the kitchen cradling her drink when I returned. I could hear Dave squawking and cursing from the other room so she must have taken the blanket off his cage.

'Hiya, boss.' Jade grinned at me from under her floppy pink fringe. She was a college student who gave me a hand at weekends and on the days she didn't have any lectures. She wanted to be a social worker but liked animals. I always felt guilty that I couldn't afford to pay her or Susie. They both put in hours of time helping me to keep the sanctuary going. Jade was supposed to be on holiday as lectures didn't start again for a few more weeks but she had a boyfriend locally and had stayed on for the summer, supplementing her income with bar jobs.

Susie didn't appear to have moved from where I'd left her. I've seen giant land snails with a better turn of speed than Susie.

'Jade, will you be around to look after the animals this afternoon? I have to go to a meeting in town.'

'Sure.' Jade swallowed the rest of her tea.

'Is there anything I can do to help you with your meeting?' Susie offered.

'No, it's a personal thing.' Nosy cow. I wasn't about to tell her where I was going. Not that it would be a secret for much longer if I didn't get the loan I needed to keep the sanctuary open. All the helpers knew we were broke, but none of them knew quite how bad it was.

'Come on then, Suze. Time we cleaned out the donkeys.' Jade pulled a bright green knitted cap from her coat pocket and set it on her head at a jaunty angle, then dragged a reluctant Susie out of the kitchen.

I jammed some bread in the toaster and refilled the kettle. A floorboard creaked upstairs.

Immi appeared in the doorway, wearing the pale blue satin pyjamas she'd sent me last Christmas. She looked wrecked.

'Coffee?'

She raked her hand through her hair, making it appear even crazier than before. 'I just want to die.'

'No, you don't.' I snatched my toast from the toaster and dropped it on to a plate.

'My life is over.' Immi flopped on to the chair Susie had recently vacated.

'Rubbish.' I started to butter my toast.

Immi winced. 'Clo, please, some of us have a headache.'

I handed her a mug and took a bite of toast as an all too familiar 4×4 pulled into the yard.

Jack Thatcher opened his car door and jumped out. I allowed myself a few seconds of pleasurable drooling while safely hidden behind the kitchen window curtain. He is the original Mr Tall, Dark and Handsome. This morning he looked particularly fine in snug-fitting dark denim jeans and a plain black sweater that showed off his broad shoulders very nicely.

The back of my house opens on to a small square yard beyond which are the animal fields and the public paths. From my kitchen window I can see any cars coming up the private lane, and I can watch the animals and keep tracks on the visitors as they go round the park. The downside to such a good view is a distinct lack of privacy. Friends, family and the volunteers all come round through the yard, although I lock the gate in the lane at night so no one can sneak in.

The front of the house faces out towards the main road and public car park. I have a tiny front lawn surrounded by a dense privet hedge and a wrought-iron gate to allow access to the narrow brick path leading to the front door.

Susie emerged from the donkey field like a woolly Exocet missile and homed straight in on Jack. She has some kind of grudge against him and is forever bending my ear with tales of his latest misdeeds. According to Susie all men are the epitome of evil and Jack is the worst, although he's always very polite and friendly to me, if anything a bit too friendly, especially lately. So, while it was tempting to leave him to her tender mercies, I supposed I'd better get out there and find out what he wanted.

Jack's main crime is that he's a property developer. He inherited the family building firm from his father and in the space of a few years he's managed to turn it into a multimillion-pound business. His company was responsible for most of the new housing in the town and for the redevelopment of the main shopping centre. I wished I had some of his business acumen: if I had then I might be able to save Rainbow Ridge.

I rummaged on the dresser for my hairbrush and a scrunchie.

'What are you doing?' Immi asked.

'Nothing. I just need to pop outside and, um . . . see someone.' I shoved my hair back so it looked a bit tidier and applied a dab of lipgloss from the almost dead tube nestling next to the cookie tin.

Immi crossed over to the window. 'Nice.'

'He's not so nice.' The words sounded sharper than I'd intended.

She gave me a curious look. 'Oh?'

'He might look okay, but he's not.' The sanctuary

stood on land that was considered ripe for development – a fact that was never far from my mind when Jack was around. We had stunning views over the open countryside with the convenience of being on the edge of town and in the catchment area for good local schools. Any houses built here would fetch large sums of money and sprout queues of chequebook-bearing yummy mummies waiting to buy them that would stretch round the block.

I'd had several unsolicited letters drop through my front door over the last few months asking me if I was interested in selling the land. Some were from developers and some were from the estate agency in town. I didn't recall seeing one from Thatcher Developments but he could have asked one of the estate agents to act on his behalf. Long Meadow, the field bordering the sanctuary, had recently been sold to Lovett Properties and they had been granted planning permission for a housing development.

Jack was good friends with many of the local councillors and I was under no illusions about his ability to pull strings if he needed to. I'd come to know him quite well from the various functions and fundraisers we'd both attended over the last few years. I knew he'd been involved in a bidding war with Lovett's for Long Meadow and recently he'd started to show a more personal interest in me.

'And that's why you've slapped on the lippy and tidied your hair?'

I ignored Immi and headed outside, giving the back

door a very satisfactory slam as I left. She considered herself to be the expert on men. I suppose compared to me she probably was, although given her recent adventures with Kirk, the homemade-porn enthusiast, I had my doubts.

Susie had Jack pinned up against the side of his car and appeared to be yattering into his face. She was probably giving him a lecture on carbon emissions, although if I hadn't known she was such a man-hater I might have suspected that she secretly fancied him. I could see her arms flailing about like a demented windmill while she talked.

'Here's Clodagh now.' He broke away from Susie's interrogation and strode towards me with a relieved expression.

Stupidly, my heart rate went up a notch as it always did when I was close to Jack. He was drop-dead gorgeous. I mean *seriously* gorgeous – every female I knew from tots to grannies fell for his crooked smile and the dimple that appeared in his right cheek. However lovely Jack might be, though, I always had to remember that he was the enemy. Unusually, that was something both Susie and Jade agreed on.

'You left your jacket at the pub last night. I had to come this way to work today so I said I'd drop it in for you.' His dark eyes burned into mine and I swallowed hard.

'Um, thanks.' I took my denim coat from his outstretched hand. I'd been doing a bit of illicit bar work down at the Frog and Ferret. It gave me some pin money and I could watch the TV in the lounge between pulling pints. I wished I'd been watching Immi's chat-show disaster – at least then I would have been prepared for her arrival – but instead the channel had been tuned to TV Gold.

The Frog and Ferret was the last place in the world I'd expected Jack to frequent. It was a real working men's pub, all lager and pork scratchings. I'd have thought that with all his money he would have gone somewhere much more glamorous and upmarket. But he'd arrived with a group of friends, male and female, a little before closing time and they'd all stood around near the wide-screen TV, chatting and laughing. I'd assumed they had been on their way back from somewhere posh, judging by the way they were dressed. Jack had leaned on the bar chatting to me for quite some time. When I'd left they were still there, Jack deep in conversation with Frank, the pub landlord, and his wife Jenny.

'Are you working at the pub again tonight?' Jack asked.

I was conscious of Susie still standing by the car with her arms folded and her ears flapping. 'No. I just help out when they're short of staff. It's more of a favour really.'

Frank paid me cash, no questions asked, so I didn't want anyone to think my being there was anything other than voluntary. I could have died last night when Jack had arrived as I was finishing up. We'd met socially a few times before when I'd been out touting for sponsorship at various business functions. Lately, however, he'd taken to stopping by the sanctuary on various pretexts, dropping off a rotary club invitation, asking advice about getting a guinea pig for his niece, all sorts of things. Jade thought he fancied me but Susie, like me, was suspicious of his motives.

Melhampton is a small place so everyone knows everyone else, although as a fairly recent incomer I hadn't fully worked out all the relationships yet. It would take longer than the seven years I'd lived here to do that. It was the kind of town where everyone went back at least three generations before they were considered a resident.

Talking to Susie and Jade was helpful; they seemed to know everything about everyone. Susie had lived locally for years and although Jade was an incomer like me, she had some kind of family connection to the town. Other than my fear of making some frightful social gaffe, I didn't mind too much about being considered an outsider. It suited me to be on the edge of things.

'I wondered what you were doing behind the bar.' A lock of dark hair fell across his brow as he tilted his head to smile at me.

'A girl has to have some social life.' Heat built up in my cheeks. Jack was the last person I wanted to know about my financial problems. He might be gorgeous and sexy but he was also the man who wouldn't hesitate to take the sanctuary and its land away from me if he spotted an opportunity. I had read and heard plenty of stories about his ruthless commercial streak. Jade and Susie had both been quick to fill me in on tales of Jack Thatcher and his ability to sniff out a business that was in trouble.

'I wondered if you wanted to come out for a drink with me tonight.' He waited for my answer.

What to do? The girly part of me wanted to say yes, but unless my interview at the bank could secure the sanctuary's future the sensible part of me had to say no. I didn't have much confidence around men and Jack was way out of my league. He'd asked me a few leading questions at the pub last night about my plans for the sanctuary, and I couldn't shake off the uneasy feeing that he might be circling, vulture-like, about my business. I also had the new problem of Immi. I didn't want to leave her alone in the house, especially if she wasn't feeling good.

'Um, Clodagh?' Jack was still waiting.

'I'd better not. I've a lot of things I need to get done.' My excuse sounded lame even to me. He'd asked me out before and my excuses got worse each time. I think there was only the old chestnut about needing to wash my hair that I hadn't used yet.

'Some other time, maybe.' His tone was stiff and it was more of a polite response than a genuine suggestion.

'Great.' I forced a smile and tried to sound keen, as if by imbuing one word with hearty enthusiasm I could remove the awkwardness hanging in the space between us.

'I'd better get going. See you around.' He turned and walked back towards his car.

Bugger. My social life was even more in the toilet than my finances. I should have agreed to go for a drink. I waved as his car pulled away but he didn't look back.

'What did he want?' Susie bore down on me before Jack had even left the yard.

'I left my jacket somewhere and he was passing so he dropped it in.' I kept my answer as vague as possible.

'Humph. You do know he has his eye on this place?' Susie glared at the gate where Jack's car had left a rapidly dispersing dust-cloud on the dirt track.

'That's just a rumour, Susie. Besides, the sanctuary is not for sale.' At least it wasn't for sale *yet*.

'Good. You wouldn't want to sell to him, anyway. He'd just shove a load of executive houses on here. You know that's what Lovett's are going to put on Long Meadow?' She waved her arms for emphasis and looked even more like a mad bag lady than usual.

'It's not going to happen.' I crossed my fingers inside my jacket pockets.

She scowled. 'Well, why else does he keep hanging around like a bad smell? That's three times in the last fortnight he's popped up here on some pretext.'

Well, excuse me! It's not entirely out of the realms of possibility that he might actually fancy me. Naturally, I didn't say that to Susie. Instead I mumbled something about paperwork and scuttled back to the kitchen, where Immi was waiting for me.

'Well, come on then, spill the beans on Mr Hunky.' She seemed to have perked up considerably during the time I'd been outside.

'There's nothing to spill.' I hung my denim jacket on the hook on the back of the pantry door and picked up what was left of my almost-cold coffee.

Immi folded her arms. 'Clodagh, you are as transparent as a pane of glass. You have a thing for him, don't you? So who is he and why did he have your coat?'

Good grief, between her and Susie I would probably go nuts. 'I do not have a thing for Jack. He had my coat because I left it at the pub last night. He was simply doing me a favour by dropping it off on his way to work.'

'Yeah, right. A really yummy-looking bloke goes out of his way to trek up here just to bring you your manky coat, but you aren't interested in him or him in you?' She leaned back with a smug expression on her face.

'It's not that simple.' My cold coffee tasted foul so I tipped it down the sink.

'I bet he didn't only come here to give you your coat.'

'Oh, okay, he asked me to go for a drink with him tonight.' I rinsed my mug under the tap, glad of an excuse not to meet Immi's triumphant smirk.

'Ha!'

'And I said no.' I plopped my mug on the draining board and turned to face my sister.

'You've been living up here with these bloody animals too long. What's wrong with you?'

'He's a property developer. It's Rainbow Ridge he's interested in, not me.'

Immi rolled her eyes. 'That's crap.'

'Excuse me?' Typical Immi – she always thought she knew everything when it came to dating. You'd have thought after the recent Kirk disaster she'd have learned her lesson. After my past experiences with men – well, one man in particular – I'd certainly learned mine. At least with my animals I wasn't likely to get my heart broken.

'Look, he's a gorgeous bloke who's asked you out. It's not as if you're overwhelmed with other offers. Plus, there's no way you'd ever sell this place, so why are you worried?'

I couldn't look at her. 'There's a problem with the sanctuary,' I mumbled.

'What do you mean? What kind of problem?' She slipped her arm round my shoulders.

'It's broke. I've enough money to keep it going for the next three months but that's it.' It was a relief to tell someone. I'd kept my worries to myself for months, although if the volunteers had been counting the visitor numbers they had to know something was wrong.

'That's crazy. You work so hard here. How come you haven't any money?' She rested her head on my shoulder.

'No visitors, lack of sponsorship, big vet bills – take your pick.' I tried not to cry as I recited the list. 'Then there's been the vandalism.'

Immi moved her head to look me in the face. 'Vandalism?'

'Someone has been damaging our fences and buildings. They seem to have been deliberately targeting us. We lost a lot of the animal feed when the store was set on fire. Now the insurance company is talking about not paying the claims. If it continues I might not be able to get cover for next year.' Despite my best efforts a large round tear escaped and rolled down my cheek.

'That's terrible. Have you been to the police? Can't they do something?'

I shook my head and swiped my hand across my face to get rid of the tear. 'They've started coming round on patrol more often but haven't caught anyone yet. I have an appointment at the bank this afternoon to try to borrow more money but I've nothing left to put up as collateral, so it's not looking good.'

'There has to be something you can try.'

'I don't know. I'm running out of ideas. I'm hoping the bank will help.' I didn't have much hope, but appealing to Mr Curzon's better nature, if he had one, had seemed like the next logical step to save my home.

A commotion outside in the yard caught my attention. I rushed to the back door and peeped out. Susie was in hot pursuit of Mr Sheen, who looked as if he'd taken advantage of an open gate to ramble off to look for more food. Jade waved at me from the donkey field where she was leaning on a broom and laughing at Susie's futile attempts to recapture him.

'You'd better stay out of sight.' I hoped Jade hadn't seen Immi standing at the back of the kitchen.

'I'm going upstairs to get dressed. Can I borrow something to wear? I need Marty to bring me my stuff from the flat.' She eyed my jumper and jeans with distaste. Most of my clothes came from the dress agency or charity shops in town. My wardrobe was mostly practical with a couple of nicer things for when I was at the Frog and Ferret, plus my suit, which I needed to press before I went to the bank.

Immi's clothes were all designer brands or knock-offs that were good enough to pass as such. I wasn't worried that she might want to keep any of my things for a moment longer than she needed to. I wondered when Marty would get in touch. Immi would soon get bored hanging around the sanctuary, and since the only social hotspot locally was the Frog and Ferret, another potential PR disaster could be looming.

'Help yourself.' I turned back to the door to see what was happening.

Susie had grabbed Mr Sheen's halter and was attempting to tug him back towards his field. Unsurprisingly, the goat had dug his hooves into the dirt and was refusing to budge. I was about to go out and help when Jade took pity on Susie and appeared with a handful of treats to tempt Mr Sheen back to his rightful place.

With the goat safely back in his pen Susie trudged off, presumably to go and sit in the kiosk at the visitors' entrance. It looked as if it would be quite a nice day so with luck we might get a few paying customers to buy bags of animal feed and maybe make a donation towards the running costs.

Although it would take a lot more than a handful of visitors to solve my current financial headache.

With Susie out of the way and Immi installed under the shower, I retrieved the account books to try to work out a business recovery plan. From my vantage point at the kitchen table I could see Jade completing the cleaning and feeding chores. Immi crashed about upstairs and Dave the parrot kept up a constant barrage of abuse from the lounge. The atmosphere wasn't exactly conducive to working on a complex financial strategy, but it would have to do.

Despite the sunny weather, the paths around the animal fields remained depressingly empty. A lone mum with a toddler in a buggy stared vacantly at the donkeys and an elderly man scattered some food for the geese. My projected gate numbers looked even more pathetic as I tried to think up new and more creative ways to increase the visitor footfall.

Advertising cost a lot of money and had done very little to boost our totals. I'd tried leaflets and posters but any positive responses had been wiped out by bad luck and the miserable weather during the school holidays. Vet bills took up a huge chunk of the sanctuary income, and even though I barely drew enough money for myself to call a wage, the out totals appeared depressingly large.

The telephone rang and Immi bounced down the stairs to snatch it up before I'd even had a chance to get up from my seat.

'Hello?'

I glared at her. The house phone was for sanctuary calls.

'Yes, this is Rainbow Ridge Animal Sanctuary.' She passed the handset over with a gusty sigh.

I dealt with the enquiry about the baby rabbits we had for sale then returned my attention to my stepsister. She was frowning over my accountancy books with a thoughtful expression on her face.

'You were right, these figures are pants.'

Because Immi was blonde, pretty, and an actress, people tended to assume she must be dim. She rarely tried to correct that impression, claiming that it paid to appear less intelligent than she actually was. But apart from her lousy taste in boyfriends and fondness for alcohol Immi was nobody's fool.

She slipped into my seat and pulled the calculator towards her. I noticed she'd helped herself to my best top – the one I only wore on very special occasions – and my nicest skirt. When I moved to look over her shoulder I could smell my luxury shower gel, too. It was one I kept for those rare, almost-never occasions when I had a date; the rest of the time I used supermarket own-brand stuff even though I'd often wondered if it was just their washing-up liquid packaged differently.

'Have you used my best shower gel?'

Immi didn't look up from her calculations. 'You know I have delicate skin. I'll replace it when I can get my stuff.'

She jabbed some buttons on the calculator a few more times and altered one of my figures with a pencil. 'Whew, you were right about this place being in trouble. How are you going to persuade the bank to lend you more money?'

I moved a pile of invoices over and showed her the three sheets of paper I'd optimistically titled 'Business Recovery Plan'. There were three different options. None of them was brilliant but it was the best I could do, given my limited resources. Immi scanned through the documents before putting them down with a sigh.

'These are stinkier than your numbers.'

'I suppose you have some better ideas?' I was stung. Okay, so my plans weren't great, but they were workable and might appeal to my odious bank manager.

'We-ell . . .' She flipped one of the invoices over and picked up the pencil. After five minutes of intensive scribbling she handed me the sheet.

I didn't want to like her idea on principle but it was actually quite good. Better than good – well, better than mine, anyway.

Immi beamed at me. 'What do you think?'

'It's not bad.'

She rolled her eyes. 'All right, so it needs a bit of work. But it's not going to solve the problem unless you come up with some sustainable long-term financial input.'

'I know. I need to get some sponsors.' I'd tried lots of places already. Most hadn't even bothered to reply.

Immi's plan should bring in some money with minimum outlay – it might buy some more time, at least. A car-boot sale sounded doable and an open day with special events could be fitted in before the summer season finished. They were all better than selling off some of the land. Once I started down that route the sanctuary's days would be numbered, as I would have disposed of the only valuable asset I had.

'Maybe *I* could get some sponsors,' Immi suggested.

'I hate to burst your bubble, but after what happened on the TV show that might not be so easy.' I felt mean for bringing it up, but it was lunchtime already and I was getting worried that Marty hadn't called.

Immi's face crumpled and I thought she was about to cry. 'I know. I hoped that might have been Marty on the phone.'

'Oh, Imms, I'm sure she'll ring. A bit of controversy might work out well for you. You never know.' I tried to sound cheerful and upbeat.

The back door opened without any warning and Jade walked in. 'Oh. Sorry, Clodagh. I didn't know you had someone here.' She goggled at Immi.

'Jade, this is my sister, Imogen.' Thank heaven it was Jade who had come in and not Susie.

'I saw you on telly! You're the girl who got drunk and hit that actor.' Jade's cheeks had flushed bright pink and her eyes had rounded when she'd realised who Immi was.

'I was not drunk.' Immi had also acquired two bright spots of colour on her face.

'Wow, you're all over the papers this morning. I can't believe you're Clodagh's sister!' Jade looked at me and then back at Immi as if trying to spot a family resemblance.

'Stepsister,' Immi said. 'My mum married her dad.'

'Wow.'

'No one is supposed to know where Immi is. Could you keep it to yourself for a while?' I hoped I could trust Jade to be discreet.

Immi batted her big blue eyes at Jade. 'I won't be staying for long – only until my agent calls. It'll make things difficult for Clodagh if the press harass me here.'

'Oh, yes, of course. I don't like that Kirk bloke. He always seems creepy to me. Does Susie know?' Jade turned back to me, looking flattered at being asked to keep Immi's secret.

'No. We thought the fewer people who knew the better.' Telling Susie would be like placing an announcement in the local press.

'Cool.' Jade beamed. She clearly enjoyed the idea of putting one over on her colleague. 'I'll take her tea up to the shed. That'll stop her from coming down here.'

She made fresh drinks, pulled her cap back on, and set off outside towards the visitor car park, holding mugs of tea for herself and Susie.

'Do you think she'll say anything?' Immi closed the back door against the cool air.

'Not to Susie.' I wasn't sure she'd resist the temptation to tell anyone else, though.

The scribbled business plan Immi had roughed out reclaimed my attention. With any luck I'd have enough time to copy it out into some sort of cohesive format before my interview at the bank.

The sound of another car barrelling up the private track and into the yard was a good indication that today wasn't shaping up to be particularly lucky. This time the car in question was a trendy little hot hatch in bright red. Or, at least, it had been bright red before it got coated in dust from the lane.

I watched as Immi's agent emerged from the car wearing a peacock-blue silk suit and shoes so high they would give any normal person a nosebleed. She crushed her cigarette beneath the toe of her stiletto before opening her boot to pull out one of Immi's pink suitcases. This was not a good sign – it looked as if Immi would be staying.

'Marty!' My sister deafened me with a yelp of delight at the sight of her agent.

I left Immi in the kitchen and went to help Marty with the case. It turned out she'd packed more than one. It definitely looked as if Immi would be with me for much longer than either one of us wanted.

'Bloody awful journey. Traffic was terrible. Is she in the house? No press? Good-oh.' Marty picked up a pink vanity box and matching holdall, leaving me with the big suitcase. She strutted briskly towards the house while I struggled along in her wake. If I didn't know better I would have sworn she'd packed bricks in the thing, it felt so heavy.

By the time I had panted up the back step and into the kitchen Marty and Immi were already air-kissing and 'darling'-ing one another. I dropped the big, heavy case and put the kettle on as Immi took Marty through to the sitting room. Just before the door closed behind them I heard Dave shout some welcoming obscenities from his cage in the corner.

I'd barely had time to put the mugs on a tray when the door into the hall opened again and Immi bounced back into the kitchen.

'That bloody bird.' She whisked the tray from my hands.

'I'll cover him back up if you like. He gets lonely and he enjoys company. At the brothel he had all the working girls to talk to him.'

Immi rolled her eyes. 'I'll strangle him if he doesn't shut up.'

I followed Immi into the sitting room. Marty was perched on a chair next to the window. She'd pushed up the sash and balanced her ashtray on the sill. Dave huffed up and down his perch, cackling and bobbing his head.

'Twenty-five quid for topless!' He gave a squawk of protest as I dodged his beak to put the cover back over his cage. He'd still shout but at least the noise would be muffled.

Immi passed a strong black coffee to Marty, who promptly produced a small tub of sweeteners from her bag and dropped three tablets into the mug.

'Right. It's not looking good, Imms. People dropping you like a bad smell. Paparazzi staking out your flat. Stories all over the press. Kirk's done a deal with a Sunday rag.' Marty paused for a puff on her cigarette and a sip of her coffee.

Immi's lower lip began to quiver.

'But it'll ease up, right?' I asked. 'And this will all be sorted out?' I mean, other celebrities seemed to do quite well out of their faux-pas.

'Hard to say. Immi's public persona was based on her sweet nature. Punching the ex has torn it. Not to mention the booze. All sorts of stories circulating. Some girl claiming you pushed her in a pool when you were drunk.' Marty took another drag from her cigarette and blew the smoke out of the open window. 'Need to let the dust settle. Then look to see how we can turn it round.'

'But what am I supposed to do?' A big tear rolled down Immi's cheek.

'Stay here and lie low, or rehab. Best advice, stay here.' Marty flicked some ash from the tip of her cigarette out of the window and into my flower bed.

'*Here?*' Immi and I spoke together.

'Quiet, out of the way. If the press show up – do some good deeds. Hug a goat or something.' The sunlight glinted on Marty's auburn lowlights as she dispensed her advice.

This sounded bad. I'd thought a few days would have been more than enough time for everything to settle down.

'But for how long?' Immi asked.

Marty took a meditative sip of coffee. 'Few weeks. Then selected interviews or something. Maybe use the animals for sympathy.'

Something that sounded very much like a muffled 'Bollocks' came from the direction of Dave's cage. I felt inclined to agree with him. Immi looked shell-shocked. I think she'd been hoping Marty would wave some kind of magic wand and smooth out all her problems. To be honest I'd been hoping she'd have some neat solution all worked out.

'What about all my work?' Immi was ashen-faced.

Marty blinked at her. 'All gone. Advertisers dropped you. The soap suspended you. Two roles you were up for are a no-go. Charity gig withdrew invitation. But there's an offer on the table from a porn channel?'

'Ugh!' Immi looked affronted by the suggestion that she might do porn.

'Think that's because of the home video Kirk made.' Marty didn't appear surprised. 'Watch out for the press and stay out of the pub or anywhere with alcohol. There's one guy – very persistent, Marcus somebody, got TV connections – look out for him.' She stubbed out her cigarette, emptied the ashtray out of the window and picked up her handbag.

'What about American work?' I couldn't believe that was the best Marty could do.

She gave a dismissive snort. 'No chance. You need to be whiter than white for the Yanks. They think she's a drunk.'

Immi let out a wail that made Dave squawk in protest from beneath his covers.

'I'll be in touch. I'll do everything I can to salvage this.' She air-kissed Immi's pale cheeks and scooted neatly out of the door. Well, as neatly as a small woman on skyscraper shoes can. I walked with her to her car.

'You will try to get her career back on track?'

'Could all turn round. Got some angles to try. Need to let things quieten down first before we can fight back.' Marty opened her car door.

'Thanks.' Marty had always been very good to Immi so I knew she'd do her best.

'Keep an eye on her. Think positive. Call me if any probs and keep her away from the booze.' She air-kissed me too and ducked into her car. She paused long enough to light up another cigarette before driving away with a careless wave and a cloud of dust.

I went back inside to unveil Dave. He and Immi both looked reproachfully at me.

'What?' I wasn't sure who I was talking to.

'I'm stuck here now.' Immi sniffed.

Dave cackled. 'Show us your tits!'

Clive the cat sneaked in and headed for Immi; I knew he was about to wrap himself around her ankles.

She shrieked as he gave a satisfied purr and sat on her foot. 'And stuck with all these bloody animals!'

Since they were *my* bloody animals – and now I came to think about it, no one had asked me if I would mind having Immi to stay – I felt more than a little bit miffed.

'Well, you don't have to be here. There's always the Priory or Clouds or wherever it is that people go these days to be dried out.' I scooped up Clive, who hissed at me in indignation at his removal from a comfy place.

Immi turned big baby blue eyes on me. 'Oh, Clodagh, you're my sister – you wouldn't want me to go to rehab, would you? I'm not an alcoholic.' Her lip did that pouty quivery thing again.

'You do like a drink, though, Imms.' I knew she didn't really have a mega drink problem but it did worry me that she was on the way to developing one. It was only when she'd been drinking that trouble seemed to find Immi.

'Only when I go out. It's not as if I get shaky with the DTs or keep bottles of vodka under my bed. Please, Clo.' She put on her wheedly voice.

I sighed. 'Okay. You know you can stay here as long as you need to.' My heart sank a little as I made the offer. Whenever my sister was around for any length of time my life always got turned upside down. Still, at least it gave me the chance to pay her back for all the good things she'd done for me in the past. All the things she'd done for me after Jonathan. He'd been my version of Kirk – only worse.

'Dozy tart,' Dave chipped in. He could have meant either of us.

'Oh, fishcakes, look at the time!' I dropped Clive on the sofa and headed for the stairs. My business plan was scribbled on the back of an invoice, my suit wasn't pressed, and my interview with the bank was in thirty minutes.

I got changed in ten seconds flat, ignoring Immi's

well-meant fashion comments about my outfit as I applied some mascara and changed my earrings. My best high-heeled shoes were stuffed under the bed and I had to hook them out with a coat hanger. Once I'd buffed them up with a quick squirt of furniture polish I presented myself to Immi for inspection.

'Shoulder pads are *so* out. Where on earth did you get this suit?' She picked some cat hairs off my jacket, shoved my business file in my hand and pronounced me ready.

All I could do was hope that Mr Curzon, the bank manager, would be impressed with my power-dressed shoulders and big earrings even if nobody else was. I jumped into my battered Fiat Panda and took off down the lane towards town.

There was a strange blue car parked in the lay-by at the entrance to the private lane that led to the back of my house. I don't know what made me notice it as cars often parked there to look at the view. Not that the view would be the same for much longer. Already a signboard had been erected in Long Meadow and twin flags flapped in the breeze on either side of the gate. Lovett Properties were clearly losing no time in their race to build exactly the kind of executive housing that I suspected Jack would like to erect on my ground.

Perhaps I noticed this car because it was small, bright blue and very clean – oh, plus the male driver was quite good looking. Not that I had time to think about it too much; Mr Curzon has a thing about punctuality and I, of course, was already late.

I managed to park fairly close to the bank and sprinted down the high street as fast as I could in a pencil skirt and high heels. The elderly cashier on the information desk gave me a suitably frosty look and stared pointedly at the clock on the wall when I gasped out the details of my appointment. After being informed that Mr Curzon was a very busy man I was shown to the seat of shame in full view of a line of customers, where I had to wait for the great man to deign to see me. It was another ten minutes before he emerged from a little cubicle which bore the legend 'Customer Service Suite' on the frosted glass.

I followed him into the room and did my best to look as tall as I possibly could. I'd read an article that said tall people were more successful than short ones, and that at any formal interview a woman should wear heels to gain an advantage over the interviewer. Since Mr Curzon wasn't particularly blessed in the height department I'd thought I'd give it a shot.

The customer service suite proved to be as miserable and uncomfortable as the meeting. Mr Curzon installed me on an old-fashioned wooden straight-backed chair on one side of the desk while he took the plush comfy leather-faced swivel throne on the other. He adjusted his half-moon spectacles to maximum advantage for intimidation and began.

The interview – if you could call it that – didn't last very long. The word 'interview' implies some kind of two-way communication, but this was more of a statement, and Mr Curzon was the one making it. It went something along the lines of 'you need a large cash injection in the next three months or the bank will call in your mortgage'. I don't recall saying very much at all. Mr Curzon wasn't interested in listening when I tried to speak and I'm sure I heard him snort when I mentioned my business plan. His only suggestion was that I 'liquidise some of my assets'; in other words sell some land.

It didn't help when I emerged from the cubicle to find that the bank was deserted except for Jack, who was leaning across the customer information counter and positively flirting with the old dragon behind the glass.

'Hi, gorgeous. Bit of a change from this morning?' His eyes crinkled at the corners as he looked me up and down. My heart gave a funny little squeeze of pleasure when his gaze lingered on my legs.

Mr Curzon slithered out from behind me to shake Jack's hand. 'Mr Thatcher, delighted you could call in. Please come through to my office.'

Much to my annoyance, Jack had the cheek to wink at me as he strolled past to join Mr Curzon. 'Love that eighties vibe,' he murmured in my ear.

It was a good job Mr Curzon was between us or I would have slugged Jack with my business folder. Jack got the invite to the office; I got the customer service suite. That said everything about the difference in our status with the bank. I made my way out of the building and on to the high street. Depression began to bite so I called in at the newsagent for a large bar of chocolate and a peek at the daily papers.

My sister was front page on all the red-tops.

DRUNKEN ACTRESS GOES BESERK!

CHAT SHOW SCANDAL!

SOAP STAR KITTEN SHOWS HER CLAWS!

I read through as many as I could. No wonder Marty had instructed Immi to lie low. It had struck me as odd that Marty hadn't brought copies of the papers to show her when she'd called this morning, but now I knew why she hadn't. Poor Immi would be shattered by the vitriol in some of the articles, although I thought the photograph they'd used of her was nice.

The newsagent was giving me dirty looks so I put the papers back, paid for my chocolate and ambled back into the street, deep in thought. Would Jade be able to keep quiet about Immi's being at the sanctuary? Even if she did, how long would it be before anyone else saw her there? Maybe her presence might draw more visitors . . . A fleeting image of Immi labelled as an exhibit next to the guinea pigs brought a smile to my lips.

Marty had seemed to think that I could give Immi the breathing space and shelter she needed till the furore died down. I wasn't sure it would be that simple, but it might work. Tomorrow was Saturday, usually one of our best days for visitors. Sunday was quieter, and on Mondays we were closed to the public. Provided I could keep her out of the way over the weekend, by Tuesday the press wagon should have rolled on to the next big thing.

I halted outside the estate agent's. One window was full of Lovett Properties with a large poster urging people to register interest in the five-bedroomed luxury houses intended for Long Meadow. It made me feel ill just to look at the plans and artist's impressions. The display on the other side was full of Thatcher

Developments. Waterfront apartments down by the river, factory units on the big new industrial estate, and executive homes on the far side of town. Jack had been a very busy boy – it was no surprise that Mr Curzon had given him the VIP treatment. I bet he got offered coffee in a china cup and a plate of fancy biscuits.

'We have to stop meeting like this.' As if my thoughts had conjured him up, his voice tickled my ear. I could see his face reflected next to mine in the plate glass of the window.

'Are you following me?' I pretended to study the properties while trying to ignore the crackle of awareness that ran across my skin.

A slow, lazy smile appeared in response to my accusation. 'Do you want me to?'

'No.' My heart gave a thump as I told the fib.

'Come and have a coffee with me.' He indicated the tea rooms on the far side of the road. 'If you won't let me take you out tonight you could at least have enough mercy to come for a cappuccino.'

'Okay. I suppose I can spare you a few minutes,' my mouth agreed before my brain could put the brakes on. I found myself crossing the high street with Jack and heading for Tea for Two.

The café was fairly quiet, with only a few tables occupied by the blue-rinse brigade. It was one of those pleasantly old-fashioned tea rooms with chintzy lace drapes. I usually took my stepmother, Gloria, there for tea when she came over to visit from her new home in the States. Thinking of Mum, I wondered if Immi had called her since the TV show. It would be awful if the press tracked her down and Immi hadn't spoken to her.

I took a seat at a corner table while Jack fetched the drinks. He returned with two mugs of coffee and two large slices of apple pie and cream. My plan of a quick drink and a fast escape had been sabotaged.

Jack picked up a fork and dived into his pie. 'What's the matter? Would you rather have had an éclair?' He popped a chunk of apple into his mouth and watched me intently while he chewed.

'No, it's okay. I like apple pie.' It was true, I did love apple pie. Now I came to think of it, I didn't remember eating anything at lunchtime and I was pretty hungry. My recent chocolate bar hadn't done much to fill the gap.

'How are things at the sanctuary?'

A pastry crumb stuck at the back of my throat so I picked up my coffee to take a covering sip. I'm not good at telling fibs. I have what Immi calls 'an expressive face'.

'Okay, so-so, you know.' I wondered if Mr Curzon had said anything about the purpose of my visit. It had to be a breach of the bankers' code or something if he had.

'How long have you been there now?' Jack had finished his pie.

'Five years.' It seemed as if my suspicions about Jack's motives for asking me out were correct. I could almost hear vulture wings flapping. My piece of pie suddenly didn't taste so good and I laid down my fork.

'It must be hard work, looking after all those animals.'

'It's all I ever wanted to do.' I've always loved animals, ever since I was little. I can't stand the thought of an animal being hurt or in pain. When Dad died just as I finished uni he left the house to Gloria and a big chunk of cash to Immi and me. I used my money to get the sanctuary; Immi spent her share on a deposit for a flat and acting lessons. Even though Gloria is fantastic and I love her to bits I still miss my dad.

'What about you?' I asked. 'Have you always wanted to build things?'

A dimple flashed in his cheek as he smiled. 'I suppose so. When I was small I used to ride with my dad in the front of his lorry. I had my own yellow helmet with my name on the front.'

I couldn't help smiling as a picture of a little Jack in a mini hard hat popped into my mind.

'You look so pretty when you smile, Clodagh.' He reached across the table to take my hand in his. 'I wish you smiled more often. You always look so serious, as if the worries of the world are on your shoulders.'

My heart gave a squeeze at the emotion in his eyes and my body felt boneless and jellified at his touch. 'Do I?'

For one long-lasting wonderful minute I thought he was about to kiss me. Then my handbag began to ring and broke the spell. I pulled my hand away from his and grabbed my mobile.

'Clo, where are you?' It was Immi.

'I'm, um . . . having a coffee with a . . . friend. Why?'

'There's a message on the answerphone about a dog and a strange man is prowling around the yard.' Immi sounded majorly stressed.

'Okay, I'll be back in ten minutes. Where's Jade?' The strange man could be anyone from a member of the public to the vet. I couldn't tell if it was her drama training making her exaggerate or if she was really scared.

'She's gone to catch the bus. The public entrance is locked and this guy is peering through the windows. I'm the only one here.'

'I'm on my way. If he tries to get in, call the police.' I leapt to my feet with the phone still clasped to my ear. This man could be the mysterious saboteur who'd been causing all the damage.

'What's wrong?' Jack stood up as I closed my phone and slid it back inside my bag.

'I have to get back. My sister is in the house on her own and someone's prowling round the yard.' I bolted for the door.

'What sister?' Jack was right behind me as I hurried down the street to my car.

'My sister, she's staying with me.'

He caught up with me as I opened my car door. 'I'll follow you.'

I drove off without a backward glance or a reply. My mind worked overtime all the way to the sanctuary. Should I have called the police? Why had I told Jack that Immi was staying with me? Was Immi all right?

The yard looked deserted when I arrived. I screeched to a halt and jumped out of the car armed with my can of de-icer. I know it's not much of a weapon but it was all I had to hand. The back door opened and Immi peered out, wearing a huge pair of sunglasses.

'Are you okay? Did you call the police?' I hurried up to her as fast as my stupid skirt would allow.

'He disappeared right after I rang you. I don't know where he went.'

Jack's Range Rover pulled into the yard next to my Fiat.

'Oh, shit. It's the hunk from this morning.' Immi pulled her pale blue hoodie over her hair as Jack jumped out of his car and jogged over to meet us.

'Is everything all right?' He blinked with surprise when he saw Immi looking like an extra from a rap video.

'We think the prowler's gone.' I waved the de-icer towards the front of the house.

Jack grinned. 'What were you planning to do with that? Hit him or defrost him?'

'Funny. We should have a look around.' I put the can down by the back step.

'I'll go.' He gave another curious glance at Immi. 'You girls stay here.'

As soon as he was out of sight Immi wasted no time in stating her opinion. 'He is hot with a capital H. That's the friend you were sneaking coffee with, then?'

'I wasn't sneaking anything. I ran into him at the bank and again on the high street.'

'Yeah, right. I thought you said he was the bad guy.'

'He is. I was being polite.'

'Do you think he recognised me?' She pulled the hoodie closer around her face.

I didn't have time to answer as Jack jogged back over to us.

'I couldn't see anyone. There are a couple of cars in the car park but nobody inside them.'

'Thanks for checking.' This felt awkward.

He stared at Immi again. 'Have we met before?'

'No, I don't think so.' She retreated back into the doorway.

'My sister lives in London; she doesn't get a chance to visit very often.' I had to get him away from the sanctuary.

'She looks familiar.'

I put my hand on the sleeve of his jacket and tugged him towards his car.

'Whoa, Clo, what's the rush?' He halted a couple of feet away from the back door. 'Where did your sister go?'

I glanced round; Immi had seized her chance to slip out of sight.

'She's not feeling very well.' I would have crossed my fingers to offset the lie but my hand was still on his arm – something I became all too aware of as I felt his muscle tense beneath his leather jacket. 'I, um, should go and see if she's okay.' My brain told me to move, but my body didn't seem to be paying attention.

Jack glanced at the closed door. 'I'm sure she's all right.'

My heart rate kicked up a notch when his arms wrapped snugly round my waist to pull me closer. I could smell the earthy scent of his cologne as his lips brushed mine. He tasted of coffee and Jack. Somehow my hands began to stroke his soft dark curls and I lost myself in the pleasure of his kiss.

The sound of the donkeys braying in their field broke the spell. I was snogging the enemy!

'I really do have to go.' I stepped out of his arms. My heart was beating like a drum and my lips tingled from his kiss. I took a step towards the house but his voice stopped me in my tracks.

'Wait. I just realised who your sister is.'

'She's that actress, the one who advertises mouthwash and plays the daughter in that daytime soap. The one who turned up pissed on the talk show last night. Her picture is all over the papers today.'

Fishcakes.

I turned back round to face Jack. The back door squeaked open again; Immi must have overheard him.

'You'd better come inside,' she said.

She'd sorted out her face and hair while I'd been at the bank, because she slipped off her hood to reveal gleaming blond locks. Then she took off her dark glasses to bat a set of long dark eyelashes in Jack's direction.

He followed me into the kitchen. 'You two are sisters?' He shook his head in apparent disbelief as Immi closed the door. 'You don't look very alike.'

'Stepsisters. Her mum married my dad,' I explained.

Immi and I had been chanting that fact for years. She had been nine and I'd been thirteen when our parents got married. Dad had been a widower; I don't remember my mum, who died in a car accident when I was only a few weeks old. Immi's mum had been a divorcee, and since Dad's death she'd remarried for the second time. Now she lives in California with Burl, a very nice retired US air force sergeant. We speak on the phone every week and email each other regularly. I'm very fond of my stepmother.

Jack leaned back against the sink unit while Immi and I sat down at the kitchen table.

'I bet every journalist and reporter in the UK would like to find *you* right now.' He looked at Immi. 'I saw a clip of the show on breakfast news this morning. You really packed a punch.'

I put my head in my hands.

'It wasn't one of my finest moments, but my kickbox training did prove rather useful,' she agreed. 'By the way, you won't tell anyone I'm staying here, will you? I know it'll get out eventually but I'd rather it was in a few days' time when the fuss has died down.'

A glint of mischief appeared in Jack's eyes. 'Mmm. Need to think about that.'

Uh oh. I knew that look, and my sister was never one to pass up a challenge.

Immi's chin tilted up in defiance. 'Keep quiet and Clo will go out on a date with you.'

'Immi!'

My protest went unheeded.

'What makes you think I'm open to bribery?' Jack grinned.

'Most men are,' Immi observed.

'Excuse me, don't I have some say in this discussion?' Much as I hated to break up their witty rapport I felt they were missing the point – which was that I hadn't agreed to a date with Jack. One quick kiss didn't mean that I wanted to spend a whole evening in his company. Judging by the way my emotions were still busy waltzing arm in arm with my hormones it would be far too risky.

'You can choose where we go,' he suggested.

'I don't think—'

'Great!' Immi beamed at us, interrupting my protest.

I hoped Clive would sick up a fur ball on her bed.

Jack grinned at me. 'I'll come back and pick you up around eight.'

'But what about Immi?' I didn't like the idea of her being in the house alone – especially after the scare with the prowler. He could well be the mystery saboteur.

'I'm not playing gooseberry to you two. And besides, I have to lie low, remember?' Immi pulled out a nail file and began to inspect her French manicure. 'Clo, it'll be fine. I can call the police if there are any problems.'

'But . . .' I wasn't happy. My sister was too fond of ordering my life for me.

'I have some calls I want to make.' She filed an imaginary snag and admired the result as if everything had been decided.

'Okay, Clodagh, I'll see you at eight. Think about where you'd like to eat.' Jack winked at Immi and let himself out of the back door.

I pulled off one of my chunky earrings and hurled it at the door. It hit the wood with a satisfying thud before rolling away under the sink unit.

'Feel better?' Immi held out her hand to check the results of her manicure once more.

'Not really.' I pulled out my other earring and dropped it into the half-open cutlery drawer. 'You stitched me up.'

Immi tucked her file back into a ritzy little pink make-up case. 'You and Mr Hunk of Burning Love were snogging the faces off one another when I peeked out through the window. I didn't think going on a date would be a hardship for you.'

'Well, you were wrong.' I flopped back down on the chair opposite Immi.

'Clo, not every bloke you meet is a ratbag.'

I gave her a look – like *she* was the great expert after beating up Kirk on national TV!

'It's true,' she protested.

'Face it, Immi, we are both crap when it comes to dating. You dated Kirk and I dated Jonathan.'

The mere mention of his name brought a bad taste to my mouth. Jonathan had been my perfect bloke. I'd changed everything for him: my hair, my clothes, my friends – even the things I ate and drank. Only my desire to show him how clever I was had saved my academic career.

He had been one of my tutors at uni. I'd thought I was so special when he'd started to single me out. It wasn't until I discovered that he'd bonked half the first-year students that I'd seen him for what he really was: a sad middle-aged lech who desperately wanted to be Peter Pan and retain his youth by sleeping with young girls.

Unfortunately, it had taken something terrible to show him in his true colours and by then it was too late. My confidence nosedived and since then I'd focused my life on caring for animals rather than men.

Immi frowned. 'I know, babe, but our luck has to change some time. Mine can't get any worse and Jack does seem keen on you.'

'Maybe.' Personally I had begun to think that Sister Philomena, the head of our old school, might have had a point when she'd talked about joining the convent. Remembering Jonathan always had that effect on me.

Immi yawned and stretched her arms above her head, arching her back like a cat. 'Where are you going to go with Jack?'

I nibbled at the skin on the side of my thumb. 'Dunno.'

'Where's really nice round here?'

I had no clue. My social life centred around the Lucky Dragon Chinese takeaway and the pub. The last time I'd been on a proper date Simon Cowell's teeth had still been their original colour. How sad was I? Twenty-eight years old and an evening at the Frog and Ferret was the highlight of my week. I kicked off my heels and padded over to the recycling box to retrieve last weekend's free newspaper.

Immi watched me spread it out on the table and hunt out the entertainment section.

'You are bloody hopeless.' She shook her head in disbelief.

'I don't have the time or the money to go anywhere fancy.'

'You don't go *anywhere*.' Immi smoothed the page to study the adverts with me.

That stung. It made me sound like some sad middle-aged hermit. 'I do go out.'

'The Frog and Ferret does not count as a night out. When did you last hit the clubs or go out with some mates to a wine bar or the cinema?'

'I went to a do at the community centre a couple of weeks ago.' Okay, so it had been to do some bar work at a wedding for extra cash, but Immi didn't need to know that. I hadn't been to a club for years; I wasn't even sure if Melhampton had such a thing. Since Jonathan I'd stopped doing all sorts of things that I used to love. Sometimes I felt years older than Immi, almost as if I'd bypassed being young and stepped right into middle age. Conversations like this make me remember why I like her better when there are more miles between us.

She rolled her eyes but bit her tongue.

'What about here?' I pointed to a review of a restaurant in a converted barn a few miles away. It didn't look so posh that I'd feel uncomfortable there, but it was a definite improvement on the Lucky Dragon.

'It's okay, but this would be better.' She pointed to an advert for an upscale organic restaurant on the far side of town.

'They probably charge fifty quid for a stuffed mushroom.' Oh, God, I would need money. I couldn't expect Jack to pay for everything. Just the thought of having to cough up cash I didn't have made my chest tighten, and I started to hyperventilate.

Immi tipped some apples out of a brown paper bag. 'Breathe.' She helped me hold the bag over my nose and mouth until I calmed down.

'I thought you were over these panic attacks, Clo.' She knelt by my feet, concern showing in her big blue eyes.

I'd thought I was over them too. Guess I was wrong. I hadn't had one for ages – after the Jonathan episode I'd had them all the time. At one point I'd become almost agoraphobic. I'd avoided leaving the flat except to attend lectures. I'd had panic attacks that were so scary I thought I had a heart problem.

Like Jade, I'd been a volunteer at a small animal shelter near the university, and animals became the sole point of sanity in my life, the one thing that kept me going when the bottom had dropped out of my world. Animals love you unconditionally. They don't judge you by your clothes or your job or how much you weigh. I can't stand cruelty or mistreatment of any kind and when I saw the state of some of the poor little creatures coming into the shelter I was determined that I would do something to help.

When Dad died and left some money I knew it was my chance to make a real difference. It was also my chance to start a new life. At the time, Rainbow Ridge was owned by an elderly couple who wanted to retire to Spain to be nearer their daughter. They sold me the house and the land for a price that was below market value because, more than anything, they wanted someone to carry on their work. I've been here ever since, quite happy in my little bubble of the countryside with my animals.

'I wouldn't have pushed you into going out with Jack if I'd thought it would make you ill again.' Immi straightened up.

'I'm okay, really. You're right – I don't go out much.' I dropped the paper bag on the table.

Someone rapped loudly on the knocker at the front door. Immi's face paled instantly.

'I'll answer it. You stay out of sight.' I slipped into the hall, closing the kitchen door behind me. Through the old-fashioned frosted glass in the front door I could make out a male figure. Cautiously, I cracked the door open.

'Hello. I called earlier to ask if you could look after Nigel?' The plump middle-aged man standing on the doorstep had a huge hairy Irish wolfhound on a piece of string. A pair of sad brown canine eyes gazed into mine.

'He's my dad's dog. I'd take him in myself while Dad's in hospital but the wife's allergic.' The man held out the piece of string. 'Dad's seriously ill and it would break his heart if anything happened to Nigel. I know he'll be all right here with you, and we'll pay for his keep and everything. The RSPCA said you'd be able to help.'

Nigel gave a piteous little whine.

'How long is it likely to be for?' I asked, though I already knew I would take him. How could I not?

'Just a week or so. I've put my name and address along with fifty quid in this envelope. I wish I could give you more.' The man fumbled inside his jacket pocket with his free hand and produced a grubby brown packet.

I took it – and the piece of string with Nigel on the other end – from the man.

'I've got his basket in the van,' he said, and bolted for the public car park with relief written all over his florid features.

I waited on the doorstep and looked through the contents of the envelope. I knew I would come to regret this; I always got far too attached to my temporary residents. The man came panting back with a big dog bed in his arms.

'I've put his toys and some food in this bag.' A large carrier dangled from his arm. 'I couldn't find his lead.'

'He's not on any medication or anything?' I'd had people dump epileptic cats and diabetic dogs on me before – unexpected medication bills were one of the main drains on my finances.

'No, he's fit as a flea. Not that he's got any fleas, mind. And he's been wormed.'

I double-checked the contact details. 'Okay, I'll ring you every week for an update.'

The man dumped the bed and the bag on the step next to Nigel. 'I'm proper grateful to you. It'll put Dad's mind at rest knowing the dog's in good hands.'

He scurried off. I led the enormous dog along the hall and into the kitchen.

'What the hell is that?' Immi's eyes rounded in surprise. 'That's not a dog. It's as big as one of your gay donkeys.'

'Pasquale and Miko are not gay. Donkeys are happiest when they live in pairs and this is Nigel. He's an Irish wolfhound.' I untied the string from Nigel's collar. The dog flopped down on Immi's feet with a heavy sigh. I petted the top of his large head and was rewarded with a lick on my chin.

'I take it this was the subject of the phone call from earlier?' Immi shuffled her feet free from Nigel's weight.

'Unless you promised anyone else that I'd take their dog, yes.' I collected Nigel's bed from the front door and put it next to the kitchen radiator. Once his ball and squeaky bone had been added, Nigel sauntered across the lino, his claws clicking, and lay down on his blanket.

'Will I have to do anything with him while you're out with Jack tonight?'

'You could take him for a walk before bed.' I turned away to pull on my coat so she couldn't see me smirking. Immi has never shared my love of animals.

'Har-de-har-har, very funny.'

'I'd better make sure the ducks and geese are in. A fox has been seen near the field.' I toed my feet into my wellies.

'Well, you'd better get a move on. Jack will be back for you soon and at the moment you look like a cross between Joan Collins, the *Dynasty* years and Worzel Gummidge.'

I satisfied myself with sticking my tongue out at her before heading out to finish off my chores for the day. This was the time I loved best – evening, when everyone had gone home and I had the place to myself. I shepherded the poultry into their shed and checked the barn where the small animals, the rabbits, gerbils and guinea pigs, lived. Mr Sheen, the goat, nodded to me through the open top door of his house; the donkeys were already inside their shed.

There was a nip in the air and it was almost dark by the time I made my way back across the yard to the house. Immi had drawn the faded blue and white checked kitchen curtains, and light spilled from round the ill-fitting edges in bright yellow stripes.

The sensor by the back door picked up my movement and the security light clicked on, illuminating the yard. In that moment I could have sworn I saw something, or someone, moving near the darkened corner of the house.

'Is anyone there?' I picked up the can of de-icer from where it still stood on the step. Nothing moved. I debated going to see, but my common sense kicked in and I scuttled back inside.

Nigel gazed up from his basket as I closed the back door and pulled the bolt across. The kitchen smelt not just of dog but also of burnt bread, so I assumed Immi had made herself some supper and gone into the front room. It didn't seem a good idea to mention to her that the prowler might still be around. It wasn't as if I'd actually seen anything anyway.

I peeped into the front room to see her curled up on the sofa, munching on some cheese on toast and browsing through the free paper. Clive the cat lay spread out on the hearth and Dave was happily occupied with spitting sunflower seed husks from his cage.

Immi looked up. 'Oh, you're back. Can I use your computer? I need to send some emails.'

'Sure. I'm on dial-up, though, so it'll be slow.' I'd wondered how she planned to occupy herself while I was out. She'd probably Google herself and then get all hot and bothered when she read the press reports.

'I didn't realise the council had given the green light to developing the fields down the road from here for housing?' She held the page up for me to see.

'Yes you did, I told you about it ages ago. It isn't Jack's company, though. Some firm called Lovett Properties are going to build there. There was quite a bidding war apparently between them and Jack's company.' I'd received even more offers for the sanctuary's fields since the story had broken – some from national building companies. No wonder my bank manager kept suggesting I sell up.

'You'd better get a move on. Lover boy will be here in half an hour.' Immi dropped the paper back down on to her lap.

'Want a shag?' Dave kicked in.

'I'm going.' I ignored the parrot and went in search of something suitable to wear for dinner.

Immi had returned my best top and skirt now that she had her own stuff. My wardrobe wasn't very inspiring, but I had a couple of dresses to wear when I went to various business functions to tout for sponsors. I fingered the hem of the black one and wondered if it would look a bit too much for dinner with Jack. I didn't want him to think I'd tried too hard, but at the same time I didn't want him to think I hadn't tried at all. On the other hand, re-reading the news story about the plans for the fields bordering mine had raised fresh doubts about my agreeing to go out with Jack in the first place.

Immi rapped on my bedroom door before pushing it open. 'Do you want to borrow this?' She held up a lovely pale green silky halterneck top. 'You could wear it with your black trousers.'

'Could I?' My sister had always been incredibly

generous with her stuff. Even when we'd been younger and she and her mum had first moved in with me and Dad, she'd never been petty about sharing.

I'd been a thirteen-year-old tomboy and she'd been a dainty nine-year-old princess with pretty dresses and a suitcase full of cuddly toys when Dad remarried. Immi crept into my room the first night after the wedding and tucked her favourite teddy under my duvet. She'd perched on the side of my bed like a small blonde fairy and hugged me tight while she told me how happy she was now that she had a sister.

Ever since then we'd been close. She could drive me bonkers with some of the things she did but I knew that when it mattered she would be there for me. And now that it mattered for Immi, I would be there for her too.

'Well, I know you haven't a big choice in clothes.' She shook her head at the contents of my closet.

'Thanks, Im.'

She grinned. 'Just remember to sort your undies out, too. You don't want to have a Bridget Jones moment.'

Luckily for her, she ducked out of the room before I could lob something at her. Jack was not going to get anywhere near my undies. Even so, I did decide to wear my best knickers. A girl needs to feel confident, right?

Jack arrived while I was still attacking my hair with Immi's straightening iron. I heard her let him in and the deep timbre of his voice as he said hello; then I burned the tip of my finger in my haste to finish my hair. I yanked the plug from the wall, did a quick lippy check in the mirror, and hurried downstairs.

Butterflies flapped around in my stomach when I saw Jack. Freshly shaven and smelling gorgeous, he'd changed his jeans and sweater for a crisp white shirt and plain dark blue trousers. He let out a low whistle of approval as I descended the stairs, making my cheeks burn with embarrassment.

'Immi, are you sure you'll be okay? Can you keep Nigel away from Clive? I forgot to ask if Nigel was cat-friendly. I'll take him out when I get back. And please talk to Dave because he gets lonely, or you could play him some music.'

Immi and Jack were both staring at me.

'Clo, it's all fine. Stop blabbering. Jack, please take her away and make her enjoy herself.' Immi prodded me in the small of my back.

Jack smiled and my heart did a double backward somersault with half-pike flip. 'I promise I'll do my best.' He held up his hand in a mock scout's-honour-style salute.

'Since when were you ever a boy scout?' I went to get my denim jacket from the back of the pantry door but it wasn't there.

'You wound me deeply.' Jack clasped his chest and put on a hurt expression.

Immi handed me a pretty sparkly shrug. She must have hidden my jacket. 'It's cool outside. You can wear this.'

'You won't forget to talk to Dave?'

'Go already!' Immi gave me another push. 'I promise I'll look after the menagerie till you get back. It'll be my penance for slugging Kirk.'

Jack helped me into the borrowed shrug and Immi locked the door behind us.

'I take it your sister doesn't like animals quite as much as you do.' He opened the car door for me.

'You noticed, huh? No, she puts up with them but gets fed up when she finds the cat on her bed or Dave spits seeds over her favourite top.'

Laughter rumbled low in his throat as he closed the car door. 'Your chariot awaits, fair maiden. Where would you like to go?' He plugged in his seat belt and put the keys in the ignition.

I tried to remember the name of the place I'd seen in the paper. 'There's a place in a barn not far from here.'

'The Apple Loft – good choice.' He started the engine. 'I didn't tell you how great you look.'

'Better than the suit?'

'Hey, I liked your suit. You have great legs.'

It was too dark to see his face properly but he didn't sound as if he was cracking a joke.

'Thanks.' I wasn't used to getting compliments. Jonathan's compliments had always had riders attached to them.

You look all right, Clodagh, although I think you would look gorgeous in a longer skirt. Or, *That's a very pretty dress, but a little loud perhaps. Navy is always a good look on a woman.*

I'd always taken Jonathan's comments to heart. Over time I had changed my appearance to make him happy. I'd let my hair grow, stopped getting it highlighted, swapped my denim jeans and miniskirts for floaty floral things and sedate day dresses in sombre colours. I'd looked more like a forty year old than a girl of twenty, but I'd been blinded by love.

'Have you been here before?' Jack asked as we zipped along dark country lanes. The yellow glow of the car headlights carved a tunnel between the hedgerows on either side of the road. The interior of the car felt secure and intimate.

'No. I don't usually go further than the Lucky Dragon Chinese takeaway. Have you?' I would have been surprised if he hadn't. Melhampton wasn't a huge town.

'A few times, but not for a while. The food was good.'

I wondered who he'd gone with. Perhaps the same group of friends that had accompanied him to the pub. I didn't want to think he'd been there on dates.

Before long, Jack swung the car into a small gravel car park. The Apple Loft was a converted red-brick barn, lit round the outside under the pantiled roof with pretty white lights. Next to the entrance stood a large stone mill wheel that was also illuminated; somewhere in front of it water burbled in a never-ending cycle. Jack held the car door open for me. My fingers tingled as his hand touched mine to help me out of the car.

The evening air felt cold after the cosy intimacy of the car and I shivered, wishing I had on my denim jacket instead of Immi's flimsy shrug. Jack draped his arm casually over my shoulders as we crunched our way along a gravel path lined with apple trees towards the entrance. I wasn't sure whether it was the heat from his body or the thought that he'd wanted to put his arm round me that made me feel so much warmer.

The inside of the Apple Loft was polished and wooden. Jazzy piano music played softly in the background and the air was redolent with the hum of conversation and the aroma of cooking food. Yummy but discreet wafts of vinegary chips and sizzling steak filled the room. Jack spoke to the maître d' while I gaped like a country yokel at the wine list, which was written on a blackboard at the back of the long glossy bar.

'They've a table free. Would you like to have a drink at the bar first or go straight through?' Jack murmured in my ear.

'I don't mind. Whatever you want to do.' I felt out of my depth; panic had started to rise from my stomach. My palms were clammy with sweat and the bar staff swam in and out of focus. I forced myself to focus on the breathing exercises Immi had taught me to control my fears, and steadied myself with a hand on the brass rail that ran along the edge of the bar. It was too much like the last meal I'd had with Jonathan – the one where he'd told me he planned to marry someone else.

Thankfully, the breathing exercise worked and I found myself following Jack and the waiter out of the bar and through into the restaurant area. Whereas the outside front of the building had been plain red brick with tiny slit-like windows, revealing little of the interior, the eating area was completely different. One of the walls was made entirely of glass and looked out on to a fairyland of apple trees illuminated with tiny white lights.

The tables were on two levels; a wrought-iron staircase led up to a wooden balcony where diners had a view not just of the trees, but also of the clientele below. My heart thumped like a bass drum in a rock concert as the waiter pulled my chair out and I accepted the cream vellum menu with shaking fingers.

I was scared to look at the prices. The only money I had with me was the fifty pounds that Nigel's owner had given me for his keep. I didn't dare use my credit card in case they whisked it away and shredded it in front of us – a strong possibility considering I was perilously close to my limit. I ventured a peep at the prices and searched for the cheapest things on the menu.

The thing was, I knew Jack would offer to pay. He was old fashioned like that, opening car doors and stuff, but I didn't want to feel beholden to him or make him think I took it for granted that he'd pay for me. If I chose carefully I could run to a starter, a main course and one drink – although the drink wouldn't be wine if the prices I'd seen on the board behind the bar were anything to go by.

I sneaked a peek at Jack over the top of my menu. He had nice hands, I decided: long, clever fingers with tidy square nails. I had a sudden picture of those hands touching my bare skin, stroking and caressing me – it was enough to make me feel quite flustered.

'What would you like to drink?' The deep timbre of his voice interrupted my chain of thought and I realised the waiter was standing expectantly at my elbow with his notepad in hand.

Sparkling mineral water appeared to be the most inexpensive option, so I went with that and Jack ordered cider.

'It's very pretty out there.' I waved my menu in the direction of the twinkly trees while the waiter went to fetch our drinks.

Jack looked up. 'It makes a change from looking at concrete foundations and bulldozers.' He smiled at me and my heart did that stupid fluttery thing again.

My stomach gave a little growl and I remembered I hadn't eaten very much all day. A waitress strolled by, carrying two large white plates piled high with steak and chips. My nose twitched appreciatively. Maybe if I skipped a starter I could afford the steak . . .

'What are you having?' Jack leaned back in his seat and placed his menu on the table.

'I'm not sure, it all looks nice. What have you picked?' I said to hedge my bets. If he wanted a starter then I couldn't let him eat alone. It was no use – I was hopeless at dating. A trip to the cinema would have been much easier. At least there I could have bought my own popcorn and cheerfully treated Jack to the movie tickets.

'The loaded potato skins and sirloin steak,' he replied.

Bugger. 'I think I'll have watercress soup and then the chicken caesar salad.' My stomach gave another little moan at the thought of passing up a nice juicy sirloin while having to watch Jack eat his.

He didn't comment on my choices. The waiter returned with our drinks and we ordered the food. My pulse rate settled down a little and the panicky feeling faded.

The maître d' had seated us in a corner near the glass window. Our circular table was illuminated by three candles in a simple silver holder, lighting the white linen cloth in a cosy glow while the rest of the restaurant remained in shadow. Only the flickering of the candles on the other tables lit the soft embrace of the surrounding darkness. I was so out of practice at all this.

Memories of the disaster date with Jonathan danced back in front of my eyes. He'd taken me to a little Italian restaurant way out of town. I'd thought it was because I was special but really, looking back, he had probably picked it because he was afraid someone might see us or – even worse – I might cause a scene when he gave me his news. I had worn the dress he liked me in best, a demure navy silk wrap-over, and had my hair up in a classic chignon.

I'd even thought for a few blissful minutes that he was about to propose. How stupid was I? He'd been thinking of a proposal all right – but it wasn't for me.

'Clodagh, are you feeling well? You look really pale.' Jack's voice snapped me back to the present.

'I'm fine, just hungry. I haven't had much time to eat today; it's all been a bit hectic.' I forced a smile, though secretly I was still shaken by the rush of bad memories.

Jack didn't look convinced, but then the waiter reappeared with our starters so, amid much clattering of cutlery on my part, his attention was diverted. The soup was delicious, and I'd emptied my bowl and eaten my bread roll before Jack had finished his potato skins. I felt better with something in my stomach.

Jack put down his fork and surveyed me with a quizzical expression on his face. 'Why are you always so jumpy around me, Clo?' His dark eyes locked into mine, sending a delicious shiver of fear mixed with desire down my spine.

'I wasn't aware I was.' I went to pick up my glass of water and splashed some of the contents on to the pristine tablecloth, the action giving the lie to my words.

He placed his hand over mine as I attempted to mop up the spill with my napkin. Heat sizzled into my flesh and my pulse quickened at his touch.

'I don't bite.' His voice was soft and my resolve turned mushy.

'I don't have much luck with men.' I wondered if my voice sounded as husky to him as it did to me.

'Maybe we can change that,' he murmured, and he leaned forward to brush my lips with his.

For a split second I forgot we were in a restaurant, forgot Immi, forgot the sanctuary – forgot everything. There was just me and Jack.

'Wow.' He breathed, rather than spoke, the exact word I had in my mind.

The waiter bustled over to clear our plates and Jack took his hand from mine, leaving me feeling shaky and suddenly bereft. I was scared to look him in the face in case my own expression revealed too much of my feelings. My hormones thought Christmas had come early and were throwing a party with my libido.

I took a long, deep breath to calm myself and picked up my glass to take a cooling sip of water.

'You know I've liked you for a long time?' Jack spoke as soon as the waiter left.

My face felt as if it was on fire. 'I . . .' I swished the ice cubes in my water round while I tried to get my brain to come up with an intelligent response.

'I've liked you since we first met at the mayor's fundraising supper. Do you remember?'

I remembered all right. The mayor's supper was the big annual event in Melhampton. It was held at the town hall, and the great and the good were all invited to donate prizes, buy tickets and generally show up in best bib and tucker. The idea was that the mayor selected a local charity each year and all the profits raised from the dinner went to that charity.

When I'd first met Jack I'd been fairly new in town and had only taken over the sanctuary a year before. It had seemed like a good idea to go to the supper so that I could network and meet a few people. There had also been the vague possibility that the mayor might choose the sanctuary as his charity for the year. I'd gone on my own – it had been a big step for me but somehow, because I didn't know anyone and no one knew me, it hadn't been that scary. Immi had loaned me a dress that she'd worn to a red-carpet premiere only the week before and I'd had my hair and nails done specially for the event.

Jack had been there with a stunning blonde. The room had been so full of people and I'd shaken hands with and smiled at so many strangers that I hadn't seen him until it was time for the raffle to be drawn. He'd been one of the donating benefactors and had been invited to draw a ticket. Not every man can wear a tuxedo without looking like a waiter at a cheap wedding, but Jack had looked astonishingly good in his.

'I won one of the raffle prizes,' I said to Jack as I placed my glass back down on the table. I never normally won anything but he had miraculously managed to select my ticket from the drum. I had gone home clutching a very expensive GHD hair-styling kit which I'd promptly given to Immi for Christmas.

The feel of Jack's hand shaking mine and the warmth

of his smile had stayed with me much longer than the hair-styling kit had done. My body warmed at the memory and I was secretly a little touched that he too remembered our first meeting after such a long time.

The waiter returned with our main courses and I tried not to dribble into my pathetic salad as the lovely smell of Jack's succulent steak reached my nostrils. Don't get me wrong, I'm not a huge meat-eater, but I do love steak and it had been a very long time since I'd been able to afford one.

Jade and Susie both think I should be a vegetarian. Susie is constantly harping on about the 'poor ickle lambs' and I swear she snoops in my recycle bins on a daily basis to make sure I'm saving the planet. I like the idea of being vegetarian but I love steak – and bacon butties.

'Would you like some of my chips?' Jack offered.

I tried not to look ravenous as he forked some of them on to the edge of my salad plate.

'How are things going at the sanctuary?'

His question took me by surprise and the happy glow of shared memories and chips evaporated.

'More visitors and sponsors would be good.' My instincts flared on to red alert. This was the second time today he'd asked about how well the sanctuary was doing. Jack might be a good kisser – okay, a *great* kisser – but he was also a businessman with a ruthless reputation.

Only twelve months ago the local papers had been full of stories about how he'd acquired the town's old steel mill. Hundreds of people lost their jobs when the factory closed. A luxury apartment complex was now rising, phoenix-like, from the ashes with 'Thatcher Developments' all over the building-site awnings and flags.

'You have a good piece of land there. How large is the acreage?' He carried on eating his meal and looking as if butter wouldn't melt in his mouth – or, in his case, prime sirloin.

'I'm not sure, exactly. I let some of the fields to a local farmer. Of course, if we were to take in more large animals I may need to revisit that arrangement.' I tried to sound casual and indifferent. I knew precisely how much land the sanctuary had. In my darker moments over the last few weeks I'd even thought about selling one of the fields at auction. Mr Curzon had been very keen on the idea when I'd had my ill-fated bank interview.

'I take it the development business is good?' I lobbed the ball back into his court, although considering the estate agent's window this afternoon had been full of Thatcher Developments it was a pretty foolish question to ask.

'Not bad. We're always on the lookout for new possibilities for sites. Melhampton is a growing town. We were very disappointed when Lovett's managed to acquire that field near you for housing. I underestimated how high they'd be prepared to go at the auction.'

I couldn't believe he was being so blatant. Anger bubbled inside me like acid and all my pleasure in the beauty of our evening at the Apple Loft was ruined. How could I possibly have allowed myself to be turned on by such a manipulative monster? I had been right about him all along, and so had Susie when she'd warned me that

Jack was only interested in my land, not me. This was a business meeting with frills – not a date.

'You mean looking out for the possibility of sites like Rainbow Ridge, Jack?'

He looked surprised when I put my knife and fork down neatly on my plate with my salad barely touched. 'Is something wrong?'

'Why should anything be wrong?' My voice held the tiniest of wobbles. 'Rainbow Ridge is not for sale.' I picked up my bag and pushed my chair away from the table. 'Excuse me for a moment.' I left him gaping after me and headed for the Ladies to recover my wits. The harsh lighting above the powder-room mirror revealed my flushed face and glittery eyes. I whipped out my mobile and called Immi.

'This is a disaster and it's all your fault!'

There were a few seconds of silence on the end of the line. 'What did he do? Refuse to have pudding, so you couldn't order any?' I heard her sigh – presumably with exasperation at my social incompetence. 'Where are you, and why is it so terrible?'

I turned my back on my reflection and leaned against the washbasin. 'He wants to get his hands on the sanctuary. Taking me out for dinner is simply a way of getting what he wants.'

'Well, where is he now?'

'Eating a steak, which I hope chokes him. I'm in the loo at a place called the Apple Loft.' I suddenly realised there was a weird noise on her end of the line. 'What's that racket?'

'That racket is that bloody great dog. He's howled non-stop ever since you left. It's like living with the Hound of the Baskervilles.' Immi didn't sound very happy. 'You aren't planning on doing a bunk through the window, are you?'

I must admit the idea had flitted across my mind, but as the Apple Loft was plunk in the middle of nowhere I suspected a getaway vehicle might prove tricky to find.

'No.'

'You were, weren't you? Bloody hell. Listen, go back to the table and I'll ring you in a couple of minutes with an "emergency".'

'Brilliant.' I'd be able to get out of the rest of the date without losing face.

She rang off and I took a few seconds to refresh my lippy and calm myself down before returning to Jack.

'Is everything okay?' he asked as I resumed my seat.

'Fine. Was your steak good?' I picked up my fork and made a half-hearted stab at my salad. I hoped Immi wouldn't wait too long to call. The lettuce tasted like sawdust in my mouth.

'It was very nice.'

I shifted uncomfortably on my chair. Immi was the actress in the family, not me.

'Clodagh, you know you could always come to me if you need sponsorship for the sanctuary. I'd be happy to help.'

The intensity of his gaze made me squirm a little more. Like I would ask him for money! If I took money from Jack it would be the thin end of the wedge. Once the sanctuary was in his debt it would only be a matter of time before he managed to wheedle his way in by using his financial muscle and eventually take over. Ha! I was wise to his game.

Right on cue, my handbag started to ring. I dived to rescue my mobile under the disapproving glares of my fellow diners.

'Okay, it's me. Tell him you need to come back now as the prowler is about again.' Immi's voice sounded breathless in my ear.

'The prowler?' I repeated as dramatically as I could.

Jack lifted an enquiring eyebrow.

'We'll come back straight away.' I raised my voice slightly.

'Clo, I'm not faking. I actually did hear a noise that sounded like someone trying to get in. I think that's why the dog's been howling.'

Immi sounded very convincing. Her acting lessons must be paying off.

'I saw torchlight in the front garden, too,' she added.

Jack folded his arms and stared at me with an expression of profound disbelief. I tried to ignore him.

'Someone was outside with a torch?'

'Clo, I'm serious.' Immi's voice took on a sharper tone.

'Okay, we'll be back as quickly as we can. Check the locks and don't go outside.' It dawned on me that maybe she wasn't acting. The mystery shadow I'd seen in the yard and the intruder Immi had spotted earlier could both be one person, and he or she might still be hanging around.

I clicked off my mobile and dropped it back in my bag.

'You know, if you wanted to go home you only had to say,' Jack drawled.

I looked around for the waiter. 'Immi heard someone scrabbling at the window and she's seen torchlight in the garden.'

Jack lifted his arm and a waiter came trotting over.

'Could we have the bill, please?'

I slipped on my borrowed shrug and delved back inside my bag for my purse. 'Jack, I'm serious, Immi might be in trouble – it's not an excuse.'

The waiter reappeared with a slip of paper balanced on a small plate. Before I could stop him Jack had picked up the bill and handed it back to the waiter along with a small bundle of ten-pound notes. Damn it, I could have had steak.

The man scuttled off before I even got a chance to open my purse. I gritted my teeth and grabbed hold of Jack's arm, virtually towing him out of the restaurant.

'Slow down. We can be back at your house in about ten minutes.'

I released his sleeve and he opened the door of the Range Rover. My heart was pounding with a mixture of concern for Immi, annoyance that I'd allowed myself to be coerced into this date, and, strangely, desire for the man who was standing so close to me in the moonlight.

'I'll give you the money for my share of the meal.' I opened my bag.

'It doesn't matter.' Jack's voice sounded surprisingly gentle considering the way I had behaved.

His mouth closed on mine and somehow my arms found their way round his back. His lips traced a line along my jaw to my earlobe and my insides turned gooey with longing. I tried to focus and remember that I was mad with him.

'Jack, we can't . . . We need to get back.' My words came out as a mumble. What was I doing dallying under the stars when my sister could be in danger?

He lifted his head and his eyes met mine. 'Then we'd better go.'

My legs shook for a good five minutes after we'd set off towards Rainbow Ridge, driving in silence down the deserted lanes. I guess neither of us wanted to talk about what was going on between us.

As we neared the edge of the town, guilt compelled me to speak. 'I did call Immi from the loo, but I don't think she's pretending about there being a prowler. Before you picked me up tonight I thought I saw someone in the yard.'

Jack flicked a glance at me as we zipped through a set of traffic lights. 'I don't understand. What changed between our arriving at the restaurant and your urgent desire to escape from me?'

He turned into the private lane that led to the sanctuary yard. The blue car was back in the lay-by.

'It's complicated.' I didn't know how to explain. I didn't want to explain. 'You had steak and you didn't let me pay.' I had the car door open before he'd even turned off the engine.

Jack followed me out of the car. 'Wait up, Clo. What

do you mean, I had steak and you didn't pay?'

The sensor light above the back door clicked on. Immi must have been looking out for us because the door opened and Nigel came loping down the step barking his large furry head off. Before I could grab him he'd galloped off down the path by the donkey pasture.

'Nigel. Heel!'

Fishcakes. I set off in pursuit of the dog. Behind me I heard Jack shout to Immi to bring a torch.

I caught up with the runaway hound as he sniffed around the silage bales. In the distance I heard a faint shriek that sounded like Immi and some more masculine cursing that I presumed must be Jack. It didn't sound good; heaven knows what they'd found. My imagination ran wild and I wished I'd got my mobile in my pocket in case there was trouble. I managed to get Nigel away from the bales and with a bit of persuasion on my part we headed back to the yard.

All I could see as Nigel and I puffed our way up to the back of the house was Jack and Immi standing next to what appeared to be a man's body.

Or a pair of legs, at least.

'What happened?' I asked. 'Is that the prowler?'

Jack and Immi stood over the body of a strangely familiar figure clad in designer clothes: a man, who lay groaning and holding his head. What appeared to be a very expensive camera lay on the gravel by his side.

Jack stooped to pick it up, while Nigel sniffed at the stranger's inert legs.

'Worse than that. Paparazzi.' He gave the victim a scathing glance.

'What happened?'

Immi shuffled her feet and I noticed my rolling pin on the ground not far from her feet.

'I saw a shadow skulking at the side of the house,' she said defensively.

'Is he badly hurt?' I wasn't sure if we should be calling an ambulance instead of standing around in the yard. Visions of the police arriving hot on the heels of the paramedics and hauling Immi away in handcuffs flashed through my mind. Not to mention a lawsuit and more media attention. It looked as if Immi was well and truly up the creek without a paddle – and just when I'd thought things couldn't get any worse.

'He's okay. We'd better get him inside.' Jack scooped the man up from the floor and half carried, half dragged him into the house. Immi and I followed them. I discreetly picked up the rolling pin and disposed of it in the kitchen sink before joining the others in the sitting room. Clive the cat took one look at Nigel and bolted upstairs. A panda screensaver flitted across the screen of my laptop, left on the arm of the chair where Immi had been sitting before she'd unbolted the door. Dave the parrot cackled under his cage cover at the unusual intrusion.

Jack arranged Immi's victim on the sofa. In the brighter light from the wall lamps I recognised the man and remembered where I'd seen him before. He was the handsome owner of the blue car that had been parked in the lay-by – the one I'd passed earlier in the day when I'd been on my way to see Mr Curzon. Now he had a duck-egg-sized lump on his right temple where Immi had beaned him with the rolling pin. He didn't look happy.

'What the bloody hell happened to me?' He glared around at us.

'Bloody hell! Naughty boy! Dear oh dear,' Dave echoed.

'I think you must have tripped and banged your head.' Immi batted innocent blue eyes at him and ignored the parrot. 'You know, in all the confusion when the dog got out. It's understandable you're confused. I'll go and get you a cold compress for that nasty bump.' She slipped out of the room before Jack or I could say anything to contradict her.

'What were you doing skulking around in Clodagh's yard anyway?' Jack demanded.

The man groaned and made a feeble attempt to raise his head from the cushions.

Immi returned clutching a small bag of frozen peas wrapped in a tea towel. 'I think the answer to that is pretty obvious. He was snooping around for photo ops.' She slapped the peas down none too carefully on his head, making him wince. 'Maybe you should call the police, Clo. He could be a peeping Tom.'

'I'm not a peeping Tom.' He sounded about as happy as he looked. 'I was just doing my job.'

'Peeping Tom!' Dave let out a wolf-whistle, which made me jump.

'Prowling about on private property? Spying on vulnerable young women and taking photographs? Sounds like a peeping Tom to me.' Jack took a seat in the armchair opposite the sofa and gave the mystery man a hard stare. 'Who are you and who do you work for?'

Immi perched herself on the arm of Jack's chair and crossed her long, slim legs while we waited for the man to answer.

'My name is Marcus Gilbert. I'm a freelance photo-journalist.' He adjusted the makeshift compress. 'I don't remember tripping over anything. My head feels more as though someone's hit me.'

Immi locked gazes with Marcus and I wondered who would blink first.

'I'm not quite sure what happened,' she said. 'I opened the back door when I heard Jack's car and Nigel, the dog, rushed outside. Clodagh ran after Nigel and I saw something shadowy at the side corner of the house. The next thing I knew, you staggered out holding your head and swearing, then you collapsed on the gravel.' Immi held up her hands in a fluttery helpless gesture, suggesting that she was at a complete loss to explain what had happened. 'Did you see anything, Jack?'

I swallowed hard and waited to hear Jack's response to my sister's blatant fib.

'Yep, what Immi said. She was by the back door and you fell out of the darkness at the side of the house on to the gravel. You must have missed your footing and knocked your head on the wall.' Jack's voice was as bland as his expression.

My heart thumped with fear as Marcus looked slowly from Immi to Jack. It was pretty clear that whatever Marcus suspected might have happened to him couldn't be proved. He wouldn't get very far if he tried to say Immi had assaulted him if Jack continued to back up her story, although I was sure he knew as well as we did that Immi was lying through her bleached-white porcelain veneers.

'Where's my camera?' Marcus asked.

Jack waved it in front of his nose. 'It's here, but you can forget about taking any photographs of Immi. I presume she's the reason you were prowling around the sanctuary?'

'Who are you? Her minder or something?' Marcus

scowled, then just as quickly winced as the movement hurt his head.

'How did you even know I was here?' Immi asked.

'I researched your background. I know your mother lives in the States so I had my mate watching the airport terminal at Heathrow, but I had a feeling you were still in the UK so I looked up your sister.' He glared at me, then glanced back at Immi. 'Then I got a lucky break when I spotted your agent leaving your flat with all that pink luggage in her car.'

'You followed Marty?' It was the first time I'd spoken.

Marcus shifted his position on the couch. 'Yeah. So now I'm here, how about an exclusive?'

'Give me one good reason why I should talk to you,' Immi said.

Marcus attempted a smile. 'If I could find you it won't take long for others to follow me. Once you've signed for an exclusive story they'll have no choice but to back off. Plus, it'll be a nice little earner and a chance for you to put out your side of things.'

'I think you should discuss this with Marty.' I could see some sense in what he was saying, but I didn't think it would be as simple as that.

'What if I say no?' Immi folded her arms defensively.

Marcus gave a small shrug of his broad shoulders. 'Then it'll be open season on you and I'm sure you've already discovered that the media aren't exactly on your side at the moment. My way you'll still get people after pictures but you'll have control over some of the images and be able to put your spin on things.'

'I still think you should talk to Marty first.' Somewhere in the back of my mind a big brass bell clanged a warning. Something to do with Marty mentioning a Marcus when she'd dropped off Immi's bags.

'Clodagh's right, Immi,' Jack added.

Immi stood up. 'Okay, I'll go and phone her.'

Marcus dug inside the breast pocket of his rather muddied shirt. 'Here, take a business card. She can check out my credentials.'

Immi accepted the card from his outstretched fingers and went to the kitchen to make her call. The rest of us sat looking awkwardly at one another while Dave muttered and cackled in his cage.

'What is that thing in there?' Marcus asked.

I explained about Dave's past life in the brothel and his issues with bad language. By the time I'd finished both Jack and Marcus were grinning.

'It really isn't funny, you know.' I don't think they appreciated how annoying it was to live with the foul-mouthed bird.

'Wankers!' Dave shrieked and both men burst out laughing.

'What's the big joke?' Immi wandered back into the room with her mobile in her hand. 'Marcus, Marty wants to talk to you.'

Marcus levered himself up from the sofa and went back to the kitchen with Immi, leaving my semi-defrosted peas in a slushy puddle on the coffee table. Jack and I were alone for the first time since we'd arrived back at the house.

'Going out on a date with you isn't for the faint-hearted,' Jack observed as he leaned back in his armchair.

'Yeah, well, maybe that's why it's not a good idea.'

Nigel raised his huge head from my feet and sighed gustily in agreement.

'Is this to do with the steak thing?' Jack frowned at me. He sat bolt upright again and caught hold of my hand, taking me by surprise. A shiver of awareness crept up my spine at his touch.

'Kind of – it's complicated.' That was an understatement. My stupid traitorous body would have been quite happy to allow Jack to shag me senseless on the sofa, but my head told me it would be much more sensible to steer clear of him until I'd revived the sanctuary's finances. My brain also reminded me of what had happened the last time I'd allowed my hormones to have their own way when it came to a man. Only Immi knew the full story about me and Jonathan, and she'd been sworn to secrecy.

I pulled my hand free. 'I'm not ready for a relationship just yet.'

Jack sighed and ran his fingers through his hair. 'I see.'

I knew he didn't see at all, but after the questions he'd asked earlier about the sanctuary I figured he couldn't be that broken-hearted. Taking me out on a date had obviously merely been a means to an end, so I expected that now I'd said I didn't want to know he'd probably drop out of my life. It was my land he was interested in. Getting me into bed would be an added bonus. The thought was rather painful but I'd already learned the hard way that it would be better to have a little pain now than a full-scale broken heart further along the line.

Marcus opened the door to the lounge and flopped back down on the couch. He looked a bit green about the gills from the effort of moving around and I tried to remember if I had a spare bucket under the sink.

Immi sauntered in behind him. 'It's all settled. Marty's going to sell the story and I'll retain editorial control. Marcus gets his scoop and we all get a bit of money for our trouble.'

'I feel sick.' Marcus bolted from the room and we heard the sounds of retching coming from the kitchen, followed by running tap water. I hoped he'd taken the rolling pin out of the sink.

'I think he's got concussion. Maybe we should take him to hospital?' For all I knew he could have a fractured skull, depending on how hard Immi had hit him.

'He'll be fine. It was only a little bump on the head.' Immi didn't sound very concerned.

'Playing a minor role in *Holby City* does not make you a medical expert.'

She stuck out her tongue. 'I know, but when I was resting last year I had to do a first aid course when I had that job at the print works, remember?'

Immi had gone through a spell with no acting work last summer before she'd landed the soap job and had been forced to take a temporary position at the works to pep up her finances. Of course she'd told everyone it was research for a role.

Marcus staggered back in. 'Sorry. God, my head's throbbing.'

'I'll get some paracetamol.' Immi left the room and started opening and closing the kitchen cupboards, making Marcus wince with every thump and bang. She returned with some tablets and a glass of water.

'Where are you staying?' Jack asked him.

Marcus grimaced as he swallowed the pills. 'Nowhere. If I'm on a stakeout I usually kip in the car.'

'Well, you can't stay in your car tonight.' I felt guilty enough that my sister had hit him over the head in the first place. What if he slept in his car and didn't wake up in the morning?

'You could stay with me,' Jack offered.

Marcus took a sip of water. 'Thanks, but when I'm working I prefer to keep my subject in sight. You wouldn't believe how many celebs agree to a deal then scarper or sell out to the opposition the minute your back's turned.'

Immi looked indignant but, personally, I didn't think she could really object to Marcus's questioning her integrity. 'Then you might as well stay here. I'm sure Clodagh won't mind you kipping on the sofa.'

I didn't want a member of the paparazzi camping in my sitting room, but I didn't want him kicking the bucket from an untreated head injury in his car, either. 'You're welcome to stay, if you like.'

Jack didn't appear very happy about the arrangement, judging by the way his jaw tightened. 'I'd better go then.'

He stood up and I walked with him to the back door, leaving Marcus to Immi's tender ministrations.

I felt awkward given the short conversation we'd had before Immi and Marcus had come back from the kitchen. Jack waited while I opened the back door to let him out into the crisp evening air.

'Are you sure you and Immi will be okay with Marcus staying here?'

It was hard to read his expression in the gloom. I hadn't bothered to switch the kitchen light on and the outdoor sensor hadn't been tripped so the room was bathed in cool, silvery moonlight.

'We'll be fine. It's just for tonight. Marty is coming back in the morning to supervise the interview and photo shoot.' Part of me couldn't help hoping that this might turn Immi's fortunes round. My sister could resume her life and I could focus on the sanctuary. The publicity might even help raise some money for the animals.

'I suppose she could always hit him again if he gives you any trouble.'

We were murmuring our conversation in the open doorway so as not to be overheard by Immi or Marcus, and every part of my body felt attuned to Jack's. Awareness seemed to crackle in the narrow space between us and I knew if he were to kiss me again now all my earlier resolve would disappear.

'I suppose she could.' It took a major effort to force out a coherent reply.

We exchanged mobile numbers, and then time felt

suspended as we stood there almost toe to toe, neither of us speaking.

'I should go.' Jack was first to break the silence.

'Yes.' This was crazy. How can a person want something but not want something all at the same time?

'I'll be off, then.' He didn't move.

'Yes.' I didn't move either.

'Goodnight, Clodagh.' He turned abruptly and strode away across the yard. The security light snapped on, flooding the yard with a harsh beam, and the spell was broken. I closed and bolted the door with shaky fingers before putting the kettle on to make myself some tea.

Early the next morning I tiptoed along the hall and peeped in through the sitting-room doorway to check on Marcus's recumbent form. Judging from the snores he was still in the land of the living, which came as something of a relief. Immi had stayed downstairs for quite a while last night talking to him, but I'd made a cup of tea and gone up to bed after Jack had left. I'd actually slept quite well considering everything that had gone on yesterday.

I opened the kitchen curtains to a bright September morning. Blue sky stretched beyond the pastures and a heavy dew sparkled on the cobwebs that were spread between the rails of the fencing.

I made myself a mug of coffee and a slice of toast before setting off to feed the chickens. With luck I'd be able to get most of the early chores completed before Susie showed up. Jade tended to come later on Saturdays. I think she and the boyfriend went out most Friday nights, from little things she dropped when Susie asked about her spare time. Susie's spare time was mostly filled with making things: cards, knitted sweaters and, more recently, home-made soap. She was a one-woman cottage industry.

I led the geese and the chickens out into their runs and filled the feed and water trays. Next came the guinea pigs, hamsters, gerbils, mice and rabbits. Once they were fed and watered I moved on to the donkeys, the sheep, Mr Sheen the goat, and Rosie the pig.

I usually tackled the sweeping and cleaning of the pens after my second cuppa of the day. By then Susie would have arrived and if I was lucky I might have a bit of help from her before the general public started to trickle in. She usually did what I thought of as the faffing-about chores, like refilling the soap dispensers at the handwashing stations or making up paper bags of feed ready to sell at the gate. Strangely, she never showed much enthusiasm for mucking out the pigsty.

The morning air was cool but the clear sky held all the promise of a beautiful September day. I pulled a few straggly weeds from the flower beds and noticed that either Marcus or Immi had snapped a branch clean off one of my flowering shrubs during the events of last night. A late rose had opened on my special bush, the pale pink head drooping under its own weight. I reached out to stroke the soft velvet of the petals, smelling the rich perfume and remembering the past, before I continued along the narrow path leading to the front garden.

As I opened the small gate marked 'Private' I noticed there were more footprints in the clay soil of the borders. Some of them clearly belonged to Marcus, because the imprints were large and masculine. Others appeared to be smaller – a more feminine shape. At first I thought they must belong to Immi, but common sense dictated that my sister would never go trampling about in a flower bed in her designer shoes. There would be no reason for her to go through the gate, anyway. We rarely went round the front unless we were gardening and Immi wasn't fond of getting her hands dirty.

The discovery left me feeling uneasy as I made my way back to the kitchen a few minutes later with Nigel padding along at my heels. He was a very sweet dog and I'd already become quite fond of him. Thankfully, there had been no more howling after I'd returned yesterday evening and he'd spent the night sleeping peacefully in his basket under the kitchen counter.

Clive, however, remained wary of the new arrival. He'd slept on my bed all night, which Immi would have a fit about if she ever found out. She's a firm believer in not permitting animals in bedrooms – something about its being unhygienic. It was one of the many points on which Immi and I agreed to differ.

I heard noises from the sitting room when I returned to the house. I assumed Marcus must be awake, so I made him a cup of tea and took it in to him. The lump on his head had turned a rather unlovely shade of green but at least the rest of his complexion was back to normal.

'What time is it?' He squinted at his watch as I placed his tea down on the coffee table.

'Ten to eight.'

He groaned and slumped back on to the sofa. Nigel

gave his ear a sympathetic lick while I opened the curtains to allow more light into the room.

'How's the head?' I uncovered Dave's cage and checked the seed box to see if it needed filling.

'Still aching.' Marcus picked up his tea and took a tentative sip.

'Screw you!' Dave remarked, and spat a sunflower seed at my guest.

'I'll get you some more painkillers.'

He was sitting on the edge of the sofa when I came back. He looked slightly incongruous with his bare chest wrapped in a pink floral quilt and Dave giving him the evil eye from the top perch of his cage. As paparazzi or 'spawn of the devil' (as Immi calls them) go, he was very good looking despite the large bruise marking his temple.

'Thanks.' He took the tablets and picked up his mug. 'This is all a bit of a contrast for your sister, isn't it?' He glanced around the room.

I followed his gaze and saw my home as he and Immi must see it. Nigel was sprawled out on the faded hearthrug. Dave's cage took up a big corner of the room and had sunflower husks all over the carpet beneath it. The early morning sun gleamed on the ginger cat hairs that decorated the old-fashioned armchair where Clive liked to lie during the day. Stuffed along the mantelpiece were old brochures and clippings on animal care.

I'd only been to Immi's flat a couple of times. It was what estate agents usually describe as compact or bijou but it had a good address – something that Immi assured me was very important. It was furnished in modern minimalist style, all polished wood floors, chrome, and off-white walls. Suddenly I felt old and frumpy and poor.

'Immi's always been very supportive of my work here.' I felt compelled to defend my sister – and the state of my surroundings. It was true, anyway. Immi might not understand why I ran the sanctuary any more than I understood her need to be famous, but at least she cared about me being happy.

'Should get some nice pictures of her mucking out your animals, then,' Marcus remarked. I assumed he was being sarky. He'd probably guessed that Immi was about as fond of doing practical work around the sanctuary as Susie was of cleaning out the large animals.

'Immi's a very sweet person.'

'She didn't exactly show her sweet side when she attacked Kirk Drummond.' Marcus took a gulp of tea.

'Kirk's a nasty piece of work. If I'd have been on that show I would probably have hit him too.' I tried to keep my tone calm and unruffled.

Marcus looked surprised. 'It didn't help that she'd had a few, either.'

'She was upset. What happened with Kirk doesn't make her a lush.' Privately I had my own concerns about Immi's drinking but I certainly wasn't about to let on to Marcus, of all people. Immi's issues with alcohol often cropped up in the conversations I had with Gloria when she rang from her home in California.

The back door banged and I heard Susie cooee a greeting, followed by the sound of mugs clinking.

'I have to get back to work. The bathroom's upstairs and there's bread in the kitchen for you to make some toast.' I edged towards the door.

'Piss off!' Dave huffed along his perch.

Susie had already helped herself to tea by the time I entered the kitchen. Her eyes were agog with excitement behind her specs.

'You never told me your stepsister was that soap actress – the one who got drunk on the telly the other night!'

I resisted the urge to jam her woolly hat down hard over her beaky nose. 'You knew I had a sister, Susie.'

'I didn't realise that was her, though. It wasn't till I got home and saw the picture of her on the front page that I recognised her from when she was here last Christmas when Jade was off with flu. I thought she just acted in little plays or was in the chorus line. Everyone is looking for her. That poor man she attacked on the show is on the front page of the paper today. He says she needs help.'

I was tempted to do an Immi and whack Susie with the rolling pin, but the woman is so thick-skulled that I doubt she would even have blinked. 'You shouldn't believe everything you read. Kirk behaved appallingly towards Immi and he isn't a nice person.'

Susie sipped her tea. 'Well, she must be feeling guilty all the same. Why else is she in hiding? She hasn't been in touch with you, has she?'

Her beady eyes gleamed with curiosity and I knew she would dob in Immi in a heartbeat if she found out she was staying here.

'Actually, Susie, Immi *has* been in touch.'

Susie almost spilled her drink in excitement. 'What did she say? Where is she?'

'She's staying not far from here and she's fine.' Well, it wasn't actually a lie. Susie didn't have to know that 'not far from here' was code for 'upstairs'.

The kitchen door creaked open and Marcus appeared. He leaned on the door jamb still wrapped in the floral quilt and brandishing his empty mug.

'Sorry to bother you, Clodagh, but is there any chance of another cup of tea?'

I thought I would have to get hold of Susie's tongue and roll it along the kitchen lino to get it to fit back in her mouth.

'Sure.' I took his mug and switched the kettle on. I tried to pretend I had gorgeous half-naked men appearing in my kitchen all the time while Susie, unusually for her, appeared to have been rendered speechless. I couldn't quite suppress the secret wish that it had been Jack standing there bare-chested and asking for tea.

With his mug refilled, Marcus vanished back into the lounge.

'Who was that?' Susie clutched at my arm in her excitement.

'Marcus.' I placed the dirty crockery in the sink.

'Where did he come from?'

I set off out into the yard. 'Not sure. I picked him up

last night.' With a small smile I increased my speed and scuttled off to the donkey shed before Susie could ask me anything else.

The next hour was spent dodging Susie. Fortunately, she was distracted by a now fully clothed Marcus emerging from the house to collect his car from the lay-by. On his return he was followed along the track by Marty in her little sports car.

I shut the back door in Susie's face as I led them inside the house. Judging from her expression there was a good possibility that she might expire from curiosity before the day was out. Immi was up, dressed, and looking very glamorous as I showed my unlikely guests into the sitting room. Marcus excused himself to shower and change his clothes before the meeting began. I noticed Immi eyeing him up as he left the room. Marty lit a fresh cigarette.

'Bit of a bugger, Marcus finding you. Still, could be advantageous if he does a positive piece.' Marty looked resplendent in head-to-toe vivid pink. Her heels were as vertiginous as the previous day's and I wondered how on earth she managed to drive in them.

'I think it'll work out from the way he was talking last night. We had a little chat after Clodagh had gone to bed.' A satisfied smile played about Immi's lips and she gave her hair a flick.

'It's a bit unorthodox. Not what I would have chosen – this route. Can't trust these buggers.' Marty didn't appear convinced.

'Has he said what kind of article he's thinking of

doing?' I was uneasy about the whole thing. I mean, Marcus could have said anything while he was concussed.

'We're going for the helping-the-animals angle. Might do you a favour, Clodagh. Get some more people through the gates. I've got promises of an exclusive with a big-name magazine and a red-top daily. Can't say too much. Confidentiality.' Marty flicked her cigarette ash out of the open window into the nasturtiums.

I suppose every cloud has a silver lining, but since most of my visitors tended to be mums with toddlers I wasn't at all certain that they would want to visit somewhere that was associated with Immi. If they took the same view as Susie they might boycott the sanctuary instead.

I left Immi and Marty discussing strategies and took Nigel outside for a quick walk. It was almost time to open and it looked as if Susie had gone up to the public entrance to get things started. The sun warmed my back as I jogged along with Nigel, checking the pens and making sure everything was in order. At least there had been no fresh vandalism overnight.

A trickle of people were already making their way along the paths and down towards the donkeys. It was more visitors than I'd seen for a long time and they weren't from the yummy-mummy brigade. This did not look good. Nigel woofed with happiness as I increased my speed to beat the pack to the house. These 'visitors' were the dreaded paparazzi.

By the time I reached the back door there must

have been twenty or thirty people hot on my heels. I ignored the shouts and the clicking of the camera shutters until I was safely inside the house with the door bolted behind me. It seemed the press had found Immi. I hoped Susie had remembered to charge them all admission.

Marty, Marcus and Immi seemed unfazed by the media circus that rapidly surrounded the house. Marcus continued to record an interview with Immi while Marty barked out vetoes to certain questions. They'd redrawn the curtains so the paparazzi couldn't peer through the windows and snatch a picture. Apparently that would break the exclusivity agreement Marty and Marcus had negotiated with the big-name magazine. Dave wasn't impressed by the interruption to his routine and shrieked obscenities from his cage throughout the interview.

I left them to it and went back to the kitchen. Someone had taken the phone off the hook. I soon found out why when I attempted to replace it – it immediately started to ring non-stop with journalists wanting to talk to my sister. It seemed sensible to take it back off the hook again, so I did.

A glance through the window showed me the yard was now packed with people, most of them armed with cameras. When a film crew from the local TV station pulled up I closed the kitchen curtains. I could hear them calling for Immi to come out and people were pounding on the front and back doors. Nigel had started to add to the noise by howling like a banshee. I was worried about how all the disturbance would affect the animals.

Marty had already smoked her way through one pack of cigarettes and my sitting room was a smoky hellhole when I went back in to ask how much longer the interview would take. Marcus was taking a picture of Immi holding a reluctant Clive when I opened the door. Poor Dave was sulking and pretending to cough.

'Few more minutes,' Marty snapped and closed the door on me.

I would have said something about its being my house but my mobile started to ring.

'Clodagh, is everything okay? The road to the sanctuary is jammed solid with cars and your landline isn't working.' Jack's voice rumbled in my ear.

'The press have found out that Immi's here. It's ridiculous.' I wanted to cry. Marty, Marcus and Immi might be all right with being besieged by the press, but I wasn't. My beloved animals were being disturbed and I could feel the old, familiar tide of panic rising in my gut.

'Sit tight. I'm coming to get you.'

I closed my phone and sank down on to the bottom step in the hall. Through the frosted glass of the front door I could see people trampling my garden and hear the pounding of fists on the woodwork. I couldn't see how Jack would manage to get anywhere near the house, let alone get me out. Nigel snuggled up to me, his big brown eyes full of trust as he laid his shaggy head across my knees.

'I'm not a celebrity – get me out of here,' I muttered

as I hugged the dog and waited for an errant knight in a Range Rover to come to my aid. Tears poured down my cheeks on to Nigel's fur.

Only last night Jack had been the enemy. Now he was my only hope.

I don't know how long I stayed in the hall huddled up against Nigel, but it felt like an eternity. My feet were cold and my legs had cramped from sitting in one spot. Immi remained closeted in the lounge with Marcus and Marty. I had no idea what they planned to do about taking photographs of Immi with the animals, or how they were going to disperse the mob surrounding my house. All I could manage to do was focus on my breathing and concentrate on the mantras to stave off my panic attacks. I'd learned from the psychologist I'd seen after my break-up with Jonathan that keeping calm was key to my staying in control.

In the distance I heard sirens wailing, and I wondered if it was a police car or an ambulance. I hoped there hadn't been a traffic accident because of the chaos caused by the press; Jack had said the road was jammed. Nigel whined in my ear as the siren grew louder. I hoped it was the police and that they might clear the paparazzi away so everything could go back to normal.

My mobile had been pinging with texts. Most were from Susie to say she was trapped in her shed at the entrance and had run out of change. At least she had taken gate money, so some good might come out of all this. Jade had texted me, too – she was stuck on the bus on the main road in a traffic jam. Unless Jack chartered a helicopter I couldn't see how he could possibly get to me.

The banging on the door stopped and the voices began to sound more distant. I thought I could hear an authoritative voice ordering the crowd away from the house and back to the public areas of the sanctuary. Nigel nuzzled my cheek while I waited to see what would happen next.

'Clodagh! It's me, Jack.' The letter box rattled.

I crept across the Victorian tiled floor and lifted the internal flap to see Jack's eyes looking at me through the narrow slot.

'The police have moved the press away. It's okay, you can let me in.'

I opened the door on the security chain, my fingers clumsy and stiff with fear as I turned the lock. To my relief I saw Jack, broad-shouldered and solid on my step. Just beyond him I could see PC Holmes, our local beat bobby, in a yellow hi-vis vest waving the press pack back to the public car park.

The next thing I knew I must have released the chain. I stumbled into Jack's arms while Nigel barked an enthusiastic greeting beside me.

'How did you get here? It's horrible. I've been so frightened.' Words tumbled out of me. I'd never been so glad to see anyone in all my days. How my sister copes with that kind of pressure in her everyday life I'll never know.

'The police were on their way here to get the traffic flowing again, so I caught a lift with PC Holmes. Apparently your sister's agent had called them too.' Jack continued to hold me close to him. I could smell the scent of his skin mingled with his cologne. 'I was worried about you.' He stroked my hair gently back from my cheek.

It struck me that I probably wasn't a very pretty sight with my eyes red-rimmed from crying and my skin all blotchy. The door to the sitting room opened and Immi popped her head out.

'Hello, Jack. We're just going to make a statement and take some photographs.' She behaved as if everything was perfectly normal and this kind of media frenzy happened to her all the time. She didn't appear at all surprised to see Jack in the house or that I was in his arms. 'Clodagh, we're going to take some pictures of me with the donkeys, as Marcus thinks they'll be the most photogenic. Is that okay?' She didn't wait for my reply but walked off towards the kitchen with Marcus and Marty following in her wake. Clive emerged too, arching his back and giving a hiss of disgust when he saw Nigel at my feet.

I felt as if all the bones in my legs had been replaced with rubber. If Jack hadn't been holding me I would probably have fallen down. I heard the back door open and people calling Immi's name.

'They must have gone outside.' Jack released me. I

swayed against the wall as he strode off along the hall. Nigel licked my hand and I forced my legs into action to follow Jack. I heard Dave cackling with glee in the sitting room at the departure of the intruders.

Jack had closed the back door and he, like me, peered through the kitchen window to watch my sister in action. Immi was in the donkey pen, posing for photographs between the two patient and gentle inhabitants. I noticed she'd borrowed my work wellies and my denim jacket to wear over her designer jeans and skinny T-shirt.

Jack turned back to me. 'Are you all right?'

I nodded. Now that the crowd had moved away from the house my panic had subsided, and I suspected the rapidity of my pulse had more to do with the way Jack was looking at me than my fear of the paparazzi.

He raked his hand through his dark hair and looked awkward. 'Will things settle down now, do you think?' His head tilted in a questioning gesture towards the window.

'I don't know. Immi always attracts attention wherever she goes. Usually when she comes here it's on a flying visit so I've managed to steer clear of the limelight until now.' I sank down on to one of the kitchen chairs as the realisation dawned that now I would always be known in town as Immi's sister. The lovely anonymity of being the girl who ran the animal sanctuary was shot for good. Now I'd be Imogen Martin's unfamous, dowdy sister.

'Does that bother you? I know it was overwhelming

just now but the up side is that it might get more attention for the sanctuary.' He pulled out the chair opposite mine and sat down.

'It's hard to explain, but I suppose I want people to come here because they care about the animals, not because they want to get a glimpse of my sister. You'd think it would help raise more money but it probably won't work out like that. People will assume that if Immi is successful then I must be, too. They'll think I don't need the sponsorship or that I'm playing at running the sanctuary as if it were a hobby.' I traced my finger along an old groove in the tabletop, frowning as I attempted to rationalise my fears. 'Attendance will go up in the short term, but it won't be the people I really want: the mums and tots or the school parties. Instead I'll get star-struck groupies looking out for Immi and teasing my poor animals for amusement while they wait.'

It occurred to me that I was maybe being ungrateful; with the dire state of the sanctuary's finances I should be welcoming any kind of cash injection that came my way. The way I felt right now, though, the price for saving the sanctuary looked pretty steep.

Jack placed his hand on top of mine, stilling my nervous movement. 'Clodagh, I was serious last night about offering to help you financially.' His hand felt warm on mine, his long fingers gentle against my skin.

'I know.' I couldn't bring myself to look at his face. His touch alone was playing havoc with my senses.

'Why won't you accept, Clo? I've got eyes; I can see the sanctuary is struggling. Some of the animal pens need replacing and the vandalism that's been reported in the paper must have hit you hard.'

I moved my hand from his and rested it on my lap. 'Jack, I can't.' I sneaked a peep at his face.

'Why not?'

I hesitated while I tried to do the grown-up thing and decline politely without getting all emotional. A tricky task, since I was torn between wanting to cry and wanting to be back in his arms. 'I think it would be a conflict of interests. Your business is property development and I know the sanctuary land is valuable. I'm very careful about who I take money from. Lovett's have already approached me about buying the ground.'

'You don't trust me. You think I'm after your land.' Jack's voice took on a hard edge.

'I didn't say that.' I'd thought it, though, and he knew I had.

He rose to his feet so abruptly that Nigel gave a woof of surprise. 'You didn't have to. This is what was on your mind when we were out last night, wasn't it? That's why you did your disappearing act to the Ladies.' His eyes were flinty and his jaw was tight with suppressed emotion.

I felt my face heat up under his gaze and although I automatically opened my mouth to deny his accusation the words died unspoken on my lips.

'That's what I thought.' The door banged and he was gone.

I rushed to the window and watched as Jack strode away through the throng of people surrounding Immi at the donkey pen.

The strength of his reaction baffled me. I could understand his being upset about my rejection of his offer to help, but the way my words had affected him seemed extreme. If he just wanted to get his hands on the sanctuary land I would have expected him to argue his case a bit more. It was as if I'd hit a raw nerve somehow. Either way, it didn't make me feel very good.

Jade's perky face suddenly appeared in front of me. She pointed towards the door, signalling me to let her in.

'Wow, it's crazy out there. Susie is under siege at the entrance and the police have only just cleared the traffic on the main road.' She rushed into the kitchen clutching her duffel bag. 'Oh, what a lovely dog.' She patted Nigel's head.

'Would you like a drink? You must be thirsty after being on the bus all that time.' I moved automatically towards the kettle, my mind still busy with thoughts of Jack.

'I'm fine. Luckily, I'd got my bottled water and my lunch with me.' She patted her bag and peered over my shoulder through the window.

Immi and her entourage were at Mr Sheen's pen. I hoped he wouldn't try to eat anything too expensive, like a camera lens. Immi appeared to be giving a brief interview to the news crews. Her face was the perfect picture of concern as she posed next to the goat. If you didn't know better you would think she lived and breathed animal welfare.

'Hey, Jack Thatcher passed me on my way in. He almost knocked me over. Looked as if something or somebody had rattled his cage good and proper.' Jade switched her attention from Immi to me when I groaned. 'What happened?' She opened her bottle of water and took a gulp.

'It's a long story but basically Jack offered me sponsorship money for the sanctuary and I turned him down. He said it was because I didn't trust him.' My shoulders sagged when I remembered how hurt he'd seemed.

'Oh.' Jade bit her lip and I could see from her face that she was weighing up whether to say something.

'What?'

'Jack can be a bit touchy about people trusting him.' She shrugged. 'At least, that's what I've heard. You don't know about his dad, do you?'

'His dad?' I'd thought his father was dead.

Jade rested her bag down on the table. 'There was a big scandal a few years ago, before you came here. Jack's dad had the business then. I forget the details, but it was all to do with embezzlement and shady dealings. The firm almost went under.'

I had to hold tight to the back of the chair to keep myself upright. 'What happened?'

'Jack's dad stepped down and Jack took over. I don't think it went to court but the firm lost a lot of business. Lovett's took a lot of trade from Jack. I suppose that's why he was so peeved to lose out to them in the auction for Long Meadow.' Jade gave another apologetic shrug.

'And now Jack thinks I think he's dishonest.'

'Sounds like it. Jack's dad was never the same after

the scandal. He died from a stroke twelve months after Jack took over the firm. I'm sorry, Clo.' She gave my arm an awkward pat.

'It's okay. You've helped make sense of a lot of things. I think I owe Jack an apology.' Poor guy, he'd put himself out and battled through the crowds to come and rescue me. All I'd done was give him the brush-off; and, worse, he probably thought I knew all about his past and thought he was trying to pull some kind of scam.

My guilt chip had been on overload before hearing what Jade had told me, but now I felt horrible, like the worst kind of person in the world. I'd let my bad experience with Jonathan colour my view of any man who tried to get close to me.

'Well, I'd let him cool down a bit first. He didn't look very happy when he pushed past me,' Jade suggested.

She had a point, and anyway, I needed to think of what to say. I wasn't very good with words. Maybe when Immi had finished with the press pack she might have some good advice for me. For all my sister's faults she did have considerably more experience with men than I did. Perhaps she could help me figure out how to talk to Jack.

Jade picked up her bag. 'I'm going to go and take over from Susie. It looks as if the crowd's dispersing and you'll need to bank the takings.' She nodded towards the window.

Sure enough, the paparazzi were showing signs of packing up. The film crew had gone and Immi and Marcus were walking back to the house. I couldn't see Marty anywhere. As the crowd thinned I saw that her car had gone from its space, as had the police patrol vehicle.

'Thanks, Jade.'

She left as Immi and Marcus came in. Immi kicked off my wellies with a grimace of relief and flexed her feet. Marcus was busy checking his camera.

'Phew. Glad that's over. I could murder a drink.' She perched gracefully on a chair and massaged one of her recently liberated feet. 'I'd love to be a fly on the wall when Kirk sees the press.'

'Well at least someone is happy.' I switched the kettle on even though I knew Immi had been hinting at something stronger than a cup of tea, but the last thing we needed was a snap of her with alcohol in her hand. Not after all her efforts today with the carefully posed pictures and the sympathetic interviews.

'I need something from my bag,' Marcus muttered. He wandered out of the kitchen towards the sitting room, sparking a flurry of welcoming abuse from Dave.

The mugs clattered in my hand as I clumped them down on the counter. I knew it was petty to take my frustration and upset out on the crockery but I couldn't help it.

'Clodagh?' Immi peered at me.

'Do you want tea or coffee?' I asked, and burst into tears.

Immi was on her feet in an instant. She padded across the kitchen and placed a contrite arm round my shoulders.

'Oh, Clo, I'm sorry. I got so swept up in everything that was going on I didn't think.' She prised the mugs that I was still clutching from my fingers, and set them down on the counter before leading me to a chair. 'With a bit of luck I'll be out of your hair soon and all the madness will die down.'

'It's not only that. It's everything.' I blew my nose on a tissue.

'Jack?'

I nodded and she enveloped me in another fierce hug.

'What's happened now? I thought whatever had gone on between you two last night got sorted out when he turned up earlier.'

I told her everything that had happened and what Jade had said about Jack's dad.

'I think you need to talk to him.' She patted my shoulder.

Her mobile buzzed on the work surface, the vibration

making it dance along the counter until she picked it up and read the text message she'd apparently received.

'I need to make a call. We'll talk later.' She jabbed a few buttons and shot off into the hall.

Marcus strolled in, carrying his overnight bag and photographic equipment. 'I'll be out of your way in a few minutes, Clodagh. I imagine it's been very stressful having the press camped on your doorstep.'

'It certainly hasn't been a walk in the park.' I pulled a fresh tissue from the box and wiped my nose, hoping my face didn't look all puffy and blotchy from crying.

'I can imagine.' He sat down on the chair Immi had just vacated. 'Give it a couple of days and the world will have moved on.' He offered an apologetic smile.

'I suppose you'll be moving on to the next big story now, too?' I couldn't fathom how anyone could make their living as paparazzi. It seemed incredible that anyone could enjoy a job feeding off someone else's misery. Although judging by the number of books I saw in the shops written by people who'd suffered harrowing childhoods, people must enjoy reading about the unhappiness of others.

'Yes, there's one breaking in London. Some politician's been caught with his trousers down.'

'Same old same old, then.' I wondered if he was hanging around chatting to me because he wanted the opportunity to say goodbye to Immi. He certainly appeared interested in her and I'd noticed her checking him out more than once during the course of the day.

'Yeah. I need to cut across country to get photographs of his wife.'

Immi came waltzing through the door with a big smile on her face. 'That was Marty.' She gave a little squeak of excitement.

'Good news?' he enquired.

'The best.' She smiled and blushed.

Marcus stood and hefted his bags back on to his shoulder. 'I have to get going. It was nice working with you; give me a call if there's ever anything . . .' He let the sentence tail away.

I presumed he meant if she had some kind of scoop for him, but then again . . .

'I hope your head is better soon.' Immi smiled at him again and held out her hand.

'It's improving.' He shook her hand then turned to me. 'Bye, Clodagh – and thank you for putting me up last night. I'm sorry about the upset.'

I followed Immi's lead and shook his hand too. 'Good luck with the politician's wife.'

Immi closed the door behind him and watched from the window as he walked across the yard to his car. 'He was very nice considering he's paparazzi. Good looking, as well,' she observed.

'You seemed to get on well with him even though you whacked him over the head with a rolling pin and almost killed him last night.'

Immi turned away from the window to face me, her blue eyes sparkling with laughter. 'Now *that* is our little secret.'

I decided to pretend she hadn't admitted almost killing Marcus. 'What's the big news?'

She gave a squeak of excitement. 'I have to be at the TV studios for five thirty on Monday morning. I've got an interview with the breakfast show. They're sending a car to pick me up. What do you think of that?'

'Lovely.' If you like that kind of thing.

She was clearly delighted.

'I get a chance to put across my side of what happened. Marty's briefed me on what I'm supposed to say and how to handle the questions. It should be similar to today.' She gave a little wriggle of pleasure.

'Great.' I was pleased for her if this was what she wanted. It did sound very positive and there was a slim to zero chance of her blowing it through alcohol if it was an early morning interview.

'And here's the best part – Marty says they'd like you to go on air, too.' She clapped her hands together in glee. 'Isn't it great?'

I stared at her as she did her happy dance in front of the sink.

'Why would they want me to be on TV?' She must have misunderstood what Marty had said to her. My palms felt clammy and my heart raced just at the idea of it.

'Because you're my sister and you can talk about the animals and what my life is like when I'm here with you.' She carried on boogieing.

'Will you keep still? I can't concentrate with you whirling about.'

'Don't tell me you don't want to do it?' Immi stopped dancing.

'I don't know. I need to think.' I jumped up from my seat and headed outside. The fresh air would help to clear my thoughts, and as it was almost closing time I had to get the day's takings from Susie.

Most of the public had gone. Jade was busily shepherding the last of the stragglers towards the exit. Peace and quiet was being restored. I paused at the donkeys' fence and waited while my animals moseyed over to sniff inquisitively at my hands. I patted their furry muzzles and fed them a few titbits from the pockets of my jeans.

'What do you guys think? Should I go on TV?' I didn't expect them to answer, but somehow voicing the question aloud made the possibility of appearing in front of millions of people while they ate their cornflakes seem more real.

Sitting in a studio somewhere with Immi and answering questions sounded as much fun as having my teeth pulled. Especially when I knew she would want me to bend the truth about her visits to the sanctuary to help her repair her public image. Normally I would never even consider the idea, but the publicity for the animals was too good to dismiss out of hand. This might be my opportunity to raise a major amount of money and get my dream back on track.

Pasquale snorted and nuzzled my ear. I gave him one last pat and walked up the small slope to the wooden shed at the entrance where we issued tickets and sold animal feed, ice creams, and soft drinks. Jade and Susie were bent over the closed top of our elderly chest freezer, carefully piling coins into little heaps.

'Nine, ten pounds. We're right out of ice creams, Coke and lemonade,' Susie announced as she scribbled figures in an untidy column on the back of a brown paper bag. Her face was flushed and her hair looked as if she'd been styled by Russell Brand.

'The takings are fantastic.' Jade slid the piles of coins into plastic money bags ready for the bank. 'I think it's a record for one day.'

We didn't charge much for admission as we aimed for frequent repeat visits. My theory had always been that a pound per adult and fifty pence per child with the under-fives entering for free would encourage people to call in regularly. Mr Curzon had been scathing in his opinion of this strategy at my ill-fated interview at the bank.

'How much is there?' The cloth bank sack bulged as Jade dropped in the last of the coins.

'Five hundred and forty-three pounds.' Susie finished totalling her figures.

'Are you sure?' I couldn't believe it. Some months we hadn't taken that amount in a week.

She pushed the paper bag towards me and I checked her arithmetic. 'Wow!' We'd taken enough money to pay our outstanding bill from the feed wholesaler and to pay for the animals' medicines. It wouldn't clear everything by any means but it would avert the bailiffs for a while.

'Do you want us to drop this in the night deposit? Susie is going to give me a lift back to my flat and we have to go through town,' Jade offered. She pulled a paying-in slip from the cashbox that we used as a till and scribbled in the amounts.

'That would be great. Thank you.' I appreciated her offer. After the tumultuous events of the past two days I needed to have some time on my own to de-stress. Not that I would get much of that done if Immi persisted in bouncing about the house like an ecstatic kangaroo.

We pulled the shutters and locked up. Susie offered to collect fresh stocks of ice cream and fizzy drinks from the cash and carry in the morning on her way to the sanctuary, and I gratefully agreed. I waved them off from the entrance, locking the gates behind them.

I pushed Immi and her problems to the back of my head while I dished out medication to my poorly animals and carried out all my early evening chores. Nigel loped around the site alongside me, his hairy face the picture of happiness as he explored the paths between the pens. I deliberately dawdled as I tended to Rosie the pig and the rest of the large animals.

With my hands occupied in my normal routines my mind was free to dwell on my other problem – Jack. I shouldn't have allowed Susie's sniping about his possible ulterior motives to colour my views. Maybe his questions about the sanctuary really were an attempt to help me. He'd certainly come rushing to my aid today when the house had been besieged by the press; he'd shown only concern for me.

I sat down on an upturned bucket in the rabbit pen and one of the dwarf lop-eared bunnies twitched his nose with interest around the toe of my boot. I hadn't always been so suspicious and distrustful of everyone. The cut-throat, back-stabbing world of celebrity that Immi lived in should have made *her* the one who was less trusting and less open. Instead, she was always urging me to give people a chance.

Nigel whined outside the pen, pawing at the wire to urge me to get a move on. I finished taking care of the small animals and locked the barn where they lived.

'Come on, Nigel, we're going walkies.' I fastened rope to his collar and we set off along the lane leading out of the sanctuary. The air felt cooler and held a hint of the end of summer. The fields surrounding us were blond with stubble where the combines had been busy. Swifts darted and dived ahead between the hedgerows as Nigel and I trudged along the track. Traffic hummed along the main road in the distance, mixing with the fat drone of the bees in the verges.

There was something remarkably soothing about strolling nowhere in particular with a dog at my side. It was tempting to keep on walking and never look back, but I knew Immi would get worried. The flesh on the tops of my arms began to goosebump in the evening breeze as the light deteriorated and so, reluctantly, I turned round.

Immi was in the kitchen when I got back. Two large black dustbin bags full of rubbish were outside the back door and she was armed with a pair of yellow Marigold gloves and a determined expression.

'What are you doing?' My kitchen appeared to have

been raided. Never the tidiest place at the best of times, it now looked as if a whirlwind had passed through it.

'I don't know how you stand living like this. Your cutlery drawer is full of junk, your fridge is like a scene from a mad scientist's laboratory, and I found dried dog food in your saucepans.' Immi waved her arms about.

'The bag burst. I had to put it somewhere.' Okay, so I'd been a bit overwhelmed with everything lately, but it wasn't that bad. I hated it when Immi went on a mission. She used to have turns like this when we were young. Her bedroom had always been a pristine pink paradise. Mine had been stuffed with old copies of *Smash Hits* magazine and dirty socks.

'The only edible food in the cupboards is animal food.' She thumped a tin of Pedigree Chum down on the worktop to prove her point.

'I haven't been shopping yet.'

She rolled her eyes. 'It's always the same when I come to stay, but this time the house is worse than ever.'

She had a point. The state of the house had started to depress even me, which was another reason why I'd spent more time at the Frog and Ferret lately. I'd been so overwhelmed with worry about my finances that I'd allowed my usual sloppy standards of housework to slide from scruffy to yucky. 'I suppose it could do with a clear-out.'

'Suppose? Clodagh, if there were hygiene police you'd be arrested and sent to jail for ten years.'

'Now you're exaggerating.' I wished I'd spent longer on my walk.

Nigel lapped some water from his dish and sank down in his basket as if baffled by the behaviour of the crazy humans.

Immi rummaged in the drawer of the dresser. 'Am I?' She rattled around in the contents and pulled out a tin of tuna. 'Expired three years ago.' She delved again. 'Three odd earrings with no fasteners, a chipped glass paperweight, a pair of pliers, and a packet of chocolate buttons that have all melted together.' She plunked each item down on the dresser top with a bang as she recited the contents.

'Okay, so I'm untidy.' I'd been looking for those pliers the other day.

She braced her hands on her hips. 'You've always been untidy but this is scary, Clo. I know I'm a selfish cow and I just flit down here whenever I've got problems and then bugger off again, but I do care about you.'

Tears prickled at the backs of my eyes. I knew she cared about me. For all my mutterings and mumblings about Immi, I owed her big time. When Jonathan dumped me it was Immi who had dropped everything to be with me, Immi who had comforted me in the black, horrible weeks that had followed. The weeks that even now we didn't talk about.

That was the real reason I would do the television show. Not for the sanctuary, although I had to do it for my animals too, but for my sister. To pay her back some of the debt I owed her for all the things she'd done for me.

Immi and I stayed up late cleaning out the kitchen and polishing the sitting room. Dave wasn't pleased with our bustling around his domain and tidying things up. He was still sulking about the invasion of his personal space earlier in the day. When he'd lived at the brothel he'd been kept in a small room the madam used for booking clients and providing phone-sex lines.

He'd been rehomed five times since Madam had been sent to prison but, like a boomerang, he kept coming back. I was attempting to retrain him by keeping him in a calm atmosphere and not using any bad language around him. Unfortunately, it didn't seem to be working, judging by the ripeness of his comments when we moved his cage to clean up.

'One more word and I'll turn you into a feather duster,' Immi threatened.

'Up yours, stupid tart!' Dave huffed up and down on his perch, eyeing her malevolently before firing a chunk of fresh apple at her head.

While we cleaned, we talked, taking a short break in the middle to ring Gloria and check she was okay.

I'd been worried that she might have been hassled by the press for comments or put under pressure to reveal Immi's whereabouts. Fortunately, she was fine and sounded quite philosophical about Immi's problems.

'Keep an eye on her for me, Clodagh. She's promised me she won't drink but you know what she's like. She means well but she's weak-willed like her father.'

I gave her my promise. Gloria rarely spoke about Immi's real dad. They'd divorced when Immi had been a toddler and I knew he'd died of alcohol poisoning shortly after Gloria and my dad had married.

One of Gloria's fears was that Immi might have inherited her father's fondness for drink. Immi always denied she had a problem and most of the time she was fine, but then she'd go and have a drop too much, as she'd done on the chat show, and then everything would go pear-shaped. I hoped this current fiasco might prove to be her wake-up call.

I would have overslept the next morning if Tom hadn't hammered on the back door for the key to the equipment shed. Tom was semi-retired and came every Sunday to cut all the grass, do small repairs around the place, and tackle any jobs that required a bit of brawn. His wife, Val, also gave a hand on the gate, looking after visitors and generally helping out.

I staggered down the stairs, bleary-eyed, and mumbled an apology as I opened the door.

'Your sister still here, then? I hear there was quite a commotion yesterday. We were on a day trip to Weston with the senior citizens' club and missed the excitement.' Tom peered round me as if he expected Immi to come wafting towards him. I hadn't the heart to tell him that my sister wasn't usually an early morning kind of person.

'Yes. She's asleep.'

'Blimey, been having a tidy-up, have you?' Surprise was etched on his wizened face as he took in the sight of my freshly cleaned kitchen. 'Fair improvement, this is.'

'Well, it was about time.' I pulled my dressing gown round me a bit more tightly. The morning air felt nippy on my pyjama-clad legs.

'By the way, I noticed somebody has been having a go at the sign up on the main road again. Spray-painted it, they have.'

My heart sank. I'd already paid a small fortune for the brown tourist-destination road signs that directed people to the sanctuary. I'd also invested in another sign, equally costly, on the main road showing a picture of the donkeys and giving our opening times. The cost of repairing the sign would probably wipe out all the money we'd taken yesterday. First impressions were important, however, and it would have to be done.

'Great. Some people are such idiots.'

Tom took the keys to the shed and wandered away, after I'd promised to bring him a cup of tea once I was dressed. A couple of hours later, with the chores taken care of and Tom merrily mowing the picnic field, I headed back into my shiny kitchen to search for something for breakfast.

Much to my surprise my sister was up, dressed and seated at the table sipping a mug of tea.

'You're up early.' Immi usually got up late and went to bed late, whereas I usually got up early and, unless I had a shift at the Frog and Ferret, was knackered by eight in the evening.

'We've a lot to do today.'

'We?' What was the 'we'? She hadn't mentioned anything last night during her *How Clean is Your House?* episode.

'You need groceries, new clothes and, should the hairdresser down at the shopping mall be open, a haircut.' She ticked the items off on her fingers as she spoke.

'And how do I pay for those, O wise one? And who looks after the animals while I'm getting them?' Resentment began to bubble in my stomach. My warm feelings of gratitude towards Immi from yesterday began to evaporate.

'Marty spotted me some cash yesterday before she left, and isn't that annoying woman in the beanie hat coming again today?'

I guessed she meant Susie. Jade had Sundays off. Usually Susie and Val were around to look after the entrance and keep an eye on things.

'I suppose so. Anyway, what's wrong with my clothes?' As soon as the words had left my lips I wished I could take them back. I knew perfectly well what was wrong with my clothes.

Okay, so I had a few nice things, but the suit I'd worn

for the bank interview was a case in point. Immi had told me I looked like Melanie Griffith in *Working Girl* when I'd put it on. And although Jack had said he liked it, I suppose he might have been fibbing. As if by magic my memory conjured up the warm look that had been in his eyes when he'd admired my legs, and my body heated. No, he'd been telling the truth.

'If you have to ask me that then you're in worse shape than I thought.' Immi finished her tea. 'Besides, you're going to be on national television tomorrow and people will know you're my sister.' She rose and plonked her empty mug on the sparkling clean stainless steel drainer.

'What's that supposed to mean?'

She paused in the doorway and turned to face me. 'It means I want you to look good. You have a really pretty face and under those horrific jeans you've got legs most women would kill for. This interview is about the sanctuary as well – you do want more sponsorship, don't you?'

She sailed off down the hall before I could respond.

'By the way, you'd better hurry and change if we're going shopping.'

I caught a glimpse of her mane of blond hair as she hung over the banister to shout her instructions. Nigel gave a little whine from his basket under the counter as if he understood that I would be leaving him for a few hours. I sympathised. I'd have liked to whine and hide under the counter too, but I was pretty sure my sister wouldn't let me.

Mutinously, I traipsed upstairs and swapped my work

jeans for clean ones and my checked work shirt for a fitted pink T-shirt. My lack of interest in all things sartorial had started when Jonathan had dumped me. He'd dictated my clothing choices for so long that I couldn't make decisions any more. Everything I had owned he'd chosen or influenced, so Immi had made a ceremonial bonfire of my wardrobe. Ever since I'd had no desire to look nice – I'd simply wanted to be invisible.

Tom agreed to walk Nigel while I was out and Val said she'd look after the gate. I knew they would be fine with everything but I still felt uneasy about leaving. Susie hadn't yet arrived with the fresh supply of ice cream when Immi dragged me to my car and shoved me inside.

There were a few paparazzi hanging around the entrance when we swept past in the car on our way to the shopping centre. Immi was fully prepared in her obligatory 'celebrity shades'. I, on the other hand, probably resembled someone with thyroid trouble thanks to the popping flashbulbs.

'Why are they using flash in daylight?' I asked as I turned on to the main road.

'The interior of the car might be too dark for the photos to come out, dummy. They take some pictures with the flash and some without to see which ones work best.' Immi settled her shades a little more firmly on the bridge of her nose.

'Oh.' Well, excuse me for asking.

The car park at the shopping centre was fairly quiet as the doors had barely opened for business when we rolled up. I grabbed a space near the entrance and switched off the engine. 'What do we do if people recognise you?' Immi was pretty famous now thanks to the kerfuffle on the chat show. I had visions of us being mobbed in the lingerie department of Marks and Sparks. The prospect of it brought me out in hives.

'I'll smile, sign autographs and keep moving.' She checked her lippy in the mirror on the sun visor.

'We'd better get going, then. I'd like to get back as soon as possible in case Val and Tom get swamped.' I wondered what the odds were of managing to escape from the shops in under an hour.

Immi swung her long legs out of the passenger seat. 'The sanctuary will not fall apart simply because you are taking a little time off.'

I hurried after her as she strutted through the entrance. The shops were virtually deserted and Immi swept along, apparently oblivious of anyone who gave her a second look. She halted outside the hairdresser and waited for me to catch her up.

Unease clawed at my insides. I usually went to the small, old-fashioned salon on the outskirts of town. Not that I had my hair cut very often, as I tried to save money where I could and looked after my hair myself with the aid of the kitchen scissors. This one seemed shiny, scary, modern and expensive.

My sister commandeered the services of the rather bored-looking girl with the trendy hair sitting at the reception desk. The next thing I knew I was swathed in a caramel-coloured nylon gown and having my hair washed while my sister discussed styles with the 'artistic director'.

Immi settled herself on one of the squashy cream leather sofas with a celebrity magazine as the stylist chopped pieces out of my hair. I had to admit that by the time they were done it actually looked quite good. How I was going to keep it looking the same way I wasn't so sure, but the stylist assured me that with some specialist products I'd be fine. A worryingly large number of bottles were loaded into a carrier bag, Immi peeled an equally large number of banknotes from a roll in her purse, and we headed back out of the salon.

'Now we need to get you some clothes,' Immi announced.

There were a lot more people wandering up and down outside the shops now. My sister attracted quite a bit of attention as we walked towards the department store at the far end of the arcade. I felt quite self-conscious as I trotted along at her side. Immi, however, appeared oblivious of the nudges, whispering, and head-turning as we made our way towards the ladies' fashions.

'Couldn't we go home now? I'm sure I've got something I could wear tomorrow.' The shopping centre always made me feel claustrophobic. I usually shopped in the more run-down area of town near the street market. The prices were lower and it was outdoors. Here, with a little knot of people trailing in our wake, I could feel the panic starting to flutter in my stomach.

'You're already wearing the best things in your

wardrobe.' Immi started rattling clothes hangers along a shiny rail of tops.

'I am not.' She had started to seriously annoy me.

'Okay, so I'm exaggerating, but you do need to find something nice for the show.' She abandoned the designer tops and moved instead to a rack of jeans. I blinked at the price tags. The cost of one pair of jeans would keep Nigel in dog food for the rest of his natural life. My idea of a designer label was Florence and Fred at Tesco.

'Won't the TV studio be able to find me something from wardrobe?' I suggested.

'You really don't want to be seen in the weather girl's cast-offs.' She sniffed.

A couple of young women approached Immi, and I watched from behind a carousel of skirts while she signed autographs and chatted to them.

'We need to find the personal shopper for the store,' she said after the girls had walked away, giggling excitedly as they peered at the snaps Immi had posed for on their mobile phones.

As if by magic a store assistant appeared and we were shepherded to a part of the store that I didn't know existed. We were installed in a small private room complete with clothes rail and complimentary coffee and biscuits. Immi issued instructions to a very pleasant lady in a suit while I nibbled on a shortbread finger and wondered if I was having some kind of mad dream.

I made one last try. 'Immi, I'm not sure about this. I could have gone to Primark and picked something up there.'

She flicked her hair back in a careless gesture. 'You are such a killjoy. Relax and have some fun, will you? You need a new outfit and I need to pick something up for myself. The photo shoot we did yesterday may well haul my arse out of a crisis, so do me a favour and enjoy yourself. Oh, and *I* do not shop at Primark.'

Seeing the determined set of her chin and the steely glint in her eyes I knew from past experience that further resistance was futile. I was doomed to a morning of enjoying myself – Immi-style.

The personal shopper staggered into the room, barely able to see over the pile of clothes in her arms. She hung the clothes along the rail, grouping them in sizes and colours.

'I'll go and fetch the other things while you look through the selections.' She flashed a beaming smile at Immi and a slightly doubtful one at me as I slopped a bit of coffee down the front of my T-shirt.

'She's bringing more?' I hissed at Immi as the door closed behind the assistant. There couldn't be that many items left in the store.

Immi took no notice and began to sort out the contents of the rail, discarding garments on to the spare armchair with cheerful abandon.

'Too bright, too tight, too boring . . . oh, my life, what was the woman thinking? Too cheap, hate the buttons . . .'

By the time the assistant came back clutching yet another pile of hangers Immi had already dismissed two-thirds of the original selection. I waited while they conferred and the shopper left to take the rejected clothes back into the store.

'Right, I've found you some tops and some jeans and trousers. Go and try them on.' Immi thrust a bundle of garments into my arms and pointed me towards the curtained changing area at the end of the room.

As I stood in the middle of the mirrored walls of the changing area I remembered why I didn't like shopping for clothes. Immi peeked round the curtain.

'What's taking you so long?' She eyed me critically. 'That's hideous. Try the indigo Levi's and the pale blue top.'

She closed the curtain and I pulled a face in the mirror. She did have an eye for clothes, though. I had no confidence about what I should wear, hence my hodge-podge wardrobe. I figured since I worked with animals it didn't matter too much. Plus, I really didn't want people to notice me.

An hour or so and several carrier bags later we emerged back into the shopping centre. Now we were definitely beginning to attract attention. Several people snapped Immi on their phones and, more worryingly, others started to follow a few steps behind us in little groups. I could hear the buzz of excitement over the ghastly piped muzak.

'Time we left.' Immi quickened her pace until we were outside the entrance and inside my little car.

'Get your toe down before any of these cretins try to block us in,' she instructed. She wedged the carriers on her lap and slipped her shades back in place, even managing a regal wave as I reversed out of the parking space. Thankfully, I didn't hit anyone and we were free.

'That wasn't so bad, was it? What shall we do next?' she asked.

'We're going home.' I'd had enough of Immi's media circus. My hands were clammy with sweat and I must have aged ten years with anxiety.

'We need groceries. Unless you want to call in somewhere for Sunday lunch?'

'Marty said you had to stay out of anywhere with alcohol, remember?' No doubt someone would run to the press if we visited the local pub for lunch. Even if Immi stuck to lemonade – which was doubtful, knowing Immi – there would be the implication that she couldn't keep away from drink. 'Why don't I take you back to the house and then I'll do a run to the supermarket,' I suggested.

She pulled a face. 'I'd rather come with you. We only need to do a quick trolley dash.'

I hesitated. I'd rather have dropped her off and gone on my own, in case we attracted the kind of attention that we'd suffered at the shopping centre.

'It's on our way home,' she wheedled. 'We'll be in and out in two minutes.'

'Okay. Two minutes.'

I should have known better. Immi pushed the trolley

inside the store while I rang Tom on my mobile to check if everything was okay back at the sanctuary. Apparently Susie had restocked the ice creams and drinks and the gate was doing brisk business.

'Val's hardly had a minute to knit the ribbing on my new sweater what with selling all yon animal feed and fizzy pop,' Tom informed me.

Normally the gate was so quiet that Val could finish a whole Fair Isle jumper without breaking a sweat while she sat there. It sounded positive. We might even take enough to pay for all the shopping Immi was likely to want.

'I'll be back soon.' I dropped my phone inside my bag and scooted off to find my sister.

Immi didn't shop like a normal person. Normal people go into a supermarket and mooch up and down the aisles dropping stuff into their trolley as they go. If they are especially organised they have lists. These people have not shopped with Immi.

Unless you've ever seen her in action it's hard to explain what she does. She zigzags around the store, distracted by every new sign and shooting off in different directions, quite often abandoning her trolley while she goes to collect something from the other side of the shop and then spending twenty minutes trying to find it again. In short, it's a nightmare.

True to form, while I'd been talking to Tom, she'd disappeared. Muttering under my breath I set off down the fruit and veg aisle to look for her. I caught a glimpse of her heading towards the bakery and quickened my pace.

'Oof.' In my haste to catch her up I hadn't paid full attention to where I was going.

'Clodagh!'

Uh-oh. I'd cannoned right into the one person I didn't want to meet right now – Jack. Ever since he'd walked out of my house I'd been visualising various scenarios in my head about what I'd say to break the ice between us again. Most of them had involved me writing a note or leaving a message on his voicemail. None of them had involved crashing into him in front of the melon stand at Tesco.

He still had his hand on the top of my arm to steady me. 'I, um, was looking for Immi.'

He released my arm as if surprised to find himself still holding on to me. My skin tingled from the gentle pressure of his fingers. 'Yes, of course.' He frowned. 'You look different.'

'I've had my hair cut.' I'd had awkward conversations with Jack before but this felt excruciating. All around us people ambled past with trolleys and baskets, or leaned in to pick up fruit from the racks behind us. 'I, um, wanted to apologise for yesterday.' An elderly woman rammed my ankle with her shopping cart, sending me hopping inelegantly towards a display of tomatoes.

The crease on his forehead deepened as he took hold of my arm again and steered me to a safer position in a quiet corner next to the mushrooms.

'I thought you made your opinion perfectly clear yesterday.' His voice was cool.

'I don't think I did.'

He moved back to allow a man in a flat cap to pick up one of the packs of mushrooms from the shelf.

'Clo, do we need fruit juice?' Immi skidded her trolley to a halt at my side. 'Hello, Jack. Has Clo told you we're going to be on breakfast telly tomorrow?' She broke the end off a stick of French bread that had poked out of the shopping in her trolley and nibbled at the crust. 'God, I'm starving.'

'We could use some orange juice – and you shouldn't eat stuff until we've paid for it.' I wished she'd buzz off. It was hard enough to talk to him with other people reaching around us all the time without having Immi crash the conversation as well.

'Orange juice, gotcha.' She zoomed off down the aisle.

I took a deep breath and tried again. 'I was attempting to apologise.'

A shelf-stacker pushed a silver metal cage loaded with trays of vegetables next to Jack and started to refill the shelves.

'This is ridiculous. Could we go somewhere for a minute, so we can talk without being interrupted?' I waited for Jack's response. If he was still upset with me he'd say no. I desperately wanted him to say yes and at least give me a chance to redeem myself.

'I suppose we could go to the coffee shop.'

My heart did a crazy little skip of relief. At least he was going to give me the opportunity to explain and put things right.

The in-store coffee shop was next to the entrance so it wasn't far away and luckily there appeared to be plenty of empty tables. We sat down at the nearest one without bothering to go and buy anything. I couldn't read Jack's thoughts. His usual ready smile had vanished and I didn't know the sombre-faced man opposite me.

'Okay, spit it out.' He leaned back in the narrow plastic seat, his eyes half closed as if he wasn't really interested in what I might be about to say.

'I didn't mean to upset you or imply that I didn't trust you when you offered to sponsor the sanctuary. It's true I wasn't sure about your motives for wanting to help me, but that didn't mean I thought you were dishonest.'

He opened his eyes. 'Go on.'

'I'm not very good at trusting people. I should have asked you about your interest in the sanctuary instead of jumping to conclusions. Like I said, I'm sorry. I . . . I didn't know about your dad till someone told me.' I waited for his reaction.

A small muscle jumped in the corner of his jaw. 'I see people are still gossiping, then.' His tone was icy, completely unlike the warm, fun-loving man I'd started to get to know.

'It wasn't gossip. I couldn't understand why you were so upset. I don't know any of the details of what happened and I haven't tried to find out. It's none of my business.' I didn't mention Lovett's or any of the other information Jade had shared with me.

His gaze never left my face. 'This isn't the time or place to tell you about my dad.'

'You don't have to tell me anything at all.' Once one person shared a secret, in my experience, they expected the recipient of the secret to share something in return. I wasn't sure I was ready to do that – or if I would ever be able to tell anyone else my secret.

'No, I think maybe we haven't done enough talking – not about the things that really matter.' Jack said.

'Maybe. The date at the Apple Loft wasn't very successful, was it?' I felt he had a point.

For the first time since I'd crashed into him the corner of his mouth tilted in a faint smile. 'It was memorable.'

A rush of desire swept through my body.

'This is a customer service announcement. Would Clodagh Martin please come to the customer service desk? That's a call for Clodagh Martin. Thank you.'

The in-store PA system boomed out over the music and infomercials that had been playing in the background.

'That'll be Immi. Oh, dear God, please don't let her have caused a scene or got herself arrested for something.' I shot to my feet. My mind raced with all the potentially illegal or crazy situations my sister could have landed herself in while I'd been talking to Jack. Taking a swig from a bottle of alcopop or eating grapes before she'd paid, perhaps. Knowing my sister it could be anything. I had visions of her being escorted from the store in handcuffs under a blanket to avoid photographers.

'Clo, wait, I'll come with you.' Jack's hand closed warmly on mine, offering me instant reassurance. My pulse speeded up a notch at this proof that he still appeared to care about me.

There was a crowd around the customer service desk. A bemused security guard appeared to be directing people away in an attempt to dispel the throng.

'Your sister has a gift for attracting attention,' Jack muttered as we jostled our way towards the counter.

Immi, of course, was at the centre of the commotion. She posed and signed autographs on the backs of various boxes and packets from people's shopping. Thankfully she didn't appear to be chained to a store detective. She spotted us making our way through the crowd and waggled her fingers in greeting.

'I'm going to kill her.' In no time at all my sister had managed to draw a crowd and throw the supermarket into chaos. How I was going to extricate her and our shopping I had no idea.

The customer service woman looked as if she would quite like to kill Immi too, judging by the murderous expression on her face. She picked up the mike and made another appeal.

'This is a customer service announcement,' she boomed. 'Would the crowd in front of the customer information desk please disperse? In the event of an emergency you are blocking the exit. This is a breach of the health and safety regulations.'

There were people with baskets and trolleys everywhere. Some were trying to get to Immi, others had simply stopped to see what the fuss was about. Either way it all served to add to the mayhem.

'You'd better go and get her.' Jack shook his head at the chaos.

I battled my way to Immi's side, getting a sharp dig in the ribs from an obese woman with a wire basket full of salad for my trouble. 'What are you doing? In and out of here in two minutes, you said.'

'It's not my fault. I was recognised in the yoghurt aisle and before I knew it I was trapped. The security man got me here and then they put out the announcement.' She scribbled her name on a box of cornflakes. 'Everyone's been very nice to me but it's a bit mad.' She smiled for a teenage boy who wanted to snap her with his phone.

'What happened to the shopping?'

'Oh, the security man got the staff to take it through a till so it's all bagged and paid for. You just need to put it in the car and then we can go.'

'And how do we get past everyone?'

She smiled sweetly for another picture. 'Put the groceries in the car and come back. The security man says he'll get some of the lads from the warehouse to keep people back while we leave. Jack can always help. He's pretty muscled.'

I caught a glimpse of Jack working his way towards us. He appeared to be trying not to grin at Immi's blasé instructions and presumably her description of him. I gritted my teeth and struggled the few feet to the counter where the customer service assistant pointed me to the mound of shopping bags in a trolley behind the desk.

Jack took charge of the trolley and forged a path out of the store to the car park. I tagged along behind him knowing just how Dorothy must have felt when she was swept up by a tornado and deposited in Oz.

'Why do I let her talk me into these things? I knew I should have taken her back to the sanctuary and come out on my own.' I wrenched the boot open and started to throw in the carriers.

Susie would have a fit if she saw the plastic bags. My Christmas present from her had been four natural cotton reusable eco-friendly bags. Of course, being me, I kept forgetting to use them and had to remember to hide the supermarket carriers. Jade, on the other hand, had given me some lovely and surprisingly expensive lipgloss which had been far more useful. Val had knitted me a woolly hat and matching gloves.

Jack handed me a carrier that seemed to be full of Special K bars. 'I don't know. It's one of the things I find so mysterious about you. One minute you're confident, businesslike and totally in control of the sanctuary and the direction you want it to take, and the next moment you're lacking in any confidence at all.'

I could feel my cheeks burning as I accepted the bag from him and tucked it in the car. 'I told you, I find it hard to trust people.'

He passed over the last of the shopping. 'Do I get to find out why?'

I pulled the boot shut and caught hold of the handle of the trolley to push it into the bay.

Jack blocked my way. 'Well?'

'I don't know.'

'I thought we'd agreed while we were in the coffee shop that we needed to spend some time talking.'

He was so close to me that I could feel the heat that

radiated from his body, sending frissons of excitement into my own. 'I suppose we did.'

'Tomorrow night?'

Oh, fishcakes. I wasn't going to get out of this. 'Okay.'

'Great. Let's go and rescue your sister.' His lips brushed my forehead with the sweetness of a vow and my stomach did a flip-flop of desire.

For a brief moment I was tempted to leave Immi to save herself so I could give in to my urge to drag Jack into the back of my Fiat and have my wicked way with him. Instead I dutifully trotted back inside the store to extricate my sister from her fans.

By the time Immi had been safely escorted to the car, Jack had gone. In all the hustle and bustle I didn't even see him leave, which left me feeling kind of disconsolate and unsettled. On the one hand I was happy that we'd chatted, but I was nervous too now that I'd committed to meeting him for a longer, more intimate encounter.

Back at the house Immi disappeared to make phone calls and send emails, leaving me to unload the grocery shopping. I didn't recognise half the things she'd bought. My usual diet consisted of own-brand staple products and cereal topped up by free meals at the Frog and Ferret when I had a shift there. Now I had a fridge full of sushi, which looked a bit odd to me. I can't say I've ever fancied eating raw fish and seaweed, despite my sister's assurances about its healthy qualities. I'd always thought it sounded like something seals would eat – give me Captain Birdseye any day.

My sister, however, had been correct about one thing. The sanctuary had survived my absence without being visited by any great disaster, and Tom and Val happily agreed to care for the animals the next morning while I was at the TV studio with Immi, so that was one thing less for me to worry about.

Nigel greeted me with barks of happiness as I staggered into the house laden with carrier bags. Clive ignored me in the way cats often do when they're a bit put out. Dave soon made his feelings known when I went to give him some fresh apple.

'About time, you dopey tart!'

I carried my new clothes up to my room and hooked the hangers carefully on the wardrobe door so they wouldn't get creased. Through the bedroom wall I could hear the murmur of Immi's voice and her laughter as she chatted on the phone. I changed out of my going-shopping clothes and into my work jeans ready to take Nigel for a long walk before evening chores and supper. Snatches of my sister's conversation wafted into my room and I wondered who she was talking to. I found out when I opened my bedroom door and overheard her say: 'I'll call you later, Marcus. Smooches to you too. Miss you.'

I crept downstairs and slipped a lead on to Nigel's collar. I hadn't seen that one coming – Immi and Marcus. I knew she'd fancied him and he'd seemed quite taken with her but I'd assumed he'd move on to the next thing once he'd returned to preying on the faux-pas of the high and mighty. I'd obviously been mistaken.

Val and Tom had locked the public entrance and completed the daily tasks of refilling the soap dispensers next to the taps, emptying the bins and picking up the litter before going home. I decided to take Nigel for a good run on the far paddock before tending to my share of the chores.

Tom had mentioned some damage to the boundary fence that he'd spotted when he'd mown the grass. I hoped it wasn't going to be anything too drastic or costly. At the moment I used the field as a place for picnics, where children could have a kick-around with a ball without disturbing the animals. If the fencing was broken I might have to keep the field closed off, since it ran alongside the main road – I couldn't risk someone getting hurt.

Nigel loped along beside me, sniffing happily at clumps of late buttercups. I would miss him when his owner recovered and took him home. It had been too long since I'd had a dog of my own. Tom had mown the field in broad swathes, leaving the cut grass to dry on the surface. The air was redolent with green scents and a cloud of tiny gnats danced in the shade of the large oak tree.

A couple of wild rabbits eyed us warily from the long grass that fringed the edge of the field. Nigel quickened his stride and they melted away into the undergrowth. I soon saw the damage that Tom had warned me about. It looked as if the phantom vandals had struck again; they'd prised off and broken several of the slats, leaving gaping holes in two of the fence panels.

Fortunately there was some strong netting in the shed so I could get Tom to make a temporary repair, but it was still annoying to feel someone was deliberately targeting the sanctuary. I scrambled through the long grass bordering the mown area to take a closer look at the damage. It appeared that someone had smashed the wood with a hammer or a large rock, judging by the shattered splinters and jagged edges.

Nigel sniffed around the hole and I held him back in case he hurt himself on the wood. Something purple caught my eye and I realised a scrap of wool had snagged on a splinter. I pulled the strands free so I could examine them more closely. The wool was a peculiar greenish mauve and I was certain that I'd seen someone I knew wearing something that colour recently.

I tucked the wool away inside my jacket pocket and carried on walking round the boundary of the field to check the rest of the fence. Once I'd satisfied myself that there was no more damage I made my way out of the paddock and back on to the path that led up to the private lane. Mr Curzon, the bank manager, had implied that the lane could be a valuable asset if I decided to sell my land as it would provide extra access to any development that took place.

There was a large metal five-bar gate that I was supposed to lock so no one could drive down into the yard at night. Lately I had been a touch lax about checking that the gate was closed and padlocked, but with the graffiti on the sign and the damage to the fence I decided I ought to be more security-conscious.

I looped Nigel's lead round the post and dragged the gate across the track, securing it with a chain so it couldn't be opened without the key. I'd need to remember to remind Immi that the TV studio car would have to collect us from the front of the house in the morning. Nigel sat and watched me, his hairy tail beating a tattoo in the dust as I hooked the keys on to the loop on the waistband of my jeans. I wasn't looking forward to accompanying Immi to the studio. Unlike my outgoing stepsister I struggled with being in the limelight. Even before Jonathan I'd been the wallflower and Immi the party girl. She had been the star of the school drama society; my job had been painting the scenery.

I plucked one of the long ears of grass from the side of the gate and nibbled the end as I walked with Nigel along the paths between the enclosures. Ever since Jonathan I'd been hiding out, content to stay in my own small world. Now, between them, Immi and Jack were forcing me out of my cosy, safe niche. I wasn't sure if I was ready.

I'd avoided relationships for over three years. On the rare occasions when I had gone on a date it had been casual and as part of a group. Jack made me feel things that I'd forgotten, stirred up old memories and emotions. Some of them – no, one of them – had been buried very deep. The only person who knew my ultimate secret was Immi. Now I had to decide if it was time to share that secret with Jack.

The cheeping of the smoke alarm as I passed the house told me that Immi had either burned some toast or attempted to cook supper. A chequered blue and white tea towel flapped smoke out of the back door.

'That stupid cooker. The back burner is like a flame thrower. Why you can't have a normal oven like other people, I'll never know.' She coughed for dramatic effect and sat down on the step.

'What have you been doing?'

The acrid smell of melting plastic filled the air. When I ventured inside I saw she'd managed to melt the handle of one of my knives by leaving it too close to the gas ring.

'I boiled some rice. I didn't see the knife was on the edge.' Luckily the smoke had dispersed when she'd opened the door. Dave was busy kicking up a fuss so I knew he hadn't been harmed by Immi's culinary disaster.

'I got distracted. There was only the stupid rice to cook; the fish is already prepared.'

I hadn't the heart to say I thought Clive's dish of KiteKat looked more appetising than the sushi.

'How did you get distracted?'

Immi flushed. 'I was on the phone.'

'Oh yes?' I started to attack the melted plastic with a metal fish slice in the hope that I could get rid of the mess before it hardened.

She scooped the rice from the pan and arranged it carefully in little decorative mounds on the plates. 'It was Marcus.'

I managed to peel off the last bit of gunk from the cooker top and dropped it into the bin. 'Really?' I felt quite proud of the note of offhand disinterest I managed to inject into my tone.

Immi looked guiltily flushed. 'I got on really well with him while he was here. Well, mainly I felt guilty about whacking him on the head so I had to be nice. Anyway, we hit it off and he's meeting us at the studio after we've finished filming tomorrow.' She rushed the last part out.

'That's nice. Does Marty know?' I washed my hands ready for supper. I wasn't certain it was nice or even if it was a good idea.

Immi placed the sushi platter in the centre of the table. 'She knew we were getting on well together.'

I thought she sounded a touch evasive. I seemed to recall Marty distinctly telling us to watch out for Marcus. He had appeared pleasant enough but he was still press. We didn't know him and he could well have a hidden agenda for wanting to get closer to Immi.

'Be careful. He's a photo-journalist, remember? One who makes his living from celebrities?' I took a seat opposite my sister.

She reached out with a fork and harpooned a couple of pieces of sushi. 'I'm not stupid. He's not like that bloke who dated Britney Spears when she had her meltdown.' There was a defiant tilt to her chin and her mouth was set in stubborn lines. It was the expression she'd always worn as a teenager when Dad had told her not to do something she'd set her heart on. Like when she'd sneaked out to go to a party at a nightclub when she was fourteen and had been brought home by the police at three in the morning when the club got raided.

'I didn't say you were stupid. Marcus is very good looking.' I chose my words carefully. I knew it would do no good to argue with her when she was in one of her belligerent moods.

'Yeah.' Her face softened a little and her eyes glazed dreamily. 'So is your Jack,' she added.

'He's not my Jack.' I peered at the sushi and tried to identify the smallest, least threatening-looking piece.

Immi swallowed her food. 'He could be yours. What did you say to him about the other day, when he walked out?'

'I told him I'd jumped the gun. He's taking me out tomorrow night. He feels we need to talk, be more honest and open with one another.' I prodded the fish on my plate and gave a shrug to show her I wasn't bothered. It wouldn't fool her for a moment but the illusion made me feel better.

Her eyes widened. 'Are you going to tell him about Jonathan?'

'I'm not sure. I might tell him some of it.' My stomach rolled when I thought about reliving those memories. Or maybe that was just the sushi.

Immi dropped her cutlery with a clatter and jumped up to hug me. 'It'll be fine. I think Jack will understand.' She resumed her seat.

I hoped she was right.

The make-up lady tutted and fussed over the dark shadows beneath my eyes as she prepared my face for my TV debut. I hadn't been asleep for long when the limo had rolled up to collect us. Immi had given me strict instructions on what to do and say during the interview.

The rather nervous-looking youth who'd greeted us in the reception area had informed us we had a three-minute slot right after the showbiz gossip and before a piece on the royal family. We'd been led away along a maze of corridors, offered a cup of tea and left to the tender mercies of the make-up lady.

Immi had been through wardrobe and was dressed and ready for the sound man to wire her up. I was still swathed in a voluminous cape with tissues tucked under my chin. The make-up artist added yet another layer of gunk to my face before declaring herself satisfied. An alien being stared back at me from the mirror. I decided not to smile in case my mask cracked and fell off.

The nervous youth appeared in the make-up room and whisked Immi off to get wired up while I got sent to wardrobe. Apparently the top I'd planned to wear was 'strobing'. I wasn't sure what that meant until the lighting guy told me it would induce migraines and motion sickness in the viewers due to the effect of the lights on the fabric. So much for my sister's attempt to make me look fashionable. It would seem I was destined to wear the weather girl's cast-offs after all.

With two minutes to go I was bundled into a borrowed top with cables hooked under my bra and tucked in my waistband. The lad, who informed me he was a 'runner', then led us along a narrow corridor and into the studio proper. By now I was practising my anti-panic-attack breathing exercises so hard I sounded like an obscene phone caller.

The studio didn't look at all how I'd imagined. The sofa where the presenters sat was in a small, brightly lit area with a backdrop behind it. Another section had a screen where the weather girl stood to do her slot. The rest of the room was in darkness. We picked our way carefully over mounds of trailing cable and waited out of shot while the presenters finished the linking piece.

The cameras panned away to the weather girl. This was the cue for Immi and me to be hustled forward to take our positions on the couch next to the showbiz reporter. People swarmed over us like ants, dabbing skin, smoothing hair and straightening wires. My heart rate kicked up another notch and my palms felt soggy with perspiration. The heat from the studio lights didn't help.

Immi seemed as cool, calm and collected as ever, presumably in complete contrast to her last ill-fated appearance on a TV show. The weather girl finished her forecast and the cameras turned on us. This was it – we were live on air.

15

The interview started with most of the questions being directed at Immi. She handled them very well, I thought, explaining that she'd been taking medication that had clashed with alcohol. The bit about the medication was news to me but I supposed it was the line that Marty had come up with to excuse her behaviour. This was the cue for them to show footage of the incident.

I tried not to appear shocked but it was the first time I'd seen it and I wanted to wince. Immi had the grace to blush, but although she apologised to the chat-show host she didn't say sorry to Kirk. I wondered if seeing herself behaving badly would impact on her drinking habits. It was probably the first time she'd seen her behaviour the way others saw it.

The presenters were quite kind in their questioning and didn't challenge her half as much as they could have done. Marty must have given Immi some coaching because she answered all the criticisms well and gave the impression that she deeply regretted the whole incident.

'And your sister turned to you in her time of crisis?' The female presenter shifted her attention to me.

'Yes. Immi and I have always been very close,' I squeaked out in response.

'A little bird has told us that you have an animal sanctuary?'

'Yes, Rainbow Ridge. We take in unwanted animals.' I managed to sound a bit more normal with my second answer. Although, I mean, duh, of course an animal sanctuary takes in unwanted animals – what else would it do? I could have done with some coaching from Marty too.

'Clodagh does a fantastic job,' Immi chimed in. 'She takes in all the animals no one else wants and if she can't rehome them they have a home for life at the sanctuary. Rainbow Ridge is open to the public and relies on sponsorship and visitor support to keep going.'

'And Imogen helps you out at the sanctuary?' The presenter's voice held a note of faint disbelief.

'Immi has always offered me a lot of support. Animal welfare is a cause close to her heart.' I felt pleased with my answer. I hadn't lied, as Immi really was soft-hearted when it came to animals. She would never hurt one for all her grumblings about my pets.

'What a shame you didn't bring one or two of the smaller ones to the studio with you,' the male presenter chipped in.

I tried to imagine Dave in the studio and managed a weak smile at the suggestion.

'I'd love to do more, but my work keeps me very busy.

However, Clodagh's planning a huge open day soon to raise some much needed funds for her animals, and obviously I'll be helping her organise everything.' Immi flashed the camera a big, beaming smile.

'Oh, that sounds wonderful! Perhaps you'd like to tell our viewers the date. I'm sure lots of people would love to come along and show you some support.' The female presenter jumped back in; perhaps she sensed my hopelessness as an interview subject. Either that or she wanted to rein Immi in a touch.

What? We hadn't set a date for an open day. We'd only talked about it briefly when Immi had been helping me draft a business plan for my abortive meeting with my bank manager. There was nothing definite.

'It's going to be held on the last Saturday of this month. We'd welcome anyone who would like to make a donation or have a stall, wouldn't we, Clodagh?' Immi turned her smile on me.

'Oh, yes.' I tried to look confident and blasé, but my head was spinning with what my sister had just done. How were we going to plan an open day with stalls, refreshments and all the paraphernalia that would be entailed in a little under two weeks? Or, I should say, how was *I* going to plan it? Immi would no doubt be safely rehabilitated and immersed back in her celebrity lifestyle by then.

'That sounds wonderful; we must send a film crew along. I think everyone would like to see the animals – and you, of course, Imogen.'

Oh, fishcakes. Thank you very much, Immi.

'There's the phone number and web address for Rainbow Ridge Animal Sanctuary at the bottom of the screen now. We wish you every success with your open day and thank you so much for coming along today.' The presenter treated us to another view of her porcelain dental veneer and moved on to link to the next film segment.

Immi and I were immediately led back across the cables where the technicians met us and disconnected us from the microphones clipped to our garments.

'There, that went well, didn't it?' Immi chirped happily as she fished the end of the wire out of her waistband and handed it to the sound man.

I didn't answer her. What I needed to say to Immi would be better said without witnesses being present. My limbs felt shaky and jellified from the ordeal of appearing on TV and with the added bombshell of the open day my mind had blanked out with panic.

We declined the offer of another cup of tea and were told the car would be ready to take us home in half an hour. The researcher then parked us in reception and disappeared. I flopped down on a chair under the blank black and white photographic stares of celebrities past and present and glared at Immi.

'Oh, look, here's Marcus!'

Marcus strode towards us. His good looks succeeded in attracting flickers of attention from the glamorous girls on the receptionist desk.

'Hello, Clodagh.' He barely had time to acknowledge me before Immi leapt up and launched herself into his arms.

'Marcus, sweetie.' She greeted him as if she hadn't seen him for months.

'How long till your limo gets here?' He kissed her on the lips.

At least he didn't seem to have a camera with him and, credit where it's due, he appeared equally happy to see her.

'Thirty mins tops.' She kissed him back. I stayed on my leather and chrome chair and tried not to look like a gooseberry.

They sat huddled together in a corner of the sofa opposite mine holding hands and whispering. The two well-groomed girlies behind the polished reception desk kept flicking curious glances at us as people scurried in and out of the building. I hoped I might spot someone famous but my luck wasn't in.

I stared out through the smoked glass walls and prayed for the car to arrive. If I didn't get home soon there was every chance that the answerphone would explode with messages now the sanctuary number had been on screen. I also needed to explain to my trusty and hardworking volunteers how come I hadn't told them I was planning an open day before it had been announced on national television.

Eventually a man arrived at the desk and one of the posh girl receptionists summoned us to our car. Marcus gave Immi a lingering goodbye kiss and we headed back to Melhampton.

'Poor Marcus is working so hard. It was nice to see him even if it was only for a little while. He's got an important meeting at the studio offices this morning.' Immi sighed and snuggled back against the seat, a beatific smile on her lips.

'I'm glad you enjoyed yourself.'

She sat up straight and adjusted her seat belt. 'What's that supposed to mean?'

'Immi, you have just announced an open day at the sanctuary in less than two weeks' time. Have you any idea of the amount of work that will entail? My phone number and website have gone out on national television! My inbox and answerphone are probably already stuffed to the gills with messages.' All my simmering indignation bubbled up.

'Well, excuse me for trying to help. Weren't you the one telling me you were broke? Weren't you the one who asked me to help draw up a business plan?' She folded her arms. 'I've even managed to get you on TV. Have you any idea how many people would kill for a slot with so much exposure?'

'You could have discussed it with me first.' I should have known. My sister was a past mistress at making me feel everything was my fault even when she was the one in the wrong. It was the same when we were teenagers. She'd been the one sneaking out of the house to meet boys and go to clubs but I'd felt guilty because I knew what she was up to.

'There wasn't exactly the opportunity, was there? And we *had* talked about it when you took your plan to the bank.'

'And how do I manage all this on my own with only a

handful of volunteers?' It was typical Immi, diving into something head first without thinking about the consequences.

'You are so ungrateful! It's not that hard to make a few calls and get some posters and adverts out.' She glared at me. 'You are so scared of taking risks or trying new things it's untrue.'

'You don't think anything through.' I was so angry I could feel my cup of tea from earlier in the day reboiling in my gut.

'Oh? Such as?'

'Do you really think it's a good idea to date Marcus? He's paparazzi.' I didn't dislike Marcus but I couldn't see how Immi could possibly trust a man who made his living photographing and selling celebrity secrets.

'You know what your problem is? You don't trust anyone. No wonder Jack walked off. What are you going to do tonight when you see him? I bet you still won't tell him about Jonathan and what happened to you.'

I stared at her. Her words had cut me to the quick, more so because deep in my heart I knew she was right.

She sighed. 'Clo, I'm sorry. What you went through was horrible and terrible and I shouldn't have said that.' She bit her lip, her clear blue eyes sending me a mute appeal for forgiveness.

'Forget it.' I turned away from her. I felt too cross to forgive her right then. Ever since she was small I'd been forgiving her for her blunders and picking up the pieces of her impulsiveness. Even if what she'd said was true it hurt too much for me to simply let it go – not this time.

We finished the journey in silence. I hoped the driver hadn't heard our conversation; fortunately the car had one of those glass screens. Otherwise he'd be busy flogging his story to one of Marcus's chums and Immi would have undone all her image rebuilding with one furious row.

A note from Tom was pinned to the back door when we got home. I took it down and unlocked the house. Nigel bounded out to greet me as if I'd been gone for years instead of one morning. The answerphone light blinked furiously while I read Tom's message.

Phone has gone mad, have left messages for you to sort out. Found a pig tied to the sign when I got here. Have put him in the spare pen. Vet will call and check him out later. T.

I dropped the note on the table and headed off to the small paddock adjoining Mr Sheen's. We used it for quarantined animals and new arrivals with unknown medical histories. Inside, fast asleep on the grass, was a very sweet little Vietnamese pot-bellied pig. Someone had no doubt bought him as a house pet and lost interest. He appeared healthy enough, so with luck I might only get billed for a call-out and not for anything more major like expensive treatment or drugs.

I left the snoozing pig and returned to the answer-phone and all the messages. Immi was nowhere in sight. From the creaking boards overhead I assumed she'd gone straight to her room. She was probably packing her case. Armed with a giant mug of tea, a packet of rich tea fingers and a notepad, I started on the messages.

Two hours later I'd deleted several pervy ones and booked a face-painter, a clown, two bouncy castles, a hair-braider, a puppet show and several refreshment vans. I'd also taken details from half a dozen would-be sponsors. There were several other calls from the public wanting to know about adopting animals and visiting the sanctuary. I scribbled those numbers down for Susie to call and get addresses so we could mail out information packs.

The voices of a girl band wafted down from Immi's room. It sounded as if she planned to stay after all. Dave screeched from the lounge so I wandered through to talk to him.

He eyed me malignantly from his top perch. 'Sod you!'

'Nice to see you, too.' I pulled out the remainder of his decaying fruit from between the bars. It paid to whip it out quickly or he would get in a sharp little nip.

'Show us your tits!' He cackled with glee when I took a seat at the table and turned on the computer.

It had barely loaded up when the vet knocked on the front door to see my latest addition. The little pig proved to be in good heath and the vet shared my opinion that he was most probably a pet whose novelty value had worn off. I decided to leave him in the quarantine field for a while before introducing him to Rosie, my other pot-bellied piglet.

By the time the vet had gone I realised it was time for

the evening round of chores. I scooted round at record speed closing things up, checking the animals and making sure everything was secure. I needed to look at my email and deal with at least some of it before Jack arrived. It was tempting to call him and cancel but a mental image of Immi smirking and saying 'Told you you'd bottle out' deterred me.

A delicious smell of chicken soup met me when I returned to the house. The kitchen table was set for two and Immi stood at the stove stirring a large pan.

'I know you're going out but I thought you might want some supper,' she said. I guessed the soup was a peace offering.

'Thanks.' My stomach gave an appreciative grumble and I sprinted upstairs to wash and change.

Jack hadn't said if we were just going for a drink or if we were eating so it wasn't a bad idea to have some soup. Immi was unusually subdued and guilt pricked at my conscience. Maybe I had been mean. If the open day came off it would be an enormous boost to my coffers. I don't know why I hadn't thought about having one before. The extra sponsorship that had been promised already as a result of the morning's appearance would be a huge help towards paying the bills.

'I'll sort out the emails while you're out with Jack, if you like,' she offered as I sat down to eat.

'That would help a lot. Thanks.' I couldn't stay mad at her. 'I'm sorry, Imms. I shouldn't have blown up at you. I know you were trying to help.'

She shrugged and prodded her spoon into her soup.

'No, you were right. I should think a bit more before I dive into things. Friends?'

'Friends.' Our old childhood formula for making up after a fight made both of us smile. 'I've put a list of who's promised what next to the computer along with a note of donation and sponsorship offers.'

'I'll get started as soon as I've cleared up. Just go out and square things with Jack. He's a cool guy and he really likes you.'

I liked Jack too but I still wasn't certain that I was ready for tonight. It had been so long since I'd allowed anyone to get close to me that I was scared. No, more than scared – petrified. While I'd believed he was the enemy I'd had some form of defence to protect my heart from getting broken; now I'd begun to know him better those defences had been well and truly breached.

We'd barely finished eating when the front doorbell rang.

Jack stood on the path, devastatingly handsome in his dark jeans and crisp cotton shirt. 'The gate in the lane was locked.'

'I should have warned you, sorry.' My heart did that stupid crazy back-flip thing it always did at the sight of him.

'Are you ready to go?' His expression was sombre and he didn't crack one of his usual smiles.

'I'll go and get my jacket.' I darted down the hall to grab my coat and bag. I yelled goodbye to Immi and closed the front door behind me. My pulse raced as I walked beside him to the car. If I could have chickened out without losing face in front of Immi I would have. Tonight I was about to do something I hadn't done for years.

Trust someone.

'You didn't say where we were going tonight.' I slid into the passenger seat of the Range Rover.

'Didn't I?' Jack quirked an eyebrow at me as he started the engine.

Oh, heck, what had he got planned? 'No, you didn't.'

'Then it'll be a surprise.' A dimple appeared in his cheek as he smiled at last, making me feel breathlessly giddy.

My stomach churned with nerves and I couldn't think of any light conversation to break the ice.

'How was the TV interview?' Jack asked.

'Apparently I'm having an open day in less than two weeks' time.' I tried to stop myself from fiddling with the charm on my bag strap.

'Immi?' He glanced at me, his lips curving in a barely suppressed grin.

'How did you guess?'

He took the road leading away from town. 'I wanted to watch but something urgent came up with work.'

'You didn't miss much.'

'It's okay, I recorded it.' His grin widened even further at the look of horror on my face.

We drove along for a few miles in companionable silence along the quiet country lanes, until he turned the car into a narrow private road with a hedge running down one side and a grey stone wall on the other. I wondered where we were as he stopped the car outside a pair of wrought-iron gates set in stone pillars on either side of a driveway.

The gates opened as if by magic and we drove through only to stop in front of a large red-brick house with a stone-canopied porch. Brass carriage lanterns glowed with a welcoming golden light on either side of the door. Virginia creeper softened the brick façade. The leaves had already started to change from summer green into vibrant autumnal splendour.

Jack turned off the engine. 'Here we are.'

The sick feeling in the pit of my stomach increased. 'And where is here, exactly?'

'My house.' He opened the car door and climbed out.

I sat for a moment gawping up at the house. This mansion was his? Now I really did feel ill when I thought about his visits to my untidy little shoebox of a home.

He opened the car door for me. 'You can come inside, you know.'

I scrambled free of the seat belt to stand next to him. 'How long have you lived here?'

'About a year.'

We crunched across the wide sweep of gravel towards the large oak front door.

'It's very nice.' My heart raced and I hoped I wasn't about to have another panic attack.

'Appearances are deceiving. It wasn't like this when I bought it and there's still a lot of work to do.' He unlocked the door and stood back for me to walk inside ahead of him.

I found myself standing in a large hall lit by a single brass lamp which stood on what appeared to be a carved oak chest at the foot of the staircase. The walls were painted a rich, dark red and a Turkish carpet covered the varnished floorboards.

'This is very lovely.' In contrast, my hall had shoes heaped by the front door and smelt of dog.

'Come through to the sitting room. Most of the downstairs is done, but I'm still finishing the upstairs.' He pushed open a panelled door that led into a large airy room with an imposing fireplace and two big, squashy, caramel-coloured sofas. Behind an intricate woven metal screen a small fire crackled in the grate. He clicked on one of the large cream-shaded lamps that were dotted about the room before moving the firescreen to one side of the hearth.

'Take a seat.' He indicated the nearer sofa. 'Can I get you a drink?'

I sat down gingerly amongst the pile of scatter cushions that had been artfully arranged along the length of the seat. 'That would be nice, thank you.' I needed some Dutch courage if I was to get through the next few hours.

'Sherry, wine, beer, coffee?'

'Wine would be lovely.'

'White or red?' he persisted.

'Red. No, white.' I figured if I spilled white wine on his sofa it wouldn't be as big a disaster as if I spilled red. Not that I expected to spill my drink, but given that I was nervous and clumsy anyway it seemed sensible to minimise the risks.

He disappeared from the room to fetch the drinks, so I took the opportunity to practise my deep breathing while I looked around. A low polished wood table stood between the two sofas. At the far end of the room French doors framed by soft green silk curtains offered a glimpse of a walled garden under a darkening sky. Everything appeared new and beautiful. I wondered if Jack had chosen the furnishings himself or if he had a designer do it for him.

'Here's your wine.'

Deep in thought, I hadn't noticed Jack's return. He handed me a glass and took a seat at the end of the sofa.

'What do you think?' He took a sip of his wine and waited for my response.

'It's gorgeous. Did you choose all the things for this room yourself?' I gripped the crystal stem of my glass tightly. My palms were sweaty and my shoulders knotty with tension from trying to make small talk.

'I knew how I wanted it to look and I have a great designer who works for me and helped me put it all together.' Jack leaned back against the cushions, resting his arm along the back of the sofa and stretching out his long legs in front of him.

In contrast, I was perched on the edge of the seat with

my knees together, clutching my wine like a life preserver.

'I wish you would relax, Clodagh. I'm not going to eat you. I thought you might feel more at ease here than in a busy pub or restaurant.'

I instantly felt guilty. 'Sorry. I get nervous. I'm out of practice with . . . you know, dating and all that kind of thing.' I wriggled in my seat till I felt the sofa cushion touch my back.

'Is it really so hard to relax around me?' He stood his glass down on the table.

'I find it hard to relax around anyone,' I mumbled, knowing that the moment was fast approaching when I wouldn't be able to dive any longer.

'Are you ready to tell me yet what happened to you?' His dark eyes seemed to burn into me.

I swallowed hard. This was it.

'I had a relationship with one of my tutors while I was at university. It was my first – my only – big relationship. I thought it was serious, but he didn't see it in the same light.' I took a gulp of wine for fortification.

Jack murmured something encouraging and I plunged on.

'It wasn't till after we broke up that I realised what a controlling relationship it had been. Jonathan used to tell me how to dress, where to go, what to eat . . . By the time we split up I had no identity of my own.'

Jack leaned forward in his seat and cursed softly under his breath.

'There's more.' My hand shook and I placed my glass

down on the table in front of me. Finally talking to Jack about what had happened to me felt strangely liberating.

'Clo, you don't have to share this with me if you don't want to. I know I said we needed to talk properly but I can see this is hard for you.' The tender concern in his voice was mirrored in the expression on his face.

'No, I've been thinking about this a lot, ever since Immi arrived. Sometimes my sister can be very good at getting me to see the obvious.' I'd been swimming along happily in my little bubble, convinced I was over what had happened to me and that everything was fine. She'd helped me see that it was all still there, just buried under the surface.

'If you're sure.' He leaned back a little, his gaze still fixed on my face.

'When Jonathan dumped me I went to pieces. I had a kind of nervous breakdown and Immi came to look after me. I hadn't felt very well for a while but then I did a test. A pregnancy test. It was positive.' I paused to regain my composure and wiped my clammy palms on the legs of my jeans. 'I didn't know what to do. One minute I was scared, then excited, then terrified. I thought I should tell Jonathan. I suppose I hoped he would tell me he'd made a big mistake and that he'd changed his mind and wanted to marry me.'

A log on the fire shifted, sending a tiny shower of red sparks into the air above the hearth.

'I couldn't have been more wrong. He blanked me completely and told me he wanted nothing to do with me. He kept me standing on the doorstep of his flat like

I was a stranger. He told me his fiancée was due to return from the States for their wedding in a few weeks' time and that I was a stupid girl.' There, it was out. Memories of that horrible black time in my life crowded in on me.

'What did you do?' Jack's voice was gentle.

'He offered me money to have the pregnancy terminated. I couldn't do that – I would never do that. It wasn't the baby's fault that its father didn't want to know. I was in such a state that I ran away and simply kept going. Poor Immi was worried sick because I was gone such a long time. I walked for miles, just wandering around the city centre. I walked so far my feet were blistered and my shoes were full of blood by the time I got back.'

'Oh, Clodagh.' Jack placed his hand over mine. 'What happened to the baby?'

'I miscarried a couple of days later and that was that.' My voice cracked as memories poured over me and I recalled the whole nightmarish experience. I remembered sitting in the bathroom crying over the loss of the poor little life that I hadn't known I'd wanted until it had slipped away from me. I recalled the cold touch of the wall tiles on my cheek and the empty, desolate psychological ache that had hurt even more than the physical pain of losing my child.

Jack enfolded me in his arms and held me close to him. With my face resting on his chest I heard the regular dull thud of his heart and smelt the lovely comforting mix of desirable male mingled with fabric softener. His lips brushed the top of my head as he murmured soothing endearments.

'I'd been trying to work out why you kept backing away from becoming involved with me. I can't begin to tell you some of the scenarios I've had running through my head.'

I hadn't known how Jack would react. The only person who knew about my pregnancy and subsequent loss was Immi. My stepmother, Gloria, had known I was ill but it all happened around the time of my father's cancer so she'd already had plenty to worry about. I'd begged Immi not to tell her.

'Immi was there for me through everything – the baby, Jonathan, my finals. Everything.' I still thought about my pregnancy as a baby. It hadn't helped to think of it as a clump of cells – one of the less sensitive suggestions from one of my therapists. One of the first things I'd done when I moved to Rainbow Ridge had been to plant a rose bush in the garden in my baby's memory. It had been Immi's idea. She'd thought it might help me to work through everything that had happened to me. She'd been right: it had helped a little, but the anniversary of my loss and the day that should have been the baby's birthday still hurt me every year as they rolled round.

Jack caressed my cheek with the palm of his hand before easing his body slightly away from me. He twisted in his seat so he could see my face.

'I understand why you didn't want to trust me.'

'It wasn't only because of my past.' I'd told him my big secret. I had to tell him about the sanctuary too. The room had grown darker whilst we'd been talking. The large shaded lamps threw soft pools of light into the room, casting strange shadows on to the pastel suede-textured walls. The flames in the fireplace flickered yellow tongues over the dwindling pile of logs in the hushed silence. 'The next few months are make or break for me. Rainbow Ridge is broke.' I held my breath and waited for his reaction.

'That's why you were at the bank.'

I couldn't read his expression – the lamplight had thrown the sharp planes of his face into shadow and made it impossible for me to see what he might be thinking.

'I was trying to get an extension on my loan.'

He slumped back into his corner of the sofa, leaving me sitting straight-backed and stranded on the cushion next to him.

'I knew you had money problems but I had no idea it was so bad. Why did you refuse my offer to help you? And the truth this time – no fudging or edging.' His face was in darkness and his tone gave me no clue to his emotions.

'The sanctuary is all I have. It's my home and my job, and my animals are my family. If I go bankrupt who would want Dave or Miko and Pasquale? The sanctuary's only asset is the land.' I couldn't look at Jack. I knew he would be a jump ahead of me by now.

'You thought I'd try to take the land and develop it? Because I'd have some kind of leverage over you and because of the auction where I bid against Lovett's?' His voice sounded flat.

'I was scared and I don't trust people easily. There are lots of stories about how ruthless you are as a businessman. Susie said—'

'Susie? The mad bag lady who helps you out?' He leaned forward and rested his head in his hands as if trying to take in the full import of my confession.

'Yes. She said you would build houses on the land. And Jade told me ages ago you built the industrial units and trading estate on the town football ground.'

He shook his head as I faltered to a halt. My explanation sounded pathetic now I'd said it aloud.

'I don't know which of us is the most screwed-up. You, because you'd sooner believe the eco-loony, or me, because despite everything you just said I'm still crazy about you.'

Jack was crazy about me. I'd trusted him with my past, the earth was still spinning on its axis, and Jack was crazy about *me*.

The glowing embers in the grate heaved a huge sigh and collapsed into a pile of ash. Jack stood and walked across to the French doors, his hands deep in his trouser pockets and his shoulders hunched as he stared out at the darkened garden. My mouth dried as I watched, anxiety displacing my momentary elation at the declaration of his feelings. He lifted his head and I saw the outline of his Adam's apple bob in his neck as he swallowed.

I folded my arms protectively in front of my body. The air in the room had cooled with the dying of the fire. 'I wanted you to know everything. You said we should be more open with one another. I'm sorry if I hurt you.' My apprehension increased with every tick of the mantel-piece clock while I waited for his response.

He turned to look at me, his silhouette black against the window frame. 'You're right. I did say that. Now I should be honest with you in return.'

A shiver ran down my spine and the flesh on my arms prickled into goosebumps when Jack spoke.

'You're cold.' He moved from the windows to the fireplace, switching on another couple of lamps on his way across the room, filling the space with warm light. Within a few minutes he'd added more wood to the fire, coaxing flames from the almost spent ashes to lick greedily at the logs in the grate.

I watched the muscles in his back move beneath his shirt as he worked and wondered what he was about to say. Presently he straightened and replaced the poker in its stand.

'You were going to tell me something?' My mouth dried.

Jack turned and paced up and down the length of the Oriental rug that lay in front of the hearth.

'Saying this isn't going to be easy, and no matter how I put it I know you're going to think badly of me.' He stopped pacing and wheeled around to face me. The trickle of apprehension that had been running through my veins increased to a torrent. His eyes burned into me and I sensed his struggle to choose the right words. 'I liked you from the moment I first met you at the mayor's supper.'

I didn't think this was a promising start. It was classic – say something nice, then hit them with the sucker punch.

'You've been honest with me.'

I braced for impact, holding my breath and steeling my body in readiness for the blow.

'And if I'm being honest with you in return, then yes, I had thought about the potential uses of some of the sanctuary's ground.'

Exhale. Still in one piece, physically, only the sick, sad feeling in my abdomen tells me I've taken the hit.

'Susie was right.' My voice sounded flat.

'Yes and no. It's my job to look at land and buildings with a view to how they're used. I do it automatically. It doesn't mean I would try to use a relationship with you to get my hands on the sanctuary's ground and build houses all over it. The rivalry between myself and Lovett's is business. What I feel for you is something else.' He swept his hand impatiently through his hair. 'I'm telling you this because I want you to know the truth, so there'll be no more suspicions or doubts between us.' He stuck his hands into the pockets of his jeans.

It felt weird to have my suspicions confirmed about Jack's interest in my property, although the part about his feelings for me sounded promising. I had to get straight in my head exactly what he'd said. 'So you do want my land?'

He sighed. 'If your ground was on the open market, then yes, I'd be looking to develop it. The point is, it's not on the market and I would never, ever try to take it away from you. Especially not just to score some imaginary points over Lovett's. I know how much the sanctuary means to you and how hard you work.'

His words hung in the air between us and I weighed them up. I wanted to believe he was sincere.

'I want you to trust me, Clodagh. I know what it's like not be trusted.'

My throat had a big lump in it that I wanted to swallow. Jack crossed the few feet between us to crouch at my feet and take my hand in his.

'My father was the victim of malicious lies that were spread about him. We suspected who was behind it but couldn't get any proof. He was accused of dishonest business practice. The police investigated and found nothing, but it was too late.'

My heart banged against my ribs at the anguish in his eyes. 'Was that when the feud started with Lovett's?'

He nodded. 'How can you fight rumours? People will always say there's no smoke without fire.'

'What happened?'

'Business associates, people he'd considered friends for years, distanced themselves from him. George Lovett was out to destroy him and all over some stupid contract that we'd won fair and square.' Jack's voice cracked and he shook his head as if still unable to believe what had happened to his father. 'Well, he succeeded. Dad's health deteriorated and he signed the firm over to me. He died a year later.'

I stretched out my free hand to stroke his hair. I knew what his pain felt like from when I'd lost my own father. Even now, almost seven years later, it still hurt. Jack raised my other hand to his lips and kissed the back of my fingers.

'I'm so sorry.' My heart ached for him.

He dropped from a crouching position on to his knees and cradled my face between his hands as he kissed me. At first our kisses were tender and tentative. The emotional roller coaster we'd been riding had taken its toll, but it didn't take long for the passion we both felt to ignite.

My hands were as swift as Jack's to remove the constraints of our clothes. Being together, making love on Jack's sofa, felt so right. It wasn't until his head lay resting on my chest and our legs were tangled together in the aftermath that I realised that neither of us had used the L word. Strangely, this didn't bother me. What mattered was that we were being truthful with one another – a false declaration of love from either of us would have been wrong.

I tugged one of the pale green cushions more comfortably under my head and admired Jack's body in the lamplight.

'Are you okay?' He raised his head to look at me.

'Yeah.' I wriggled a little to shift my position, enjoying the feel of his skin against mine.

'You're so beautiful, Clodagh.' He dipped his head to

suck on my nipple, making desire build in my stomach with every gentle tug and my flesh peak in response to his lips.

He worked his way down my body with his mouth, across my stomach and on into the more sensitive, secret areas of my body until I closed my eyes and dug my fingers into the cushions with pleasure at his explorations. I gave myself up to the moment, shuddering with desire as he brought me to a climax.

'Damn, you're good.' I waited for him to ease back up beside me while I caught my breath. The whole of my body felt tingling and alive in a way I hadn't been for years.

He smiled, the dimple in his cheek quirking at my words. Unable to resist, I slid my hand across the taut, sweat-slicked skin of his abdomen to cup him firmly with my hand. His pupils dilated at my touch and I felt him grow in response to my teasing fingers. His expression sobered as I rubbed my breasts against his chest, manoeuvring myself so I could straddle his body before making good use of another one of the condoms from his wallet.

'I have to go home.' I peeled myself away from Jack and picked my bra up from the floor. The fire in the hearth had died once more and the mantelpiece clock told me it was way after midnight.

'You could stay the night.' Jack eased himself up on to one elbow and traced his finger down the length of my spine.

'Immi will worry and I have to be there for the animals.' I fastened my bra and searched for my discarded top while trying to ignore his touch. Tiredness pulled at my limbs from my early start that morning and the recent exercise. I longed to be tucked up in my bed, asleep.

Jack sat up and plucked his jeans from where they lay in a crumpled heap next to my knickers. 'Okay, I'll run you home.' He passed me my clothes and we dressed quickly in an oddly embarrassing silence.

'Ready?' Jack smoothed his hair down with his fingers.

'Sure.' I collected my bag and slipped the strap over my shoulder.

It was strange. I hadn't been shy or felt embarrassed all the while I'd been naked in his arms but now, fully dressed and sitting beside him in the car, I felt awkward.

We didn't speak as we drove through the dark and deserted lanes back to the sanctuary. Watching his strong, capable fingers on the steering wheel brought a flush to my cheeks when I recalled the magic they'd woven on my naked body.

The car crunched to a halt in the sanctuary's public car park. Jack turned off the engine and headlights. Immi had left the porch light on for me and I could see light showing through a chink in her bedroom curtains.

'Guess I'd better say goodnight.' I had my hand on the door handle ready to make good my escape.

'I'll call you.' Jack leaned across and kissed me on the

lips. As he moved his head and I opened my eyes I saw something bright between the trees in the direction of the entrance kiosk.

'What's that?' I tugged off my seat belt and scrambled free of the car.

Jack jumped out and came to my side. 'Shit, it's a fire!'

He pulled his mobile free of his jeans pocket and hit the nines as we hurried across the road towards the entrance. Thick smoke rose rapidly as we neared the kiosk. The shed was well alight, shooting red sparks into the air as flames lapped greedily at the old timbers.

'What's stored in there?' Jack caught hold of my arm, preventing me from getting closer.

'Our fridge with the drinks and ice cream . . . a few chairs, that's all.' I hunted around for the hose that we used to fill the water troughs.

'The fire brigade are on their way.' Jack seized the rubber hose from my hands. 'Go and turn on the tap, and stay back from the shed in case anything explodes.'

I hadn't thought of that. 'Be careful!'

I ran to the tap and turned it as fully open as it would go. Jack played the water on to the seat of the flames. In the distance I heard the wail of the sirens as the fire engine raced nearer. The density of the smoke increased, making my eyes stream. A series of pops and bangs came from the heart of the blaze. Jack edged closer with the hose.

'Get back!' My heart was in my mouth as the shed made an ominous cracking noise. Then, without further warning, the roof collapsed with a whoosh.

Jack half staggered and half jumped out of the path of the burning timbers that spilled towards us.

'Jack!'

'I'm okay.' Like me, he was coughing from the effects of the smoke.

The sound of the siren reached a peak as a fire engine screeched to a halt in the lane and half a dozen yellow-helmeted firemen leapt out. Jack and I stood to one side while they quickly and efficiently extinguished the flames.

A police car pulled up alongside the fire engine. I recognised our local beat officer as he came towards us.

'What's happened here?' He pulled out his notepad.

Jack explained that we'd found the kiosk ablaze.

'Did either of you notice anything unusual when you approached the fire?' The chief fire officer joined our little group, huddled in the light that was thrown from the fire engine's blue light.

'There was a smell like petrol.' I hated to think of the possibility of arson but with the vandalism we'd been suffering from lately I couldn't ignore it. Especially as we'd already had one fire on the site, when the feed store had been burned out.

'And you were absent this evening, miss?' the fireman asked.

Jack squeezed my hand. 'She was with me all evening. I was dropping her back when we saw the flames.'

'Neither of you saw anything or anyone as you pulled up?' the policeman queried.

'Nothing.' I'd been too busy kissing Jack to look out for arsonists.

'Is anyone in the house tonight?' The policeman inclined his head towards my front door.

That was odd. With all the noise, the flashing blue lights and the smoke, Immi hadn't made an appearance. 'My sister's at home.'

Jack raised his eyebrows, indicating his own surprise at Immi's failure to show up. We walked the few hundred yards back up the lane to my garden gate. I fumbled in my bag for the key to the front door and led my strange little posse into the hall. Nigel pattered out of the kitchen, his nails clicking on the floor as he investigated the late-night visitors, his tail wagging a cautious welcome.

The kitchen and sitting room were in darkness. Even Dave was silent, his cage covered with his blanket. I left the others at the foot of the stairs and ran up to Immi's room. I could understand her not seeing or hearing the fire initially, as her room overlooked the front garden and lane whereas the shed was off to the side of the house just out of sight. Even so, surely, she hadn't slept through the mayhem of the fire engine's arrival and the firemen shouting instructions to each other?

Her bedroom door was cracked open and her bedside light was on. I peeped in to see her lying on her bed in her silk pyjamas. Her iPod was plugged into her ears and a pink satin sleep mask was fixed in place across her eyes. I couldn't be certain, but I thought her breath smelt more of alcohol than of toothpaste, so I guessed she'd taken advantage of my absence to sneak a tipple. The house could have burned down, never mind the shed, and she wouldn't have seen or heard a thing.

'Immi!' I pulled the earplug from her ear.

She sat up immediately, shoving her mask up on to her forehead and blinking crossly at me in the bright light. 'Where have you been? God, you stink like a bonfire.'

'That's because someone burned down the kiosk! There's a fire engine outside and a policeman in the hall.'

'A whole truckful of firemen, and I missed it? You can be so selfish.' She grabbed her robe and shuffled her feet into fluffy pink kitten-heel slippers.

I caught up with her in the hall, where she was already batting her eyelashes at the policeman. He seemed suitably flattered by her attention so I went to look for Jack. I found him in the kitchen making tea.

'The fire crew got called to another blaze. They seem certain an accelerant was used. Probably petrol. They'll be in touch so you can file a claim with the insurance company.' He poured boiling water into a mug and added a teabag. 'Where was Immi?'

'In bed. She had a sleep mask and her iPod on.' I slumped on to one of the kitchen chairs. It suddenly hit me that I'd been awake for almost twenty-four hours and I was exhausted.

Jack passed me a mug of tea. Streaks of dirt patterned his cheeks and his clothes were grimy from fighting the fire. 'I take it she didn't hear or see anything, then?'

'Nope.'

I heard the front door close and Immi sailed into the kitchen. 'Ugh, you two smell worse than those ferrets Clodagh had last year. The policeman says he'll call back tomorrow to check our statements.'

'I'm ready for a shower and my bed.' I knew I wouldn't get much sleep before I had to get up to tend the animals. I wasn't up to dealing with Immi. Talking to her about the fire and her drinking would have to wait.

'I should be going too.' Jack replaced the kettle on the work top. 'I'll call you at lunchtime.' He bent to kiss my cheek and saw himself out, leaving me in the kitchen with my sister.

'Looks like something good came out of tonight,' Immi remarked as she perched on the chair opposite mine. She looked all bright-eyed and bushy-tailed from her nap.

I was too tired to talk. 'I'm shattered, Imms. It's already two in the morning and I need to be up again in four hours. I'm going to hit the shower.'

'But I'm awake now,' she protested as I got up from my seat.

'Then go talk to Dave.'

I staggered off up to the bathroom, had the fastest shower on record and fell into bed with my hair still wet.

Unsurprisingly, when my alarm went off my eyes felt as if the sandman had used real sand and my hair looked as if Amy Winehouse had styled it – in the dark, with a blowtorch. I pulled on whatever clothes were nearest to hand and made my way downstairs.

The kitchen still smelt of smoke and charred wood. Nigel blinked sleepy eyes at me as I made myself a mug of coffee and shoved my feet into my boots ready for the morning chores. My limbs still felt heavy and I moved around the room on automatic pilot.

Mist rose from the fields as I pottered about the paddocks, curling around me like a gauze wrapper as I fed the geese. The air was redolent with the scent of burnt timber and ash flakes rested on the roof of the chicken house. Even the familiarity of my regular routine failed to soothe me. This latest attack was much more significant than a hole in the fence or damage to a sign. It was even worse than the fire at the feed store, which had been smaller and further away from the house.

Once I'd taken care of the animals I walked across to the entrance to inspect the fire damage in daylight. Puddles of water were mixed with the remains of the shed. The freezer stood forlornly amongst the debris, its formerly white exterior blackened and blistered by the heat. I felt too heartsick at the sight of the damage to even try to calculate the cash value of what we'd lost.

Somehow I would have to try to clean up the mess before we opened. I also needed to rig up a temporary kiosk to take admission money. The paper bags of feed that we normally sold, and all the refreshment stock, had been burned to a crisp. My heart sank when I thought of the phone call I would have to make to the insurance company with yet another claim.

In some of my madder moments I'd wondered if Jack could have been behind some of the incidents as a way of speeding up the sanctuary's financial collapse. If I couldn't get insurance and/or went bankrupt then the land would go to auction and probably be sold off at a rock-bottom price. After hearing Jack's confidences last night I felt ashamed that I could ever have thought that way.

My whole body heated with embarrassment at the thought of Jack. He had the perfect alibi for last night since we'd been busy making love when the arsonist had struck. I suppose that Jack had provided me with an alibi, too. The fireman's questions last night had made it clear that he had wondered if I'd burned the shed down myself. It was probably what the insurance company would think too when I summoned enough energy to call and tell them of the latest disaster.

I strolled over to the storage barn to collect a wheelbarrow and some heavy-duty gloves, my mind busy trying to make sense of the vandalism. There had always been isolated problems, but that wasn't surprising. Every business was subject to the odd broken window, piece of graffiti or theft. In the last six months it had felt almost as if the sanctuary was under siege. Virtually every week had brought fresh incidents. At first they had been small – spray paint on the signs, damage to the fencing – but then there had been the first fire.

Once my gloves were firmly in place I started dropping charred pieces of timber into the wheelbarrow. Looking back, the problems with the vandalism had accelerated since the neighbouring field had been sold to Lovett's. The talk at the Frog and Ferret was that Lovett's was a conglomerate from out of town. They had a bit of a shifty reputation for poor quality and high prices on their constructions. There was much muttering amongst the pub regulars of backhanders at the council. Everything I'd heard at the pub seemed to confirm what Jack had told me.

I trundled my full barrow across the yard to tip the debris from the fire safely out of sight from the public and away from the animal pens. It had to be a coincidence about the vandalism and Lovett's planned construction nearby. Didn't it?

I pushed my barrow back and carried on clearing up the mess, my mind working furiously as I lobbed rubbish into a heap. A year ago the sanctuary land would have only been valued for agricultural use. But now the precedent had been set with the green light for construction so close to me then my ground was probably a lot more valuable than I'd thought. But there was one weight off my mind, at least. Now that I knew Jack better, I believed he would never stoop to anything underhand to persuade me to sell.

'Cooee, Clodagh!'

I looked up to see Susie flapping her arm at me by the public entrance. I left my half-filled barrow and went to let her in.

'What happened? Where's the kiosk?' Her eyes boggled as she took in the damage.

'Someone burned it down late last night.'

'But didn't you hear or see anything?' She adjusted her specs and peered at the remains of our freezer as if it would confess to being a witness.

'I was out and found the blaze when I got back. Immi was in bed wearing earplugs and an eye mask. She didn't hear a thing.' I stirred a pile of ashes with the toe of my boot. There was also the matter of Immi's drinking. I'd found an empty bottle of gin hidden in the bottom of the dustbin. I didn't mention that to Susie – I still had to discuss it with Immi.

'I suppose it could have been the wiring.' She bent closer to the freezer and squinted at a melted blob of plastic that might have been the plug.

'No, it was arson. I could smell petrol.' I watched as she straightened up, bewilderment written all over her face.

'That doesn't make any sense.' She blinked and shook her head.

I decided not to share my thoughts on why we were being targeted. Right now I wasn't sure what to think or whom to trust. 'Come on, we'll go and have a cup of tea before we finish clearing up this mess.' I pulled off my gloves and put them on top of the barrow before leading the way to the house.

Immi was seated at the kitchen table munching on a bowl of Special K when I opened the back door.

'Ugh. You've been messing with the fire again.' She wrinkled her nose as we entered the kitchen.

'I've got to clean up the mess and rig up a temporary kiosk before we open.' I washed my hands under the tap while Susie put the kettle on.

'It's dreadful! I can't believe someone would do something like that on purpose.' Susie fished a teaspoon out of the cutlery drawer and bumped it shut with her hip.

Immi frowned. 'It is a bit odd. I mean, it's quite a walk to the nearest houses, although I expect that will alter when they build on the land down the road. Someone would have to drive out here deliberately to burn down the kiosk.'

Susie sank down on the chair opposite her. 'But why would anyone want to do that to an animal sanctuary? Clodagh hasn't an enemy in the world and who would want to harm these poor darling little creatures?' She stooped to stroke Clive as he ambled past with his nose in the air. He gave her the kind of look that only a cat can bestow before sitting down just out of her reach to wash his paws with neat little flicks of his tongue.

Immi exchanged a meaningful glance with me while Susie was preoccupied with Clive. I knew she'd had the same suspicious thoughts that I'd had about why we were being targeted.

I'd just finished making drinks for the three of us when there was a rap at the door and Jade walked in.

'What happened to the kiosk?' She unhitched her canvas bag from her shoulder and dropped it on to the kitchen table next to Immi's cereal bowl.

'Arson attack.' I reached for another mug from the shelf to make her a drink.

'Arson? It might have been the wiring. The freezer was pretty ancient.'

'Clodagh said there was a strong petrol smell,' Susie informed her as she took a sip from her mug.

'Really? I didn't notice anything when I walked by this morning.' Jade frowned.

'It was quite strong last night.' I passed her a mug of tea.

'Gosh.' She accepted her drink, slopping a little bit on to her sweater. Something about the unusual shade of the yarn rang a bell in the back of my mind.

'That's a lovely jumper, Jade.' I passed her some kitchen towel to mop up the spill.

She glanced down as if surprised. 'It was a present from my aunt in Canada. She's a big knitter.'

Susie's face lit up at the mention of knitting. 'I wonder if she'd have some good patterns. I'm between projects at the moment.'

'Knitting aside, ladies, we need to get the mess cleared away before we open and we'll have to rig up something to use as a temporary booth.' I wasn't sure how we were going to do that. All I wanted was to go back to bed and get some sleep.

A horn beeped outside, accompanied by the rumble of heavy machinery. I pushed past Jade, who was still showing Susie the ribbing on her sweater, and opened the back door. A yellow JCB was at the public gate, in front of a lorry with 'Thatcher Developments' written along the side. I ran across the yard.

A large man in a hard hat leaned out of the cab of the digger. 'Boss sent us to clear the debris from the fire.'

'Cool!' Immi appeared at my elbow and flashed the man a megawatt soap-star smile.

'There's a new shed on the truck, too, so if you want to open the gate, we'll get on.'

'Jack is such a generous guy.' Immi helped me swing

the large metal barrier open to allow the vehicles through.

'Humph. Probably a guilty conscience,' Susie muttered. She and Jade had followed us outside.

'What do you mean?' I had a good idea, though. After all, I'd have thought the same thing about Jack myself not so long ago.

'Well, you have to admit that the problems with vandalism have got worse since Lovett's got planning permission for Long Meadow,' Susie said. 'I'm sure Jack wouldn't want them muscling in on his territory any more than they have already. He's been sniffing around here for ages because he can smell a profit.'

Jade nodded in agreement. 'You know he hates George Lovett's guts.'

'I was with Jack last night. There's no way he had anything to do with this. Maybe Lovett's are behind it. Maybe it's a conspiracy.' I watched as the JCB driver lowered the bucket to scoop up the burnt-out remains of the freezer.

Susie and Jade were silent. From the looks on their faces my outburst had clearly convinced them that I'd cracked under the strain. Immi had gone to chat to the two men who were unloading shed panels from the lorry. My mobile buzzed deep inside my jacket pocket. I fished it out to see a text from Jack.

Thght I cld help. Call u l8r.

I sent him back a quick text to say thanks and added a kiss before slipping the phone back in my pocket. The bulldozer made short work of clearing up the mess and the workmen soon had the construction of the new shed well under way. Jade and Susie had drifted off to clean out the donkey stable and, I suspected, to talk about Jack and me.

Immi walked back to join me. 'The men said they'll get Jack's electrician to run the power back into the shed once it's up. I've promised them a cup of tea, too.'

'Thanks.'

'Listen, why don't you go and grab a nap? The punk and the bag lady will look after the menagerie and I'll supervise the workmen.' She gave the workers a cheery wave as we re-entered the house.

'I would, but I need to ring the insurance company and there are a million things to do for the open day.' My eyeballs physically ached, I felt so tired.

'Go to bed. There's nothing that can't wait. I've seen all your lists so I can do some ringing for you.' She gave me a little push towards the stairs. 'I think Jack's tired you out.'

Telltale heat shot into my cheeks, making my sister laugh.

'It's always sex with you.'

'Well, it's about time you got some.' She grinned.

'I'm going for a sleep.' I headed up the stairs with as much dignity as I could muster. From the lounge I heard Dave screech, 'Trollop!' as I reached the landing.

I think I was unconscious the moment my head hit the pillow because the next thing I remembered was Immi shaking me awake.

'What time issit?' The cotton of the pillowcase felt

damp against my cheek. I must have been sleeping with my mouth open.

'Two o'clock. I brought you some coffee.' She set a mug down on my dresser before perching herself on the end of my bed.

'The sanctuary.' I sat up and rubbed sleep out of my eyes.

'Is fine. Susie is manning the new shed at the entrance, visitors are pouring in and everything is okay.'

I pulled my soggy pillow up behind my shoulders and flopped back down. 'Phew.'

'Spill the beans, then. I take it you and Jack finally got down and dirty last night.' Her eyes held a mischievous glint.

'You're impossible.'

'Oh, come on, Clo. The man is hot and I'm so happy to see you finally shaking off the ghost of student life past.'

I picked up my drink and inhaled the coffee aroma. 'Yeah, well.' I could feel myself blushing again as I remembered making love with Jack. Parts of my body ached in places that hadn't been exercised for a very long time, and my skin tingled with pleasure at the memory of his hands.

'Talking of hot men, Marcus is arriving later today.' Immi stretched her arms above her head in a long languid movement.

I surveyed her through the steam that rose from the rim of my mug. 'Oh?'

Immi picked at an imaginary piece of fluff on the cover of my duvet. 'He's really sweet, Clo.' Her face had flushed a delicate shade of pink.

'He seems okay, but he is a member of the paparazzi.' It bothered me that Marcus made his living from other people's misery. There had been tons of stories in the press about so-called photo-journalists cosying up to celebrities and pretending to be in love with them only to dish the dirt a few weeks down the line. I didn't want that to happen to my sister.

'That's just it. He's quit.' Immi beamed at me.

I straightened up on my pillow. 'Quit?'

'He's got a new job. He was head-hunted to present a show on TV. One of those consumer programmes where they expose dodgy builders and stuff. Remember I told you he had an interview at the studios? It's been on the cards for a while but no one was supposed to know about it.' She hugged herself with delight.

'Wow.' I wasn't sure what to say. I was still a little concerned that Marcus might somehow be using my sister's fame in some way. It looked as if I would have to try harder at learning to trust people.

'He's very photogenic and he's smart. He'll be perfect on TV.'

She had a point. 'If it's what he wants then that's great.'

Immi traced a finger around the faded daisy pattern on my quilt cover. 'I was thinking about what you said earlier about the vandalism starting when the field next to yours was sold. Apart from the bank and the volunteers, who else would be likely to know that you've been having financial problems?'

I wasn't sure what she was driving at. 'No one, really. The volunteers would guess something was wrong because of the poor visitor numbers and the lack of investment. But I've tried to keep the extent of my problems secret.'

'That's what I thought.' Immi's pretty face sobered.

'Why?'

'Oh, nothing. Just thinking.'

I let it be. I still needed to tackle her about the alcohol I'd smelled on her breath when I'd woken her last night. It was vital I picked the right moment or she'd simply deny everything and blow me off.

'Is it okay if Marcus stays here for a couple of days?' She changed the subject.

'Sure.' I took a long draught of coffee. I hoped I was doing the right thing in agreeing. Maybe this learning to trust was like a three-step recovery programme. 'You don't think you might be rushing things a bit with Marcus?' Their relationship certainly appeared to be moving quickly.

The colour in her cheeks deepened. 'Maybe, but I really like him and he likes me. The real me, not the actress or the personality, but me – and that's kind of nice, you know?'

I gave her a hug. What could I say?

Step one: pick the right time to talk about the responsible consumption of alcohol.

Step two: let your sister share your guest bed with her photo-journalist boyfriend.

Step three: shake off my granny mentality and start living again.

This was going to be tough.

Immi wandered off downstairs to check her emails and Clive the cat slipped in to snuggle up next to me on the bed. If I'd followed Immi's line of thought correctly earlier, she'd seemed to be implying that one of the volunteers could somehow be linked to the attacks on the sanctuary.

I took another long drink of coffee and hoped the caffeine would help me think more clearly. Susie and Jade were my friends, and I couldn't see any of the other helpers, like Val and Tom, being the culprits. They weren't here often enough to know what was going on.

Surely Susie and Jade couldn't be in league with one another. They didn't even appear to like each other very much. Immi had to be mistaken. Even if the vandalism was connected to the sale of Long Meadow, it didn't mean that any of the volunteers were involved. Yet it seemed equally crazy to think that Lovett's might be behind my problems.

I finished my drink and kept thinking. Shamefully, I'd been only too willing to think that Jack would stoop to foul play in an attempt to obtain the sanctuary. Why was it so hard to accept that another company – whom I didn't even know personally – might be unscrupulously involved? Especially after what George Lovett had done to Jack's father.

Clive butted his soft head against my hand in a demand to be stroked. Vandalism and general annoyance might succeed in softening me up towards a sale, but it would be unlikely to work all on its own. So, no one would risk it unless they had a good idea of the extent of my financial woes. I tickled Clive on the white bib beneath his chin while my mind clicked over the problem.

Vandalism could push a failing business to the brink if the insurance premiums were increased beyond the owner's means. That, along with the damage to items such as the sheds or feed, which were expensive items to replace, might be enough to force me to close, considering my perilous financial state. Lovett's would be in a prime position to make an offer as they already had planning permission for Long Meadow.

I turned my thoughts back to the volunteers, since I couldn't see Mr Curzon, my bank manager, in the role of chief villain. Susie was always trying to snoop, but Jade had equal access to the house. She knew I was short of money, since she was the one who had suggested bar work to me when we'd been chatting a few months back. My head reeled at the implications. All this time I'd been suspecting Jack when perhaps I should have been focusing closer to home.

I'd had letters from Lovett's asking me to contact

their lawyer if I was interested in selling them the sanctuary land even before the planning consent had been granted for the neighbouring field. Naturally, I'd ripped them up and thrown them in the recycling box – somewhere Susie was always snooping. But Immi *had* to be mistaken. Why would Jade or Susie want to help Lovett's?

So much for my learning to trust people. I felt utterly confused. Everything was jumbled up in my head. I tipped Clive off my quilt and wandered downstairs to look for Immi. I really needed to talk to someone about all this.

The sitting room was empty except for Nigel, who lay snoozing happily on the hearth rug.

'Up yours!' Dave fired the husk of a sunflower seed at me.

I ducked back out and headed for the kitchen, only to discover that it, too, was deserted. There seemed to be plenty of visitors wandering around looking at the animals, though. Mr Sheen was munching away to his heart's content thanks to the generosity of a group of pre-schoolers who were offering him numerous tiny palms full of food. I guessed either Susie or Jade had made up some fresh bags of animal feed from the emergency stores in the storage barn, to replace the ones we'd lost in the blaze.

A familiar small blue car was parked in the yard next to my beat-up Fiat. Marcus must have arrived. I plunked myself down at the kitchen table and wondered where he and Immi had gone. The notepad next to the phone was filled with her untidy black scrawl. I picked it up and flipped through. More confirmations for the open day from stallholders and people wanting details about sponsorship. Something positive had come from Immi's chat-show disaster, after all.

I picked up the pen and thought hard about the vandalism incidents. Then, I made a list of the damages and the approximate dates when they had occurred. Once I'd finished I stared at it for a long minute. I pulled my mobile from my pocket and found Jack's number in my address book. I took a deep breath and pressed the buttons before I could change my mind. I had to talk to him.

'Clodagh, is everything okay?' He answered on the first ring, his voice managing to sound surprised and pleased at the same time.

'Fine. Thank you for the shed. I appreciate the help. I wasn't sure how I would be able to open when I saw the mess this morning.'

'No prob.' There was a pause.

'I wanted to ask you for some advice on something.' My stomach felt as if elephants were turning cartwheels in it.

'Okay.'

'Can you call round when you finish work?' I held my breath.

'Sure.'

I exhaled slowly. 'Thanks.'

'See you soon.'

I could feel his smile warming my heart as I terminated the call. My hands shook as I returned the phone to my pocket. I'd asked Jack for help. Asking anyone for help was completely alien to me. Ever since Jonathan I'd tried to be as self-sufficient as possible. I might ask Immi or Gloria for advice but never anyone else – even talking to my bank manager was an ordeal.

The back door opened and Immi and Marcus stepped into the kitchen. Immi's cheeks were flushed and rosy, and Marcus had hold of her hand. They looked like a couple of teenagers on a first date. I hoped the date hadn't included imbibing anything alcoholic.

'I've been showing Marcus the damage to the fence at the bottom of the far paddock.' Her colour deepened and she gave a little giggle.

As she crossed over to the sink I noticed that there were strands of grass clinging to the back of her jeans. If she wasn't careful there would be more pictures of her in the papers. This time they would show her rolling around with Marcus in a public place and that wouldn't help me build up my visitor numbers. The mummy brigade wouldn't want to expose their toddlers to Immi's shenanigans.

'Immi told me all about the fire and the vandalism.' Marcus swept a hand through his thick dark hair and I noticed that while he might be talking to me he was looking at my sister. He also appeared to have a small green grass stain on his designer jeans.

'Marcus agrees with me. He thinks there's something odd about all the problems you've had since Lovett's bought Long Meadow.' Immi turned to face me, her big blue eyes anxious in her expressive face.

I leaned back in my seat and blew out a sigh. 'I know. I thought about what you said earlier and I've asked Jack to call in on his way home.'

Immi frowned. 'You don't *still* think he's behind all this?'

'No. I wanted his advice.'

She gaped at me. 'You asked Jack for advice? Wow.'

Marcus looked bewildered. Immi smiled at him and kissed his cheek. 'It's complicated.'

Jack arrived after the sanctuary had closed. His car pulled into the deserted public car park as I returned from walking Nigel along the lane. The dog gave a welcoming woof as I hurried to meet him.

'Hi.' Jack bent his head to kiss me on the lips, sending a shiver of pleasure right through me.

'Come inside the house. We're having a meeting in the sitting room.' I felt stiff and awkward. Memories of his body lying naked next to mine sent heat flooding into my cheeks and my voice sounded all breathy. He raised an eyebrow at my statement but followed me along the front path, carrying his briefcase.

'Marcus is here too.' I thought I ought to mention Marcus's presence before we went in.

'I thought he'd gone back to London?' Jack frowned and I guessed he must have been wondering why I'd asked him to call round.

'He and Immi are having a bit of a thing. He's got a new job and Immi's asked him to stay here for a few days before he starts.'

'Oh?'

'He's working in TV on an investigative journalism show.' I opened the front door and let Nigel off his lead as I kicked off my shoes.

'Mmm,' was Jack's only comment to my last piece of information as we entered the sitting room.

Marcus and Immi were cosied up together on the sofa, sipping tea. Clive stretched from his favourite position on the armchair before stalking past us and into the hall with his tail held high. Dave shuffled up and down his perch, bobbing his head in either indignation or excitement at our invasion of his space.

'Bugger off!' He rolled his beady eyes at me as I took a seat in the armchair that Clive had just vacated.

Jack nodded his head in recognition to Marcus and took the chair opposite mine. 'So what's going on?'

'I wanted to ask you about this. The vandalism at the sanctuary has accelerated enormously since Lovett's acquired Long Meadow.' I gave him the list of damages and rough dates that I'd made while Immi had been frolicking in the grass with Marcus.

He studied the list I'd given him and his lips thinned. 'That's a lot of incidents.' He raised his eyes to meet mine.

'Immi thought there was a connection.' I swallowed and waited to hear what he thought.

'It's possible, but it could be coincidence.' He dropped my list down on the table. 'It's a very serious allegation if you think someone has organised this kind of activity to force you into closing. I thought we'd discussed this matter already.'

Ice trickled down my spine as I noticed the rigidity in his jaw. This was all going horribly wrong. Jack had misinterpreted my question. He thought this meeting was some kind of set-up. He thought I still didn't trust him even after the experiences we'd shared only a few hours ago. Tears prickled behind my eyes.

'We thought it might be someone with insider information about my finances.' Even as the words left my mouth I knew I'd made matters worse.

'If there's nothing else, Clodagh, I should get going. I've a lot of work to do tonight.' He picked up his briefcase.

'Then you think all this vandalism is random?' Immi asked. She sounded bewildered by Jack's response to my list.

Marcus said nothing, merely sat watching Jack through narrowed eyes.

Jack stood. 'I've no idea. If you think it's something more organised then I can only suggest you put it in the hands of the police.' His voice was as cold as the expression on his face. 'Now, if you'll excuse me.' He strode out of the room and I heard the front door bang before I could gather my wits.

'Go after him,' Immi urged. Her eyes widened as the penny dropped and she made the connection between Jack's reaction and what I'd told her about his father.

I scrambled to my feet and flew out of the house after Jack. Sharp bits of gravel cut into my feet through my socks but I didn't care. I had to stop him and explain that he'd misunderstood what I'd been trying to find out.

'Jack!'

He paused for a second as he opened the door of the Range Rover.

'Jack!' I'd almost caught up to him.

He climbed into the driver's seat, his gaze fixed firmly ahead, blanking me out completely. I sprinted the last few feet, almost falling over in my haste to tug open the passenger door before he could start the engine and drive away.

'Wait!' I tumbled into the footwell and on to the passenger seat, gasping for breath.

I saw a muscle jump in his cheek as I wriggled myself up straight but he didn't speak.

'Jack, you don't understand. I wasn't implying that you were involved.' My words fell out in a breathless rush. I wanted to reach out to him, to place my hand on his arm and make him listen to me, but he wouldn't even turn his head to look at me.

'Clodagh, I'm not stupid. You call me up and say you want advice. I get here and find you've made a list of criminal activity complete with dates, you have an investigative photo-journalist installed on your couch, and you ask me if I think the vandalism is connected with the development of Long Meadow. You've already accused me once of trying something underhand to acquire your property.' His profile was grim as he kept his gaze fixed on a distant group of trees.

'Jack, I thought we'd cleared all that up. I didn't ask you here tonight to accuse you of anything.' Panic clawed at my insides. I had to make him believe me.

He turned to look at me and the hurt in his eyes made my heart squeeze. 'I thought what we shared together last night was something special—'

'It was!' I interrupted, desperate to make him listen to me.

He shook his head. 'But I was wrong.'

'No, Jack.' I had to stop him, get him to see the truth.

'I think you'd better get out of the car, Clodagh.' His voice sounded cold and controlled.

I stared at him for a moment. I couldn't believe this was happening. A few hours ago I'd been naked in his arms. We'd exchanged confidences, made love, been honest with each other in a way I'd never thought I could be with anyone again after Jonathan. Now it was gone, evaporated away like the morning mist. He didn't believe I trusted him and because of that he didn't or couldn't trust me. We were both victims of our pasts.

I slid from the car seat and closed the door behind me without a word. What was the point? I stood back as he reversed the car and roared out of the car park without so much as a backward glance.

I stood on the car park in my socks with tears rolling down my face and my heart in a million pieces.

I made my way slowly back to the house without a care for the sharp stones that stabbed at the soles of my feet. The wrenching, tearing pain in my heart was so much greater. Immi stood waiting for me on the front step, her forehead creased with anxiety.

'What happened? Where's Jack?' She stepped out to meet me and placed a comforting arm round my shoulders.

'He wouldn't listen. He thinks I've set him up. That I believe he's the one behind the vandalism and that asking him to call round was some sort of trap.' My voice broke with the strain of all the conflicting emotions churning around inside me.

'What? Why? That's crazy.' Immi steered me gently back inside the house.

I shook my head. 'You don't understand. When I was at his house we talked about the sanctuary and the land, and just now I told him that Marcus works in investigative journalism. It never occurred to me that he would think I still didn't trust him.' My nose was running and I fumbled in my pocket for a tissue. 'He told me all about his father and how badly he'd been affected by what happened to him. Oh, Imms, how could I have been so stupid? I should have explained it all to him before he got here.'

She offered me a tissue, since I hadn't been able to find one in my pocket. 'You weren't to know that he'd jump to the wrong conclusion. When he's had a chance to calm down and think things through he'll realise he's made a mistake.'

I scrubbed at my eyes and blew my nose. 'I wish I could believe that.'

'Would you like me to talk to him?' She gave me a hug.

I managed a feeble smile at the idea of Immi being the voice of reason. 'I don't think it would do any good. Maybe you're right – perhaps he needs time to calm down and then I can try to explain properly.'

She gave me another sisterly squeeze.

'Where's Marcus?'

Immi's face glowed at the mention of his name. 'Making some phone calls to some of his contacts. He wants to find out more about Lovett's. There might be a story in it.'

'Does he know any of the background to this feud between Jack's father and George Lovett?'

Immi shrugged. 'Why would he? I don't know much, only the little bit that Jade and Susie mentioned. Do you think he should check it out?'

'It might be important. At least I'd know a bit more about why Jack and George Lovett hate each other so much, and what sparked off the original incident involving Jack's dad.' I trailed into the sitting room and took a seat on the sofa.

Dave greeted me from his perch. 'Get your knickers off!'

'Oh, be quiet,' Immi muttered as she sat down next to me.

'Listen, while Marcus is out I wanted to talk to you about last night.' I figured my day couldn't get any worse, so I thought I might as well tackle Immi about the empty gin bottle while Marcus wasn't around to overhear us.

'Oh?' Immi looked blankly at me.

'I found a bottle in the bottom of the bin.'

She flopped back. 'Oh.'

'Imms, I'm worried about you.'

She leaned forward again and buried her face in her hands.

'I think you need help.'

'All I had was one glass of gin, Clo. I found the bottle while we were cleaning. God knows how long you'd had it. I finished it off with some of the orange juice from the fridge. One drink does not make me an alcoholic.' Her voice sounded dull, as if she was weary of the discussion.

'The clip they showed at the TV studio of you attacking Kirk scared me, Immi. Okay, so you say you had one glass of gin, but was that because that was all there was left? Would you have been able to stop if it was half a bottle?' I waited for her reply.

To my surprise her shoulders started to shake and she gave a strangled sob.

'Immi?' I put my arms round my smart, sassy soap-star sister, who promptly collapsed sobbing on to my shoulder.

'I don't know.' She hiccoughed to a halt.

'Look, why don't I make an appointment for you with my doctor? Get you some help?' I didn't know what else to suggest. If I rang Marty then Immi would end up somewhere like the Priory and the press would have a field day.

'I don't know, Clo. I don't get the DTs or anything. I can go weeks and not touch a drop, honestly,' she mumbled into my T-shirt.

'I know. But when you do start you can't stop, and that's what scares me. Let me talk to my GP and see what she says.'

She sat up and pulled a tissue from her pocket to pat under her eyes. 'Okay, but for God's sake be discreet.'

I gave her another hug, then she disappeared up to her room to repair her face before Marcus could see that she'd been crying and ask any awkward questions.

'Show us your tits!' Dave instructed as he strutted along his perch.

'Behave!' I reprimanded him. He settled in one spot, his feathers ruffled in a silent huff.

I called my GP and managed to secure an appointment for Immi for the following afternoon. It took some doing to get past the receptionist to speak directly to my doctor, but I felt that the fewer people who knew about the consultation the better.

When my mobile rang as we were eating supper I thought it might be Jack. Instead it was Frank, landlord of the Frog and Ferret.

'Hey up, Clo, I don't suppose you could do me a favour and come down and pull a few pints for an hour tonight? I didn't know if you'd be too busy now you're a famous TV star and all, but I'm run off my feet here. The darts team are in from the Rose and Crown for a match. I can't keep pace with the pie and chip orders.'

I glanced at Immi and Marcus, who were playing footsie with each under the table as they ate their spaghetti. I decided I'd prefer to be behind the bar at the pub than playing gooseberry in my own front room.

'Okay. I'll be there in a few minutes.'

'Champion.'

I put my empty spaghetti plate in the sink and hurried upstairs to change. I decided to wear the top Immi had selected for my TV appearance – the one the technicians told me would induce migraine in the viewers. I liked it, and it seemed a shame not to give it an outing.

Frank was up to his eyes in punters and pint pots when I reached the pub. I lifted the hatch in the counter and slipped in beside him. The dull roar of the darts crowd competed with the sound of the TV and the chatter coming from the lounge bar.

'Crikey, I'm glad to see you, lass. Can you get pulling while I nip down the cellar to change a barrel? The bitter's gone.' Perspiration dripped from his round, rosy face and he looked like a small ruffled cherub.

I took over dealing with the orders. Most of the

punters were regulars so I was subject to a volley of good-natured banter about my fifteen minutes of fame on TV. By the time Frank re-emerged from the cellar I'd pulled dozens of pints and run half a dozen food orders through to Jenny, his wife, who was in charge of the kitchen.

He rejoined me behind the bar. 'Thanks for coming in, pet. Young Tony phoned in sick and I'd forgotten about this blessed match. The Rose and Crown team always bring a load of supporters.'

'It's okay. I wasn't doing anything.' It would probably do me good to get out of the house. Left at home I'd only end up talking to Dave and brooding about Jack. At least here I would be kept busy and wouldn't have time to fret.

'Well, I'm proper grateful.' Frank bustled past me to fill a wine glass from the bottle.

The next couple of hours flew past. All evening I was half hoping that Jack might call in and I'd have an opportunity to talk to him. It didn't happen, though. The only people I saw were the darts team and their wives filling up on lager and packets of salted nuts.

It was almost closing time before the crowd began to thin and I was able to take advantage of the lull to do a glass run. I nipped through the hatch to the lounge and began to collect the empties, stacking the dirty glassware on the bar ready for the washer. A large and merry party of punters called goodnight as they left, letting a blast of chilly air into the room through the old-fashioned half-glazed door.

'You've been busy tonight,' an elderly local man observed from his seat in the corner.

'Rose and Crown were here for a darts match.' I recognised him as the chap who usually called in for a pint of mild on his way home from walking his dog. Sure enough, his wiry greyhound cross lay patiently under his seat waiting for her master to finish his drink. We weren't supposed to let dogs in because we served food in the lounge, but since the hot meals service stopped at nine thirty Frank didn't mind making an exception for a regular.

'They always have a good turn-out. I suppose it might all change when Lovett's sell them swanky houses next to your place. Probably want to posh this place up. Won't be much darts-playing then.' His wrinkled face crinkled with disapproval.

'I don't know. I reckon any new residents will leave this place alone. Might not be smart enough.' I smiled at him. I couldn't picture the five-bedroom executive homeowners wanting to pop into the Frog and Ferret for a pint.

'I take it you're not selling up, then? I reckon they would have liked to get their hands on your place. George Lovett's not an easy bloke to say no to.' The old man supped at his beer.

'Do you know Mr Lovett?' I paused with my hands full of empty pint glasses.

'Aye. Used to work for him on contract from time to time. I was an electrician till I retired. I didn't do much for him, though. Didn't like his building methods. I preferred working for Joe Thatcher – proper gent, he was. It was a shame what happened with him and Lovett.'

'What *did* happen between them?' I placed the glassware down carefully on the bar.

The old man glanced round the empty room as if he suspected someone of lurking behind the cigarette machine. 'Lovett never liked Joe. He wanted to put him out of business. Didn't want him queering his pitch. There was a big row over a contract for the new hospital. Joe landed it and Lovett cried foul. Joe hadn't done owt wrong but by the time his name had been dragged through the mud he were a broken man. He died soon after. His son has the business now. Chip off the block is young Jack.'

'That's terrible.'

The old man's account tallied with everything Jack had told me. No wonder he had been so angry, especially after he'd confided to me what had happened to his father.

'Take my advice, lass. If George Lovett comes offering you big money and fancy promises, have nowt to do with him.'

'Don't worry. I've no intentions of selling. My animals are too important to me.' I wiped my hands on a bar towel.

The old man finished his drink and picked up his cap from the seat beside him. 'I'm glad to hear it. Come on, Sadie.' He gave a gentle tug on his dog's lead. 'Best be off; the missus will be waiting.' He shuffled off into the night, leaving me to finish collecting the empties.

'Me and Jenny'll finish off now, Clodagh, love, if you want to get off home.' Frank hailed me from the entrance to the kitchen.

'Thanks.' I placed the last of the empties on the counter and collected my jacket.

'I've put you an extra tenner in for tonight. Got us out of a real mess, you did.' He pulled some money from his pocket.

'Any time.' I enjoyed bar work, and Frank and Jenny were nice people who'd lived in Melhampton all their lives. 'Listen, Frank . . . do you know much about George Lovett?'

Frank scratched his thinning locks, making an errant piece of hair stick out above his ear like a piece of thistledown. 'A bit – none of it good. Why, is he after your place?'

'I had a letter the other week. I'm not interested in selling, though,' I said hastily, in case word got out about my enquiry.

'He's rumoured to be a nasty piece of work.' Jenny came out of the kitchen to join her husband. 'I thought you were walking out with Jack Thatcher. You know there's bad blood between him and Lovett? Young Jack seemed very sweet on you the other night. Right keen to take your coat up to the sanctuary he was, when you left it behind.' She grinned at me.

'Jack's just an acquaintance.' I pocketed my wages, eager to escape Jenny's scrutiny. The Frog and Ferret was a hotbed of gossip and rumour. Jack's paying so much attention to me when I'd been serving at the bar on the night of the chat show had clearly not gone unnoticed.

'Acquaintance, is it? I've heard it called some things before, but not that.'

She and Frank exchanged knowing smiles. My body heated up with embarrassment as I mumbled goodbye and fled outside into the cool night air.

Immi and Marcus didn't emerge from the guest room until almost lunchtime. I decided it was probably my break-up with Jack that was souring my disposition when they appeared in my kitchen hand in hand to get sandwiches.

'Don't forget we need to call into town later this afternoon.' I looked meaningfully at Immi. I didn't want her trying to wriggle out of our appointment. My doctor had agreed to open up half an hour early for afternoon surgery so Immi could slip in and out before everyone else began to arrive.

'I know.' She pouted as she poured a couple of glasses of orange juice.

Marcus downed his drink in a few large gulps. 'I'll catch you girls later.' He disappeared through the back door, and Nigel let out a little woof of surprise at the speed of his exit.

'He's running late. He has some appointments.' Immi leaned against the sink and cradled her glass, her eyes dreamy. 'He's so dynamic.'

I made pretend retching noises.

'You're just being childish.' She whopped me lightly on the back of my head with an oven glove, making Nigel growl.

'It's okay,' I reassured him as I scratched the top of his enormous head. 'Imogen was only playing.'

He gave Immi a doubtful look and flopped back down in his basket with a heavy sigh.

'When is he going home?' Immi asked.

'I'm not sure. His owner is still very ill. They rang yesterday and asked me to keep him for a bit longer.' I didn't wish Nigel's owner any harm but I wouldn't mind keeping the Irish wolfhound for good. I'd become very attached to him during the short time he'd been at Rainbow Ridge. Saying farewell to my animals when they were rehomed was one of the hardest things about my work.

Immi faffed about the kitchen, making lunch and wittering on about Marcus, while I sorted out my paperwork for the bank. Since our appearance on television the cheques and donations had started to flood in. There was enough money to pay all the immediate outstanding bills and even a little bit left over to help defray my humongous overdraft. Mr Curzon would be a very happy man when I deposited all this lot in his coffers.

Unusually for me, I changed clothes before we set off for town. I knew it was silly but if by any chance I did bump into Jack, I wanted to look nice. Immi raised her eyebrows when I ran back downstairs in my new jeans and a pretty top, but bit her lip when I glared at her.

'So, what's this Dr Ramirez like?' Immi settled her

sunglasses over her eyes and adjusted her baseball cap.

'Nice. She's good. Everyone likes her.' I waved to Jade as the car scrunched out of the yard and up the private lane to the road.

'And you impressed on her that my visit was confidential, right?'

'Of course. That's why she's seeing you now while the surgery is officially closed. We're to go to the staff door and she'll meet us there so we don't have to run the gauntlet of all the reception staff.'

Immi settled back in the passenger seat and blew out a breath.

'It'll be okay, Imms.' I hoped it would be. It had taken a lot of courage for my sister to admit she had a problem.

The small car park next to the surgery was deserted except for a silver Mitsubishi Shogun that I recognised as Dr Ramirez's. The modern red-brick building was at the far end of town, and apart from anyone who might be nipping to the chemist next door, the place was usually empty at this time of day. I parked near the staff door and walked the few paces with Immi to meet the other woman.

'Come through to my room.' She held the door open for us to enter.

Maria Ramirez was a plump, pretty woman in her mid-forties. She liked animals and had a framed picture of her two youngest daughters with their Labrador on her desk. She had been very nice to me when I registered at her practice. She had appeared to understand completely when I'd told her about the panic attacks and the other problems I'd had.

We sat down on the chairs in front of Dr Ramirez's desk and Immi removed her cap.

'What can I do for you today?' Dr Ramirez glanced between us both, waiting for someone to speak. She didn't appear fazed by my sister's sunglasses.

'Clodagh thinks I have a problem with alcohol,' Immi blurted.

'I see. And what about you? Do you think she is correct, that you have a problem with drinking?' Her voice was gentle.

Immi nodded, bowing her head forward to slide her fingers beneath the bottom of her sunglasses so she could wipe her eyes.

I relaxed slightly in my chair. I'd wondered if Immi would chicken out or try to deny her problem when she was actually faced with doing something about it. I was proud of her for finally facing her demons, something I was only just beginning to do myself.

'Maybe you should tell me about it,' Dr Ramirez suggested.

We finally left some forty minutes later with Dr Ramirez promising to make a referral to a counsellor to give Immi support and help. We slipped back out of the staff door and into the car.

'Are you okay?'

Immi tugged her cap back over her trademark blond hair. 'Yeah. It went better than I thought.'

I drove around to the high street so I could zip into the bank before it closed. Immi wanted to buy chocolate so she went in the other direction, towards the newsagent's. I kept hoping I might see Jack, which was crazy since there was no earthly reason why I should bump into him in town at that time of day.

The ice dragon on the bank counter actually unfroze enough to bestow a smile on me when I paid in the cheques, and she even unbent enough to ask after Immi. I was tempted to ask her if she'd seen Jack but decided that would be pushing my luck.

Immi wasn't waiting in the car when I returned to our parking spot. I hoped she hadn't caused another scene somewhere. Melhampton wasn't used to having a celebrity thrust into its midst, especially one in the middle of a scandal. The newsagent got twitchy if you spent too long looking at the magazines, so he'd probably have a stroke if the chaos that usually happened around my sister materialised in his shop.

It was hot in the car so I rolled down the windows and turned on the radio while I waited. I decided I'd give her ten minutes before I went in search of her. Three and a half songs plus the news later, Immi strolled up to the car. A bundle of glossy magazines was tucked under one arm.

'Took you a long time,' I commented.

She slipped into the passenger seat and fished in her bag before tossing me a Crunchie bar.

'I was just keeping abreast of the news and choosing something to read.'

There was something she'd left out, I could tell from

her tone. I hoped it wasn't anything alcohol-related. There was a small off-licence three doors down from the paper shop.

Susie had almost finished locking up and clearing away when we returned to the sanctuary. I'd barely had time to stop the engine when she hustled across, her nose twitching with excitement.

'George Lovett was here. In person. Asking for you.' She thrust a business card at me.

Immi clambered out of the car and came to stand next to me. We peered at his card together.

'Did he say what he wanted?' I passed the card to Immi. I didn't like touching the thing.

'He wants to meet you. He turned up just after you left. His chauffeur parked his Jag across the walkway and waited for him.' Susie scowled in disapproval.

'What did you say?'

'I told him you were out and that you weren't likely to want to sell the sanctuary so he was wasting his time if that was what he'd come about.' Susie bristled with indignation.

'I bet that went down well,' Immi murmured.

'What did he say to that?' I hoped she'd say he'd changed his mind about meeting me.

'He gave me his card and said something funny.'

'What kind of funny?' Immi took the question right out of my mouth.

'He said he was sure you would see reason and recognise a good deal when you heard it. He wants you to call him.'

Susie's idea of funny was obviously different from mine. 'Okay. Thanks, Susie.'

She gave a self-righteous wriggle of her shoulders. 'That's all right, Clodagh. I'd do anything for you and these lovely creatures.' She heaved a sentimental sigh as she gazed past me to look at Mr Sheen. 'He spoke to Jade as well, for ages, but she left to get the bus before I could find out what he said. They didn't seem to want me to overhear their conversation.'

I could tell that was the part that irked her. Susie hated not being in the loop. With her information imparted, she wombled off to drive home.

'I wonder what he said to Jade,' Immi mused as I closed the gate to the private lane. Susie had already locked the public entrance behind her as she'd left.

'Dunno. Probably the same sort of thing he said to Susie. Susie loves a drama.'

'Maybe.' Immi didn't sound convinced.

'What, you still think that one of the volunteers may be working for Lovett's?' A cool breeze blew against my arm, making me shiver.

'I don't know. But there's something not right. I have an instinct for those kinds of things.'

Immi had instincts for all kinds of things – or so she said. The trouble was that she wasn't always terribly accurate, although she was quick to claim the credit for those rare occasions when she did predict something correctly.

Marcus was in the lounge when we entered the house. We knew he'd be there because we'd seen his little blue car parked in the yard when we'd arrived. Fortunately Immi had loaned him her key or he would have had to sit on the back step until we returned from town. I heard Dave shrieking abuse at him as soon as we set foot in the kitchen.

'I'm starving.' Immi opened the fridge and peered at the contents. 'We need to do another grocery run.'

'You mean *I* need to do a grocery run. I think they may have banned you after the other day.'

She pulled out a pot of yoghurt and inspected the date. 'It's not my fault people find me interesting.' She took a spoon from the drawer and headed to the sitting room. A few seconds later I heard Dave shouting, 'Spank me, spank me!' as the door closed.

I opened the fridge and took a peek. Immi was right – it looked pretty bare except for something in the salad drawer that might pass as a science experiment.

'I'm going to the supermarket,' I called into the hall as I picked up my car keys again. I wanted to make a swift getaway before Immi could decide to come with me. Another scene like the madness of the other day might land me with a permanent ban from the store.

A few spots of half-hearted rain landed on the windscreen as I left the sanctuary. The weather had closed in while we'd been in town and as I set off down the hill I found myself driving into low cloud and drizzle.

There were roadworks along the route I usually took to the supermarket and I had to follow yellow diversion signs along unfamiliar roads. Rain pelted down on the bonnet of the car and the wipers struggled to keep pace with the deluge.

I'd been battling through the rain for a good five minutes when I realised that I must have missed one of the diversion signs, because the town was well behind me and I was heading for open countryside. Not for the first time, I wished I had sat nav. The pouring rain and road spray from the lorries passing me in the opposite lane didn't help my visibility. I turned off as soon as I could and set off along a smaller road that looked as if it would be a promising route back to town. At least I wouldn't have to deal with spray from the traffic as well as rain.

I spotted a white finger post for Melhampton and took the turn. The road narrowed into a lane and as the rain slowed I could see fields to either side of me. Further along the road the fields on one side became obscured by a grey stone wall that grew progressively taller and a prickly, eerie feeling of déjà vu crept over me.

The lane was empty of traffic except for my Fiat, so I slowed to a crawl. Sure enough, looming up in front of me was a familiar pair of stone pillars. Somehow I'd ended up outside Jack's house.

I halted in the lay-by opposite his gates and peered across to see if his Range Rover was on the drive. I don't know what I thought I might do if it was. I wasn't courageous enough to press the buzzer that was set into one of the pillars and ask for admission. Memories of my last visit rushed to the fore, making my body tingle. I backed up a little and spotted Jack's car parked in front of his house, but it wasn't alone. Through the wrought-iron bars of his gate I could see a silver Jaguar with personalised number plates. I didn't have to be a mastermined to figure out the clues to the identity of the owner. The GEO at the start of the plate was a pretty big hint. What I couldn't figure out was why Jack would be entertaining George Lovett, a man he couldn't stand.

I sat in my car for a while, staring through the rain-spattered window at the vehicles parked side by side on Jack's drive while I tried to make sense of it. Eventually I willed myself to release the handbrake and drive off. I didn't want to be found sitting there like a mad stalker if they emerged from the house.

I drove to the supermarket and wandered around the aisles in a complete daze. What was George Lovett doing at Jack's? It made no sense. Was he hoping to make some kind of business deal? I would have thought it unlikely, knowing how things stood between them.

I lobbed a bag of frozen peas into my trolley to replace the ones we'd ruined on Marcus's head when Immi had whacked him the other day. I couldn't believe Jack was hand in hand with George Lovett, considering the history between them. I *knew* that what he'd told me the night we'd made love was the truth. It had been a night for honesty and sharing secrets. He couldn't have lied to me. Frank at the Frog and Ferret had confirmed everything Jack had said, so why would Jack meet a man he hated?

I drove home along the rain-soaked roads with my head still in a whirl. When I pulled into the yard I saw Marcus loading one of Immi's pink suitcases into the boot of his car.

'Where have you been?' Immi teetered out of the house in a pair of high-heeled strappy sandals and handed her pink vanity case to Marcus before pulling up the hood of her sparkly silver jacket against the weather. 'Marty called. I need to go back to London. She's set up a whole string of interviews and magazine shoots.'

'Oh.' I'd become used to having Immi around the place and right now I could have done with someone to talk to.

'Don't worry, I'll be back in time for your open day,' she called over her shoulder as she strutted back inside the house to collect more luggage.

Marcus emerged from the boot of his car. 'I'm sorry we're dashing off like this, Clodagh. I'm still hunting up more information for you on Lovett's operations. If I hit on anything interesting I'll get in touch.'

'Thanks.' I wasn't sure what else to say. After seeing Lovett's car outside Jack's house I couldn't tell what surprises Marcus might uncover, or even if I really wanted to know about them.

Immi reappeared, this time wearing her trademark sunglasses despite the drizzle. She had her favourite oversized Chloe handbag on her arm. 'I'd written you a note in case we were gone when you got back, so just ignore it.' She enveloped me in a fierce over-the-top Immi-style hug. 'I'll ring you.'

I hugged her back, feeling absurdly tearful. 'Take care, please.'

'I will. I promise.' She jumped in Marcus's car and with a last wave out of the window they were gone.

I padlocked the gate behind them and carried my groceries inside the house.

'Looks like it's just you and me, Nigel.' An indignant squawk came from the lounge. 'Oh, and him, of course.' Nigel nuzzled my hand as if he understood perfectly.

I took Immi's note from the table and put it in the recycling box. I thought about making a sandwich but it seemed like too much trouble now that there was only me, and I'd lost my appetite after seeing George Lovett's car at Jack's house.

I checked the answerphone for messages, more in hope than expectation that Jack might have tried to call me. There was one call from the son of Nigel's owner promising to call around with more money, and another from Gloria, my stepmum, wanting to know if Immi and I were okay. Nothing else.

Outside it had started to rain in earnest again, large drops lashing against the window panes. The mist had closed in, enveloping the house in a soft, grey blanket, until I could no longer see past the boundary of the yard and the donkey pen. I drew the curtains and turned on the lamps. Nigel followed me into the sitting room, where Clive lay sleeping on the armchair as usual. Dave huffed his feathers when I sat down in front of the computer, but contented himself with making loud cracking noises with his beak instead of his usual ribald conversation.

It was no use: I couldn't concentrate on answering emails about the open day. I gave up after half an hour, once I'd messaged Gloria with an Immi update and closed the computer down. Nigel nudged my leg in a plea to go out. I slipped on my jacket and got a torch, and we stepped out of the back door into the damp and murky night.

The torch wasn't much help, its beam too weak to penetrate the mist, as we walked briskly towards the area of rough grass near the compost and waste bins behind the barn. I turned up my jacket collar against the damp air creeping insidiously round the back of my neck. I waited for Nigel to finish doing his business and prayed he would hurry up. Normally being alone around the sanctuary didn't bother me, but now I no longer knew who was friend and who was foe it felt eerie and dangerous outside in the dark.

Nigel and I soon padded back towards the house. The yellow glow of my security light illuminated the fog swirling in front of the back door. As we drew closer Nigel stopped in his tracks and gave a low warning growl. I clutched his collar and strained to see what had spooked him.

'Who's there?' I shone my useless flashlight into the opaque mist.

A tall male figure in a long dark overcoat stepped out of the gloom beyond the range of the security light. 'Its okay, Clodagh, it's me. I didn't mean to scare you.'

Jack. I loosened my grip on Nigel's collar and he bounded forward to greet the unexpected visitor with a welcoming lick.

'Where did you come from?' Stupid question. He must have parked in the public car park.

'I tried the front door and couldn't get any reply, so when I saw the yard light glowing in the fog I came round the back. The door was open and I assumed you weren't far away.' He gently pushed Nigel down from where he was attempting to lick his ears.

My hands shook and I stuffed them into my pockets. 'You gave me a fright.'

'I didn't mean to.' He came nearer, his face uncharacteristically serious as he gazed at me. 'I came to apologise for storming out the other night.'

Nigel wandered back to my side.

'Oh.' The mist moved and I shivered; the damp air was slowly seeping into my jacket. 'You'd better come inside.' His sudden appearance, so soon after my discovery earlier in the afternoon, left me feeling unnerved and jittery.

The kitchen was bright, warm and welcoming after the cold night air. Nigel bestowed a last lick on Jack's hand then curled himself up in his basket with a contented sigh. I took off my coat and hung it up before turning to face my visitor.

'I took a wrong turn earlier this evening on my way to the supermarket and ended up going past your house.'

'Then you'll have seen George Lovett's car there, no

doubt.' Jack undid the buttons on his long dark overcoat. He didn't seem unduly perturbed by my comment.

'Yes. Apparently he called here this afternoon. I didn't talk to him – it happened while I was in town with Immi.'

Jack dug his hands in the pockets of his coat and squared his shoulders. 'Where's Immi now?'

'She's gone back to London with Marcus. What's the deal with Lovett, Jack?' My heart rate quickened as I waited for his response. I wasn't about to be diverted into discussing my sister. I wanted answers.

He blew out a breath. 'I saw your sister in town this afternoon. She'd texted me and asked me to meet her.'

I remembered Immi's guilty expression when she'd taken so long returning to the car from the newsagent's. 'Why would she want to meet you?' Another stupid question. My sister had clearly been interfering in my life – again.

'She felt bad about the other night. She worries about you, and about the sanctuary, too. She explained about her suspicions that the volunteers might be involved.' He gave another sigh and looked sheepish. 'I already knew I'd made a twat of myself by blowing up at you. Immi just confirmed it.'

We faced each other across the kitchen.

My pulse gave a little jump at the contrite expression in his eyes. 'You still haven't told me where George Lovett fits into all this.'

He dashed his hand through his hair. 'Lovett turned up at my house right after I got home from meeting Immi. He must have driven to my house straight from here.'

Dread trickled down my spine like iced water – I didn't like the sound of that. 'Why would he visit you? And why would you let him in? I thought you hated each other.'

Jack shrugged. 'I wanted to hear what he had to say, especially after Immi had suggested that Lovett's lot might be behind your problems with vandalism.' His jaw tightened. 'Trust me, it wasn't exactly a friendly meeting.'

'No, I don't imagine it was.'

He reached out to take my hand in his. His touch felt warm against my skin, sending delicious skittery feelings of pleasure tumbling through my body. 'I thought we promised we'd be honest with each other. I know I blew it when I didn't listen to what you wanted to tell me the other night. Will you forgive me and trust me now?'

I gazed into his eyes and waited for my usual feelings of panic and distrust to surface. Nothing. My legacy from Jonathan appeared to have faded. 'There's nothing to forgive. I should have explained things more clearly when you arrived. I'm not surprised you thought I was trying to trick you.'

He smoothed his thumb across my hand and I swallowed hard.

'Does that mean I can stay and tell you what Lovett had to say?' A smile played on the corner of his mouth and the dimple quirked in his cheek.

'I think so.' I didn't get to say anything else for a few minutes. I was too busy kissing Jack – or he was kissing me, I'm not sure which.

Presently, he draped his coat over the back of one of

my kitchen chairs and we went through to the sitting room.

Dave pinged on the bars of his cage as we sat on the sofa. 'Cheap tart! Show us your knickers!'

Jack grinned as he slipped his arm round my shoulders. 'That bird is mental.'

I tried not to let the feel of his hand caressing the nape of my neck distract me. 'You were going to tell me what Lovett wanted?'

His expression immediately sobered and the movement of his fingers stilled. 'He wanted to know if you had agreed to sell your land to me.'

'What? Why would he ask you that?'

Jack frowned. 'He seemed to think that you were on the point of selling when Immi showed up to stay with you. I think your sister may have derailed any plans he might have been harbouring with the TV appearance and the open-day announcement.'

I wriggled upright. 'Why would he think I was about to sell?'

Jack's face gave me my answer.

'He thought I would have no choice, because of my financial problems?'

'Which supports Immi and Marcus's theory that someone close to you has been leaking information. He hinted that he had insider knowledge.'

I leaned back against Jack, revelling in the feel of his firm muscular body against mine. 'Does that mean he could be implicated in the arson attacks?'

'I don't know. It would be hard to prove.'

'What did you say to him?' I took a sideways peep at his face as he pondered my question.

'I told him I wasn't aware that you had any plans to sell. I said he must have been misinformed as to your financial situation.'

'How did he take that?' Anxiety swept through me. George Lovett didn't have a reputation for being the kind of man who would take no for an answer.

I felt Jack give another shrug. 'He didn't seem pleased. He wanted me to know that he'd top any offer I made for your land. He even suggested that if I got it from you cheap he'd pay me a sweetener if I sold it on to him rather than develop it myself. I told him what he could do with his offer, then he called his chauffeur and left.'

'Susie told him I wasn't likely to sell when he called this afternoon. She said he spoke to Jade too, but she didn't know what he said.'

Jack kissed my hair. 'Immi and Marcus think either Susie or Jade is giving out info to Lovett. You know them better than anyone, what do you think?'

My stomach gave a sick lurch. I'd hoped my sister might be mistaken but Jack appeared to be giving credence to her theories. 'I don't know. Susie is a bit eccentric but she really does love the animals. Jade is an excellent volunteer, very hard-working. I'm having a hard time believing either of them could be involved. You don't think they might have let slip the information accidentally?'

Jack's face was sombre. 'I think it's more than passing

on information. Marcus is doing some digging around. It may well be that one or both of them are involved in the arson attacks and the vandalism.'

'That's horrible.' My voice came out as a whisper.

Jack wrapped his arms round me and held me close while I tried to come to terms with what he'd just said.

'When is your open day?' he asked after a few minutes.

'Next week. Why?' I twisted round in his arms to look him square in the face.

'This open day is a big deal for the sanctuary. The media will be here in force – TV, journalists, London press, pretty well everybody. Lovett's best chance, probably his last chance, to force you into selling up would be if something was to happen to really screw up that day.'

I thought about it. It made a twisted kind of sense. If the day was a success then my visitor numbers would probably stay up for a while. I'd make enough money to clear all my debts and save some capital so I'd be secure for the next season. On the other hand, if the day was a failure the bad publicity would more than likely spell the end of Rainbow Ridge.

Before I could ask Jack what he thought I should do, we were interrupted by a commotion in the kitchen. Nigel alternated between howling and barking whilst he scrabbled frantically at the back door.

'What's the matter with your dog?' Jack followed hard on my heels as I hurried along the hall.

'No idea. The only other time he's done this was when Marcus was prowling around and Immi was in the house by herself. Remember? We had to come back from the Apple Loft?' I grabbed Nigel's collar and tried to haul the big dog away from the door, soothing him as I did so.

Jack picked up the torch from where I'd left it on the kitchen table. 'Stay here. I'll go and have a look.' He unlocked the door and was swallowed up by the foggy darkness. I realised a couple of seconds later that the security light had failed to activate.

'Jack! Come back!' Fishcakes, where had he gone? I struggled to hold on to Nigel as he attempted to escape after Jack through the open door.

Something shiny sparkled on the doorstep, twinkling in the light spilling out from the kitchen. I suddenly realised that the bulb in the security light hadn't failed. It had been deliberately smashed, leaving glass shards all over the ground. That had probably been the trigger for Nigel's barking fit.

I hesitated in the doorway. I wanted to go out to look for Jack but the mist and drizzle were so bad that I couldn't see where he'd gone. In the distant darkness near the pens I heard shouting and what sounded like feet scuffling on the gravel path. I snatched up my mobile from the kitchen counter, ready to call the police.

'Jack!'

Nigel slipped free from my grip and shot off into the night. I could hear him barking from the same direction as the scuffling noises. At least, I thought it was the same area. The fog had a strangely disorientating effect and the normal sounds of the sanctuary at night were muffled and distorted.

I shoved my feet into my wellies and scrabbled in the dresser drawers for another torch. I found an old one with a dodgy connection and headed for the back door, hoping I wasn't doing something stupid. The feeble beam illuminated a wall of white mist. I took a deep breath and plunged outside in search of Nigel and Jack. The light from the torch picked up the fence rail and I began to make my way along the path using the rail as my guide. The sounds of barking grew closer and I could hear the crunch of gravel being kicked, mixed with the sound of Jack swearing. It sounded as if there was some kind of fight going on.

I kept going, hoping to stumble across Jack any

moment, but he was further away than I thought. My torch began to flicker. Where the hell were they? I shook the torch in a desperate bid to get the beam to hold steady.

'Jack!'

Nigel responded to my shout with a fresh volley of barks. The scuffling and cursing stopped and for a split second silence fell across the darkness. Then Nigel began to howl. I stumbled along as quickly as I could, muttering a prayer under my breath. What on earth had happened?

Nigel emerged from the fog, whimpering piteously in little snatches of sound. I shone the torch on him and hunted for injuries. He didn't seem hurt and I ran forward, spotting the torch that Jack had taken lying on the ground a few feet ahead. I picked it up but it was completely dead.

'Jack, where are you?' I played my torch around, looking for clues. 'Oh, my God.' The flickering beam fell on a male shape, sprawled on the ground.

I dropped on to my knees at Jack's side. A livid gash streaked his temple and blood oozed stickily from the cut. He wasn't moving. I pulled my mobile from my pocket and dialled for an ambulance while I searched urgently for a pulse.

The ambulance seemed to take for ever as I knelt in the darkness, stroking Jack's hair and reassuring him through my tears that he would be okay. He groaned a couple of times so I knew he was alive, but I was frightened to move him in case I hurt him. The light was too poor for me to see the extent of his injuries. Nigel stayed with me, his hairy body butted up close to mine while I prayed for the medics to hurry.

Finally I saw bright lights coming towards me through the mist, and heard voices.

'Here, we're over here! Hurry, please.' My voice gave out in a sob as the paramedics and police reached us.

I handed over the key to the gate so they could bring the ambulance closer while a policeman questioned me about what had happened. I couldn't tell him anything. I hadn't seen what had gone on and I was too busy trying to watch what was being done to Jack to focus on answering the questions.

The paramedics slipped a soft collar round Jack's neck and lifted him on to a stretcher trolley.

'Please, I want to go with him.' I clutched at the sleeve of the man who was checking Jack's blood pressure.

The policeman nodded his permission and I took Nigel back to the house while Jack was loaded into the back of the ambulance. I locked the back door and jumped into the vehicle, and we set off for the hospital.

'Are you a relative, miss?'

'No, I'm just a friend.' It occurred to me then that I didn't know what I was in Jack's life. A friend? A girlfriend? We'd made love – did that elevate us to relationship status or did it mean I fell into the one-night-stand category? I answered the rest of the paramedic's questions as best as I could. Not that I knew many answers. None that might be useful, like his date of birth or next of kin.

Jack lay on the gurney looking pasty white, with a gauze dressing over the cut on his head. The paramedic kept shining a penlight in his eyes and making notes on a chart while a drip was attached to Jack's arm. We soon arrived at Melhampton General Hospital and I accompanied Jack's stretcher into Accident and Emergency before I was stopped by an officious charge nurse and sent to the waiting room.

I sent a text to Immi.

Jack in hospital. Attacked at sanctuary.

I didn't know what else to put. It was no use calling her; I knew that at night she tended to leave her phone in her kitchen in a stainless steel Alessi fruit bowl that always reminded me of a kidney dish. For all I knew she might not even be back at her flat yet.

I dropped my phone into my coat pocket, leaned back on the hard green plastic chair and closed my eyes for a moment to hold in the tears that threatened to fall. Someone had smashed my security light and attacked Jack out in the fog. The vandalism and arson hadn't been funny before, but this incident took things to a whole other level. Now I was actually scared to be in my own house.

I prayed Jack would be okay. He'd looked so pale. People died from head injuries; you read about it in the paper and saw their ages and thought how terrible it was. Anxiety knotted in my stomach. It made me feel sick, and suddenly all the pain and grief I'd felt when my dad died and when I'd miscarried my baby flooded back over me.

I tried to focus on my surroundings to distract myself

from the awful scenarios playing inside my mind. A television screen in the corner of the waiting room played a series of crappy infomercials about returning crutches and paying for parking. A young woman in a pink sari to my left sobbed noisily into a bundle of tissues and a group of drunken lads were arguing by the reception counter.

Every few minutes the automatic doors would open with new arrivals or people limping off home with different body parts swathed in plaster or bandages. I wondered how long it would be before anyone came out and told me how Jack was doing. I tried to think positively and watched an advert for a firm of local solicitors on the TV screen.

'Clodagh Martin?' A young nurse with dark hair appeared at my side. 'Mr Thatcher has come round and is asking for you.'

I followed the nurse down a long white-walled corridor, silently thanking God with every step that Jack was okay.

'He's through there.' She indicated an area screened off with dark blue curtains. 'I'm afraid you can't stay long as he's being moved to the observation ward and the police are waiting to interview him about the attack.' She gave me a doubtful smile, almost as if she suspected me of being implicated in it.

'Hey.' Jack gave me a feeble smile as I entered his cubicle.

'Hey yourself.' I took his hand. 'How are you?' The gash above his eye had been closed with what appeared to be small strips of plaster. A greenish black bruise had started to form around the cut and along the cheekbone on the other side of his face, where the harsh fluorescent lighting showed up a scrape.

'I've been better. I've some sympathy for Marcus now.' The dimple flashed briefly in his cheek.

I bit my lip in an attempt to stop myself from crying. 'What happened?'

'Two people jumped me. I tried fighting them off but two on one in the fog wasn't good combo.' He squeezed my fingers. 'I'm glad it was me that got whacked and not you.'

'Don't say that.' I sniffed. 'The nurse said the police are coming to talk to you.'

'Yeah. They want to keep me here tonight because I was out for so long.'

'They asked me about contacting somebody. I didn't know who to tell them to call.'

'It's okay. The nurses have dealt with everything.' He adjusted his position slightly on the trolley and winced at the movement. 'Listen, are you okay to go back to the sanctuary? Can you get Immi to come back or is there someone else you can go and stay with?'

'I'll be fine. I've sent Immi a text.' I crossed the fingers of my free hand inside my jacket pocket. I wasn't looking forward to being on my own at the sanctuary but the animals needed me. As soon as it was daylight I could ring Tom and Val. I was sure they would be able to help.

The nurse bustled back into the cubicle and picked

up Jack's chart. She gave me a polite smile. 'I'm afraid you'll have to leave now.'

Jack gave my hand another squeeze of reassurance before I got bundled back along the corridor to the waiting room. I rang for a cab to take me home. For the first time the sanctuary was no longer my cosy refuge from the world. Life had intruded on it big time, shattering my illusions of security and peace. I felt glad I had Nigel and grateful that he was a big dog, not a little terrier or a handbag pooch.

My phone rang while I was in the cab. The tinny tune made me jump and I almost dropped it as I fished it out of my pocket.

'I got the text. What happened?' Immi's voice was breathless with anxiety.

I told her everything.

'Oh, my God, Clodagh. Where are you? You can't stay at the sanctuary by yourself. Who were these people? What did they want?' Questions that I had no answers for poured out of her.

'Imms, it's okay.' I paid the cabbie and hurried down the path to my front door, anxious to get safely inside before he drove away and left me alone. The fog had lifted slightly and the visibility had improved enough to enable me to continue to talk to Immi while I unlocked the door. 'Look, I'm home. Nothing else is likely to happen tonight and someone has to be here for the animals.'

I didn't know if I was attempting to reassure her or myself.

'Lock the windows and the doors. Do you need someone there? I can send Marcus.'

I smiled a bit at the last part. Nigel pattered down the hall to greet me and even Clive deigned to come and wrap himself round my legs while I fastened the door chain.

'I'm fine. Marcus does not need to drive all the way back down here. Tom will be here in a few hours.' I peeped through the sitting-room door to see Dave dozing on his perch.

'I don't know. This is seriously scary stuff, Clo.' I could hear the indecision in her voice.

'Go to bed. That's what I intend to do. I'll call you tomorrow. Everything is okay – really.'

I put the cover over Dave's cage and checked the back door and the lock on the kitchen window. After a moment's thought I rummaged in the base of the dresser and found my claw hammer. I intended to sleep with some security under my pillow.

I didn't sleep very well even with the hammer under my pillow and a chair wedged under my bedroom door handle. I kept seeing images of Jack sprawled on the ground in the darkness while two black-clad, faceless people laughed at me.

In the end I rose and dressed before my alarm went off. Last night's fog and rain had dissipated, leaving a damp grey morning in their wake. My cup of tea did nothing to clear my head and I wondered if it was too early to call the hospital to find out how Jack was feeling.

The animals appeared none the worse for the night's events when I whizzed through my early morning chores. I deliberately avoided going near the area of the sanctuary where Jack had been set upon. I knew his mystery assailants weren't likely to still be hanging about, but I wasn't up to being all calm and rational while the attack was so fresh in my memory. Every time the wind blew or a leaf rustled I whirled round, thinking someone was behind me. After an hour of twitching and jumping I was exhausted by my own paranoia. Even Nigel seemed worn out by the strain.

My chores completed, I headed back to the house and rang the hospital. A brusque voice informed me that Jack had spent a comfortable night and no decision had been reached as to when he would be discharged. The latter bit of information was offered grudgingly and only after I'd phrased the question three different ways. I made myself a plate of toast and waited for Tom to arrive.

Tom had offered to come in every morning to prepare the sanctuary for the open day. Flushed with the cash boost from the TV appearance, I intended to invest in materials to make some much-needed repairs. Everything would get a coat of paint or preserver, the lawn areas were to be immaculate and everything would be in as good a shape as we could manage on the big day. Immi had been in contact with a film crew and Marty had lined up the rest of the media, ready to descend on us in their hordes.

I munched on my toast and thought about what Jack had said about someone trying to sabotage the open day. Last night, before the attack, I'd thought the idea far-fetched. Now I wasn't so sure.

My mobile rang, sending me shooting out of my seat with a yelp.

'It's me. I knew you'd be up at this ridiculous hour. I've been up ages, too – Marty has scheduled an insane number of interviews today. Is everything okay? How's Jack?' Immi's voice sounded thready and I could hear traffic noise in the background.

'They wouldn't tell me much, just said he'd had a comfortable night. I'm waiting for Tom to turn up.'

Right on cue there was a knock at the back door and Tom's face appeared at the kitchen window. I unlocked the door and drew back the bolt with my free hand. 'Imms, he's here so I'll have to go.'

'I'll call you later.' She might have said something else but the connection crackled and died before she'd finished speaking.

'Locked and bolted? What's up, Clodagh?' Tom asked.

As I explained what had happened his normally cheerful expression was replaced with a frown. 'You should have phoned us. Val would have come and stopped with you. It's not right, a young lass like you being on your own when there're thugs about. I don't know what this town is coming to.' He chuntered on about when he'd been a lad, and how the police should do more, and what happened to all the taxes he paid. It reminded me so much of something my dad might have said that I had a lump in my throat and tears in my eyes by the time he'd finished.

I finally managed to reassure him that I was okay, and dispatched him to fix the felt roof on the donkey stable. Then Susie appeared.

'Is the kettle hot? It's not so nice out there this morning.' She dumped her bag down on the kitchen table and began to unravel some of her layers.

'Jack's in hospital. He was attacked here late last night by a prowler. We don't know why. Nothing was taken or damaged that I can see, apart from the security light being smashed.' I watched closely for her reaction. Not that I could see Susie donning black clothes and a balaclava and launching an assault on Jack under the cover of darkness. Since Jack is over six feet tall and Susie about five foot two it wouldn't have been much of a contest.

'Attacked? Here?' She gaped at me open-mouthed. 'Was he badly hurt? Oh my goodness, Clodagh, what if you'd been here on your own?'

If she was feigning surprise she was a better actress than my sister. I made her a cup of tea and she took a seat at the table.

'I know, I can't stop thinking about it. It gives me the shivers.'

'Jade's late today. Perhaps her bus didn't turn up.' Susie glanced at the old-fashioned man's watch on her wrist. 'I'm surprised her boyfriend never gives her a lift. He's got a really nice car.'

'Oh?' I was surprised. I'd always been under the impression that Jade's boyfriend was a struggling student like her.

'I've only met him a couple of times. Jade never seems very keen for me to see him.' Susie slurped her tea. 'He's quite a bit older than her.'

'What does he do? I always thought he was a student.' I leaned back against the sink unit and tried to act nonchalant.

Susie wrinkled her brow. 'I'm not certain. Some kind of trade, I think. Plumbing or something.'

I stored that nugget away in my brain as Susie finished her drink and went off to start her work. Our chat had made me feel uneasy. I knew very little about my volunteers, and now it appeared that even the bits I thought I knew I actually didn't.

My mobile rang again as I started to wash up the mugs.

'Hey.'

My heart gave its usual funny little flip at the sound of Jack's voice.

'Hey to you too. How are you? I rang earlier but they wouldn't tell me anything.'

'I can come out, only there's a slight hitch.'

'What kind of hitch?' My voice was shrill; all kinds of horrors whizzed through my mind. Most of them involved blood clots on the brain and terrible psychological side-effects from the attack.

'Well, despite the best efforts of my boyish charm and good looks, they're insisting that I don't drive and that I have someone stay with me for twenty-four hours.'

I relaxed as the threat of permanent brain damage receded. 'Your car's here anyway. I can come and get you. You can stay with me.'

The connection went quiet. Maybe staying in my house was the last thing he wanted. Maybe staying with *me* was the last thing he wanted.

'Thanks, Clodagh.'

I left Tom and Susie in command and hurried off to the hospital. Jack was seated in a chair at the side of his bed. I tried not to gasp at the state he was in. The black and green bruising had extended over most of his face and his jaw looked puffy and swollen.

'I've heard the other guy looks worse,' he quipped.

I tried to muster a smile. One of the nurses gave me a leaflet on head injuries with a list of instructions about what I should do if he started having any problems.

'I'm sure I'll be in good hands,' he assured her.

We made our way out of the hospital to my car.

'Do you want to collect anything from your house?' I busied myself with fastening my seat belt and fiddling with the car key. I wasn't sure that Jack actually wanted to stay at the sanctuary.

'Toothbrush, razor, knuckleduster.' He winced as he tried to smile.

'Very funny. You don't have to stay with me if you'd rather not. You know, if there's a friend you'd rather stay with or something.' That hadn't come out right. It sounded as if I didn't want him to stay.

'I think I'd scare most of them half to death if I turned up on their doorstep looking like this.' He moved cautiously in his seat and I wondered how much of a battering the rest of him had taken.

'I'll make up the bed in Immi's room for you.'

I shouldn't have thought about his body or bed. I could feel myself getting flustered and had to open my window a crack. I half expected him to make some joke about sharing my bed but he didn't. Instead he looked thoughtful and stared out of the window. I couldn't help feeling snubbed.

I waited in the car while Jack went into his house to collect an overnight bag. I'd offered to help but he'd insisted he'd only be a few minutes.

I'd started to worry about how long he'd been inside when he emerged clutching a navy blue holdall in one hand and his BlackBerry in the other. He eased his way into the passenger seat, concentrating on the screen of his phone.

'Interesting.' He tapped a quick response to whoever had texted him and dropped the phone back in his lap.

I wasn't sure what his comment was supposed to mean, but I didn't want to look nosy by asking what the message was about.

It was time for lunch when we finally arrived back at the sanctuary. Tom had vanished and I assumed Susie was safely ensconced in the new shed with her Tupperware box of salad. There was no sign of Jade and I wondered if she'd turned up.

'Make yourself at home.' I opened the back door.

'Thanks.' Jack followed me in and patted Nigel on the head when the dog came pattering over to greet him.

We stood looking at one another in the kitchen.

'Can I get you a drink, or some lunch?' This felt awkward.

'Coffee would be fine.'

'Go on through to the sitting room.' We were like strangers together, not like two people who'd been as intimate as two people can be only a few days before.

I heard Dave swearing a welcome as I waited for the kettle to boil. It was going to feel very weird having Jack around for the next twenty-four hours. Every time I looked at his poor battered face I felt guilty that I hadn't been quicker to follow him outside into the fog last night.

I carried his coffee through to the sitting room and put it down carefully on the table.

'Give us a quickie!' Dave huffed up and down his perch, bobbing his head.

Jack was looking at his phone again.

'Are you sure you should be doing that?' I tried to remember if the nurses had said anything about reading. There had been a long list of dos and don'ts.

'It's from Marcus.' Jack glanced up at me from under his swollen eyebrow. 'He's been doing a lot of digging around.'

'And?' I sat down on the arm of the chair, risking a glare from Clive, who felt the armchair was strictly his province.

'It would seem Lovett has been getting into some murky waters. His company finances are stretched quite thinly at the moment.' Jack frowned and tapped a message back to Marcus.

'Then why would he want to spend more money on buying Rainbow Ridge?'

Jack placed his BlackBerry on the table and picked up his coffee mug. 'I think your land is important for several reasons. Not least access.' He sipped cautiously at his drink and winced as he caught his lip.

'I don't understand.' My heart squeezed in sympathy with Jack's struggle to drink his coffee.

'Your land would enable him to open up the Long Meadow site. He could build almost double the number of properties. The plans he's had passed are quite restrictive because of the road access. Obtaining the rights to the private lane would make a huge difference.'

'I see.' That was more or less what Mr Curzon at the bank had said when I'd gone for my chat with him: that it was the lane that made my land so desirable.

Jack replaced his mug on the table. Dark stubble shadowed his cheeks and smudges of fatigue showed under his eyes.

'You look beat. Go and have a rest on Immi's bed. I made it up before I came to get you.' I expected him to argue with me.

'Some sleep wouldn't be a bad idea. I didn't get a lot of it last night. And every time I did drop off they wanted to either shine a torch in my eyes or pump my arm up to check my blood pressure.' He eased up from the sofa.

'Immi's is the pink room.' I remained seated, even though I wanted to wrap my arms around him and hug his hurts away.

'Of course.' He managed a faint smile and a few seconds later I heard the heavy tread of his feet on the stairs.

'Slapper!' Dave spat the last of his pear at me.

I left Jack to sleep and mooched off round the sanctuary with Nigel at my heels. The poor weather had deterred most potential visitors and only the barn was busy with some toddlers and their parents looking at the rabbits and other small animals.

I found Susie in the shed, leafing through a craft magazine.

'Look at these lovely doilies. I must practise my crochet.' She waved a picture of a hideous woolly object at me.

'Lovely.' I hoped she couldn't tell I was lying.

'Jade called after you'd gone out and said she wouldn't be in for a few days. She said she wasn't very well.'

'She seemed okay yesterday. Does she have a cold or something?' Jade was usually as fit as a flea. It was Susie who was normally dosing herself up with herbal remedies and stinking us out with Vick's VapoRub.

'She was very vague, actually. I asked if she had a cold; I would have dropped some of my decongestants round to her house if she had.' Susie continued to flip through her magazine. 'She said she didn't feel well but that she'd be in for the open day.'

'I hope she feels better soon.' I wasn't sure whether I meant what I said, because I couldn't shake the prickle of unease that had settled between my shoulder blades.

Susie blinked at me from behind her specs. 'I expect she'll turn up when she's ready. Oh, and I couldn't get her to tell me what George Lovett said to her. I told her if he'd given her a message for you I'd be happy to pass it on.'

'What did she say to that?' You had to admire Susie's cheek.

'She didn't say anything, simply ignored me.'

'Couldn't have been anything important, then.'

'But he talked to her for ages. She looked all flushed and he looked grumpy. But he generally looks grumpy anyway. Like a bulldog chewing a wasp.' She still sounded huffy.

'I'm sure it was nothing.' I wished I could be sure, but Jade's behaviour had begun to look increasingly odd.

Susie gave a disparaging sniff and resumed the study of her craft magazine.

Nigel and I wandered back out to see Tom placing a ladder against the back wall of the house ready to replace the broken bulb in the security light.

'I thought I'd best get this done. You need to see who's hanging about, especially after what happened to your young man.'

I held the bottom of the ladder while Tom clambered up.

'I found out what those vandals were up to last night,' he called over his shoulder.

'What?'

'It looks as if they were trying to cut the wire fencing that runs along the back by the barn. I found a hole in it this morning – patched it back up, though.' He screwed in the new bulb and tucked the metal fragment of the old one safely into the pocket on the bib of his overalls.

I waited for him to descend the ladder. 'What do you think they were hoping to do?'

'I dunno. Seems a lot of trouble to go to just to make mischief. Especially as they attacked your young man for no good reason.' Tom gave me a meaningful look. It was clear he had Jack and me pegged as an item.

'There have certainly been a lot of peculiar things happening lately.'

He picked up the ladder. 'Aye, and I reckon it's a good thing you've got company in this house. Val and me never thought it was very safe when it was only you and your sister, especially with the kind of attention she attracts. Now this has happened I hate to think what could have gone on with you here on your own.'

He looked so worried that I felt quite mushy over his concern for my safety. 'I'll be fine,' I reassured him. 'I doubt if the people who attacked Jack are likely to come back. The police have promised to make extra patrols.'

'That's all well and good, but they promised extra patrols before and nothing came of it.' Tom sounded unconvinced. 'It's a good job you've got the lad staying here with you.'

I wasn't sure if Jack would be up to fighting anyone for a while, considering his present battered state, but Tom clearly felt I was safer with a man on the premises.

Once Susie and Tom had gone and the sanctuary was closed I decided to make Jack a cup of tea before starting my evening rounds. The damp grey day had given way to a drizzly evening and I wasn't looking forward to being out in the grounds alone.

Jack had drawn the curtains in Immi's room and was asleep under her pastel-pink duvet. He stirred as I opened the door, blinking at me in the gloom.

'I brought you a cup of tea.' I switched on the bedside lamp, making a pool of mellow light.

'Thanks. I think I went out cold.' He eased himself up into a sitting position. His lightly tanned bare skin was in a sharp contrast to the girly bed linen. An ugly scrape on his shoulder matched the bruising on his face. My fingers made an automatic move towards the injured skin. Fortunately, I checked myself before he noticed.

'Tom says he found a hole in the chain-link fence on the boundary by the barn.'

Jack moved his legs under the quilt and patted the edge of the bed, indicating that I should sit down. I perched on the edge of the bed accordingly.

'I remember hearing the noise of the cutters on the wire mesh,' Jack said, 'but in the fog I couldn't tell where they were. Then I saw the light of the torches coming towards me and tried to block their path. I caught hold of one of them, a hefty bloke, and we had a bit of a scuffle as I tried to hold on, but I think that must have been when the other one hit me with something heavy. The next thing I remember is waking up in the hospital.'

'And you never saw their faces?'

He shook his head. 'The one I fought with was definitely a man but I got the impression the other one, the one who knocked me out, was a woman. I definitely heard a female voice before everything went black.'

I picked at the ribbon braid on the edge of the duvet cover with my fingernail. 'That makes it worse, somehow.'

He adjusted the pillow behind his head. The combination of the stubble on his face and the unkempt lock of hair that fell across his brow made him look like a dark, sexy pirate. His bare chest was exposed, revealing the faint trail of dark hairs leading down to more intimate areas. My pulse hitched up a notch and desire pooled in my stomach. He scratched thoughtfully at the corner of his lips, right where I longed to kiss him. Fishcakes, I needed to move off the edge of his bed . . .

I shot to my feet. 'I'd better get on with my jobs. I'll cook some supper when I come back in.' I edged towards the door.

Jack watched me with a bemused expression on his face. 'Would it be okay if I used your shower?'

'Shower, um . . . yeah, help yourself,' I squeaked, then bolted from the room all hot and bothered by mental images of Jack naked in my shower.

I hurried through the outside jobs with my trusty can of de-icer tucked in my pocket. Not much of a weapon, but with the visibility decreasing as the cloud cover came in, it was better than nothing. Nigel accompanied me, his hairy face clearly conveying his opinion that humans were mad and silently asking why I wasn't indoors instead of getting wet in the rain.

Once back in the house he sloped off to the sitting room and sprawled out on the hearthrug to steam gently in front of the fire. I stayed in the kitchen, wondering what I could cook for supper. The dreariness of the evening made me feel chilled inside. I drew the blue gingham curtains against the darkening sky and turned on the radio for company. Upstairs the floorboards creaked as Jack moved around. It took all my effort to concentrate on chopping vegetables instead of indulging in lustful daydreams about my house guest.

Jack appeared in the kitchen while I was busy singing along to Wham! and prodding the potatoes with a knife as they bubbled in the pan.

'Can I help with anything?'

I stopped singing and dropped the lid back on the saucepan with a clang. 'No, it's okay. Have a seat. Everything is almost done.'

He'd shaved as well as showered and I could smell the faint scent of clean male as I placed cutlery on the table in front of him. I bustled about the kitchen, draining the potatoes and dishing up the chicken and vegetables. I'd never cooked a meal for a man before.

Jonathan had always insisted we ate out, usually somewhere dimly lit and a long way from the university. Before then I'd lived at home, so any date with food involved meant eating out or joining in with a family meal. The family meals had tended not to be very successful as my dad had interrogated my date over the starter and Immi had talked them to death by dessert.

I slid the plates on to the mats and joined Jack at the table.

'This looks nice.' He picked up his cutlery.

'Thanks.' This was crazy. I'd had sex with this man. There wasn't a part of my body he hadn't touched, and we'd seen each other naked. The evening we'd made love everything had seemed natural and right. Two people sealing a deal to be honest and open with each other. We'd shared deep secrets and feelings, not to mention our bodies, yet simply sitting in the quiet cosiness of my kitchen together and eating a meal that I'd prepared seemed far more intimate, somehow.

What was I to him? When we'd had wild rampant sex neither of us had mentioned love and that had been okay. It hadn't seemed necessary. Now I knew Jack better my feelings towards him had grown, but I still wasn't sure where I stood. I concentrated on eating my chicken and tried to muster enough courage to bring the subject up.

The background music on the radio gave way to the hourly news bulletin. I didn't pay much attention to the newsreader until I heard him mention Kirk's name. I hurried to turn up the volume.

'Breaking news this evening from Los Angeles, where the British actor Kirk Drummond has been arrested less than a week after arriving there to begin work on the blockbuster film *Deep Sky*. No further details have been given at this point but the arrest is thought to be in connection with an alleged sex offence involving a minor. Drummond hit the headlines last Thursday when he was assaulted by his former girlfriend, soap star Imogen Martin, on the popular TV chat show, *Talk About It*. Since then a number of women have come forward alleging improper sexual behaviour by the thirty-year-old actor.'

'Sounds like your sister will be in demand even more now.'

I turned the volume back down. 'I told you he was a sleaze bag.'

Kirk being slime didn't excuse Immi from getting sloshed and causing a scene for the entertainment of the nation, but it did mitigate the offence a little. We'd barely finished eating when my mobile started to ring. First there was Immi, wanting to know if I'd heard the news about Kirk, then Gloria, via text, to say it was big news over in the US too.

Jack helped me wash up while I answered the various calls. All the time I was aware of electricity building between us as we stood side by side at the kitchen sink exchanging chit-chat and passing plates.

'That's the last pan.' Jack hung the tea towel on its hook. 'What do you do for fun round here?'

'Read, surf the Net, talk to Dave. I don't have a TV.' I straightened up from putting the saucepan away inside the cupboard to discover he'd moved closer to me. 'Of course, we could go to the pub for an hour.' My voice squeaked up a notch again as I realised I was trapped between Jack and the sink unit.

'Or we could just stay in,' he murmured, and lowered his lips to meet mine.

I tried to remember to be careful of his sore mouth as the lean, hard length of his body pressed against me.

'Staying in might be nice,' I managed to pant between kisses.

His hands slipped beneath my T-shirt and under my bra to cup my breasts. As he slid his thumbs across my nipples I really couldn't think straight at all.

Jack left shortly after I'd crept out of bed to start my morning chores; his BlackBerry had rung a few minutes before my alarm with a call from one of his sites about a problem. I'd hoped he'd be able to stay so we could talk. We certainly hadn't done any talking last night. We'd been too busy doing other things until we'd fallen asleep. My plans for a cosy breakfast together were crushed when Jack ended his call and, with much muttering of bad language, started to dress in a tearing hurry. He didn't even stop for coffee. I had to be satisfied with a quick kiss and a 'See you later'.

My day turned out to be quite busy too. The weather had improved and so, therefore, had the visitor count – plus the phone kept ringing with calls about the open day, which was now only a week away. There were also a few calls from the local press who'd got wind of the attack on Jack and wanted details or comments. I let the machine take their calls. I'd learned enough from Immi not to go down that particular route.

Immi rang to say her suspension from the daytime soap had been lifted and she was to start filming again on

Monday. In fact, the only person who didn't call me was Jack. I could understand him being busy, but we'd spent the night in one another's arms . . . Surely he could have found a little time in his day for a quick call? My spirits nose-dived as the day wore on without a word from him. I wasn't even sure if he planned to come back to the sanctuary or if he would return home now he was medically in the clear.

His apparent uninterest had left me feeling more than a little cross, so I agreed to go with Val, Tom and Susie to the Chinese for supper after the sanctuary closed. If Jack were to turn up with a big bunch of roses expecting to find me at home waiting for him he would be sadly disappointed. I'd done that too often before with Jonathan, cancelling plans, putting off friends, only to sit at home all alone on the off chance that he might call me. I didn't plan to make the same mistake again.

The meal at the Lucky Dragon was good. It was nice to go out for a few hours and have some fun as a reward for everyone's hard work. Val and Tom were excited about the open day and mercifully refrained from teasing me too much about Jack. Even Susie joined in the chat and was actually quite funny after half a lager.

We didn't stay late. Val and Tom gave me a ride home while Susie headed off in the opposite direction. I checked my mobile in the back of Tom's car – still nothing from Jack, not even a poxy text. It seemed I still didn't know where I stood with him. I didn't expect him to swear undying devotion to me – although it would actually be quite nice if he did – I just wanted to feel that I meant something to him. I didn't want to be one more notch on his bedpost, somebody he slept with when the fancy took him. Maybe I'd been fooling myself when I'd said that not saying the L word didn't matter to me. Perhaps it mattered more than I'd been prepared to admit. My good mood from the night out seeped away as I put my mobile away and said goodnight to Val and Tom.

The sunshine of the afternoon had given way to a cool night with a brisk breeze. I crossed the road to the front of my house, listening to the rustle of the leaves as the branches tossed in the crisp evening air. I had to admit the crispness came as a blessed relief after the fog of the last few nights. It seemed to dispel the creepy atmosphere of suspicion and fear that had surrounded me ever since the attack on Jack.

I saw the black scorch marks and blistered paint scarring the front door round the letter box before I'd even pulled my key from my bag. My pulse leapt up as Nigel howled like a banshee from the hallway. I forced the key into the lock with shaking hands. My haste to get inside made my fingers clumsy as I struggled to unlock the door.

Nigel bounded forward to greet me, almost knocking me over as he planted his huge paws on my shoulders to pin me to the wall in his happiness at my return. The smell of cordite made me cough as I tried to reassure the big dog so I could see what had happened. I checked him over but didn't think that he was hurt.

On the doormat I saw the reason for the scorching that I'd noticed round the letter box outside. A half-spent firework had burned a hole in the mat, making the house stink of burnt coir. The cream walls of the hall were sooty with smoke and there were flash burns on the stair carpet. The Chinese I'd just eaten tried to come back up as I realised how close I'd been to having my home burned down. Thank God the fire had failed to take hold, self-extinguishing on the mat instead. I soothed Nigel, then hurried into the lounge to check on Dave.

'Sod you!' He huffed up his feathers and squawked at me.

His temper had clearly not been improved by the firework experience. Reassured that he was okay, I rang the police. Dave continued to shriek his annoyance at me till I was forced to quiet him by offering a grape, one of his favourite treats. I peered in the kitchen in case there had been any attempt to start a fire there too, but everything looked exactly as I'd left it.

My pulse began to settle now I knew the extent of the damage, but then I realised my cat had disappeared. Clive disliked any kind of loud noise and tended to go off and hide if I wasn't around. Panicking in case he'd been hurt, I checked all his favourite hiding places. I finally found him inside my wardrobe, where he'd peed on my shoes, just as the police patrol car pulled up.

It was two hours before the police finally left, complete with the firework and a statement. I threw the burnt mat outside the back door and scrubbed the worst of the soot from the walls and the hallway floor. I was overwhelmed with relief that the house hadn't caught fire and none of my pets had been hurt. A shudder ran through me when I thought about all the things that could have happened. I could have been home when the firework was being pushed through the door. Nigel could have been asleep on the doormat.

I rang Immi to tell her what had happened. Her phone was off so I left a message on her voicemail. I sat at the bottom of the stairs for a while with Nigel at my side, wondering if I should call Jack. I wanted to ring and let him know what had happened but at the same time I still felt peeved that he hadn't phoned me. If I did call him would he feel obligated to offer to come and stay the night with me? My body heated at the idea of another night with Jack in my bed and I closed the phone quickly.

I'd run around like a fool after Jonathan, and all I'd got for my efforts had been a broken heart and a nervous breakdown. I stared at the mobile in my hand, torn between wanting to hear Jack's voice reassuring me and fear that I was about to repeat the mistakes of my past. I'd taken some huge steps lately but right now it was almost midnight and my limbs were shaky with fatigue. Tomorrow, when I felt stronger – I'd call him tomorrow.

Tom, Val and Susie were all horrified when they arrived the next morning and learned what had happened while we'd been out at the restaurant.

'The whole house could have gone up.' Val's pleasant face was perturbed.

'Your poor pets!' Susie looked like she was about to cry.

'CCTV, that's what you need,' was Tom's contribution.

'I'm coming back tonight. It's the last of the interviews and shoots today. They can get lost for the rest. You can't stay there on your own.' Immi sounded as shaken as I felt when she called at breakfast time.

I didn't put up much of a protest. The thought of spending another evening on my own at the house scared me more than I'd been willing to let on. I'd spent the night tossing and turning at every alien sound. I even agreed to let Tom go off and get some cameras for the front and back of the house, I felt so nervy.

When Jack's Range Rover pulled up in the yard just before ten, the others all made themselves scarce. My terse responses to their innocent enquiries about Jack's whereabouts had tipped them off that all wasn't well between us.

His face was like thunder as he slammed the car door shut and stormed across the gravel towards me.

'What's going on? I had a garbled message from Immi on my phone this morning about a house fire. Are you hurt? Why didn't you call me?' The bruising on his face had fully developed and the cut above his eyebrow looked livid and sore.

'Everything's fine. Nothing was damaged except my doormat.' I tried to ignore the stabbing hurt in my chest that he'd only turned up now because my sister had phoned him.

'It doesn't sound very fine. I gather from Immi that someone tried to burn your house down.' A nerve jumped in his cheek.

'Look, it was late last night. The police came and by the time they'd gone it was almost midnight. Besides, *you* didn't call *me* all day.' I felt quite indignant. He'd dashed from my bed and not contacted me and had only bothered now because my sister had taken it upon herself to call him.

Jack swore and I glared at him.

'I didn't get a chance to ring you yesterday. I was on site all day and didn't get home till after eleven last night.'

'Right.' I wasn't born yesterday. Jack might know how to press all the right buttons to turn me on but I'd already had one disastrous relationship, and while I knew Jack wasn't like Jonathan I couldn't afford to let my heart get broken again. It had taken me too long to recover the first time. He could have phoned me if he'd really wanted to.

Jack glowered at me. 'God, Clodagh, you can be as stubborn as your donkeys. Tell me you're not planning on staying here by yourself tonight? What if these people try something else?'

'It's okay. Immi's coming back. You don't need to worry about me.' That let him off the hook. He didn't need to play the valiant knight any more.

He gritted his jaw. 'Then I'm sure you'll both be fine.'

He turned on his heel and strode back towards his car. From the way he spun the wheels as he left I knew I'd made him really angry.

My own anger fizzled away in the time it took Jack to vanish from sight. I knew he was cross because he cared. It was this trust business again. I should have trusted that he'd call me, that he wouldn't simply get up from my bed and leave me high and dry. Why did I keep making the same stupid mistakes?

Susie emerged from Miko and Pasquale's stable. 'He looked cross.'

'We had a bit of a disagreement.' I wasn't about to discuss my private life with Susie, so I opted for diversionary tactics. 'Any news from Jade?'

She shook her head. 'I tried to call her to tell her about the fire but I got put on to voicemail.'

There wasn't any more time to talk as a lorry arrived with the portable toilets for the paddock. The rest of the day seemed to fly past. I was glad to be busy – it stopped me from dwelling on the empty, hollow feeling inside me caused by my argument with Jack.

Immi arrived by taxi after supper. She rushed down the path to meet me, leaving the bemused taxi driver to lift her pink luggage from the boot of the cab.

'I thought Jack would be here,' she announced once she'd paid her fare and I'd hauled her bags up to her room.

'It's a long story.' I filled her in on what had happened, glossing over the sex part. 'You shouldn't have rung him.'

'Well, how was I to know what was going on? I knew

he was staying with you yet you didn't mention him being here, so what was I supposed to think? If the two of you can't decide if you're an item or not then how am I supposed to know?' Immi was indignant.

Maybe she had a point. I decided to change the subject. 'How's Marcus?'

A beatific smile settled on my sister's face. 'He's such a sweetie, but horrendously busy with his new job. You know what he found out about your friend George Lovett, of course?'

'Yes, Jack told me.'

'Oh, I'm glad you talked about something.'

I wasn't sure I liked the hint of sarcasm in her tone. 'Do you still think one of the volunteers is involved in all this?'

Immi frowned. 'I don't know. From what you've told me it doesn't sound as if Val or Tom would get involved with this kind of thing, and annoying as Susie is, I can't see that she could be, either.'

'Which leaves Jade.' I didn't want to think of Jade's being allied with people who would attack Jack and try to burn down the sanctuary and my house. But it did seem strange that she hadn't rung me herself to say she was ill and that her time off coincided with an escalation in the attacks. She knew I needed money and it appeared that I had a very different idea of Jade's lifestyle from the one Susie had described.

It could still simply be me being paranoid, though. Having someone push a live firework through your letter box and batter your boyfriend unconscious does that to a girl. I might be maligning Jade – it could just be a string of freaky coincidences that was making me suspicious.

'Mmm. Maybe we should do some snooping around.' Immi's eyes brightened.

'That might be difficult considering you're so well known.' I knew my sister had visions of us staking out Jade's place like members of *The Bill* or younger, slimmer versions of *Cagney and Lacey*.

Immi shrugged. 'It probably wouldn't tell us anything, anyway. I guess we'll have to wait and see if she shows up for the open day and keep a close eye on her.'

The weekend passed without any further incidents. There was no word from Jade and nothing from Jack. My hopes of his calling me were fading fast but I expressly forbade Immi to interfere with my love life by contacting him. She set off back to London late on Sunday accompanied by Marcus, both of them promising to return on Friday in time for the big day.

Their car had barely disappeared from view when Val and Tom arrived with a bottle of wine and a Monopoly board.

'We thought a bit of company would be nice for you,' Val said as she counted out the money.

'Aye, let anyone know as might be watching you're not on your own,' Tom added, as he decided he would be the old boot.

I knew there was a conspiracy when Susie turned up the following evening with a plastic fishing box full of craft material, claiming, 'I thought we could sell some gift cards and things on Saturday.'

I appreciated their concern but the one person I really wanted to come to keep me safe wasn't there. It had been more than two days and I hadn't heard from Jack.

Jade reappeared on Friday full of tales about a broken mobile phone and a bout of the flu. I wanted to believe her but somehow I couldn't shake that doubtful feeling. Every time I approached her she would find something to do that took her off somewhere else. She definitely didn't want to talk to me, although as I watched from a distance she appeared to have lots to say to everyone else.

The sanctuary buzzed with activity. A team of men arrived to erect a marquee ready for the open day; I thought it would be advisable to have somewhere for people to go if it decided to rain. The weather forecast still sounded a little changeable. I was kept busy all day long – managing visitors, directing workmen and trying to keep Jade under discreet observation. She didn't seem any different from usual, though, apart from wanting to avoid me and Susie, but then she always tried to avoid Susie.

Meanwhile, the universe seemed to have declared open warfare on Kirk. He was in custody in LA charged with statutory rape of a minor, since it had transpired that his latest girlfriend – not the one who had attacked Immi on the chat show – was only fifteen. Immi appeared to have been fully reinstated in the public's good books and offers of work were rolling in. I just hoped she'd stay on the wagon now that she had a second chance and Marcus to support her.

I'd given up checking my mobile for messages from Jack, even though I still got a hollow achy feeling under my ribs every time I thought about him. A few times my fingers had strayed to my mobile and brought his number on to the screen, but my courage would fail at the last minute and I'd close the phone without dialling.

Immi and Marcus were still loved up and he was, in fact, due to arrive with her at supper time that evening. I didn't begrudge my sister her happiness, but it left me feeling even more lonely than usual.

Jack was the first person I'd allowed to get close to me in a long time. I'd really thought that he and I could be good together. Physically speaking we certainly were – he only had to look at me to make me tingle with lust. That had never been the case with Jonathan. It had been what Immi called car ferry sex with Jonathan: roll on – engage docking procedure – roll off. What I'd had with Jack seemed worlds away from that.

My relationship with Jonathan had been entirely based on my neediness, something that he'd actively encouraged. It had all boiled down to him and how *I* could become what *he* wanted. I'd been young and impressionable and he'd taken advantage of my immaturity. I'd been someone he filled time with while he waited for his college professor fiancée to return home.

I closed the sanctuary to the public a few minutes early and took a tray of drinks down to the paddock, where everyone was busy working to get things ready for the next day.

'Where's Jade?' I hadn't seen her for a while – so much for keeping her under observation.

'She claimed she wasn't feeling well so she left a bit early,' Susie said. I got the feeling she wasn't very impressed by this excuse. Susie and Jade had never exactly been bosom buddies. Jade thought Susie was a bit mental and Susie resented Jade in case she usurped Susie's position as Most Dedicated Worker at the sanctuary.

'Do you think she'll be okay for tomorrow?' Perhaps Jade had lost interest in volunteering, or, if she was the mole, maybe she thought we'd rumbled her.

'She said she'd be here, although I'm sure we could manage perfectly well without her. All she's done all day is mooch about and ask questions.' Susie sipped her drink.

The old saying about pots and kettles went through my mind. Susie was always asking questions so it was a bit rich to comment on Jade. Even so, it niggled me that she could have come simply to obtain more information. It would explain her readiness to chat with everyone. Perhaps she'd thought Susie and I were suspicious so she'd kept away from us in case *we* asked the questions.

'The marquee looks nice, doesn't it?' I leaned back against the fence and admired the little flags fluttering at each end.

'You won't recognise this place tomorrow when the stalls and the rides get here,' Val said as she came over to join us.

'It's right exciting. We should do this every year, Clodagh.' Tom wiped the perspiration from his brow with his forearm.

'I don't know about that. Ask me tomorrow night when it's all over.'

'I only hope it goes off all right with all the trouble you've had lately. It would be just like some fool to try to spoil it all,' Tom remarked.

He'd voiced my worst fears. I'd been thinking about what Jack had said about someone sabotaging the open day. The police had promised to keep a high-profile presence around the sanctuary and there hadn't been any problems for a week now. I'd had another letter from Lovett's asking me to make an appointment with their solicitors and dumped it in the recycling box, but George Lovett himself had made no second attempt to call in or contact me by phone.

'We'll have to be on the lookout. The police will be here and we've Margaret and Doreen to give an extra hand.' Margaret and Doreen were two local ladies who usually helped in the high season by manning the gate and selling refreshments. They were both very elderly but liked to come and assist where they could, even though Doreen had bad eyes and Margaret walked with a stick.

'I don't know if Miss Marple and her assistant will be much good at deterring ruthless criminals,' Val mused. Her straight face sent both Tom and me into giggles. 'Margaret'll not be able to give chase down the field with her stick.'

Susie didn't get the joke.

'I'll pop back later on when I take the dog for a walk. Just to check on everything in case there's anybody unsavoury hanging about,' Tom announced.

'Then I'm coming back with you. You're not coming here on your own at midnight. If they could knock out young Jack then they'll make mincemeat out of an old fool like you.' Val tugged her cardi round her voluminous bosom in a determined fashion while Tom rolled his eyes.

'I'm sure everything will be fine – and I don't want anyone turning into a vigilante.' I gave Tom a warning stare.

We finished our drinks amicably. I collected up the mugs and said goodbye to everyone before securing the gates behind them. The sanctuary looked lovely. The fences were coated, the outbuildings and stables were all repaired and shipshape, the signs on the paddocks were clear and, most important of all, the animals appeared loved and cared for. I hoped all our efforts would succeed in securing the future of Rainbow Ridge.

Immi and Marcus had promised to bring pizza with them when they arrived, so I didn't have to worry about cooking. Instead I showered and changed before taking Nigel for a walk along the road. Lovett's men had started work on Long Meadow and clods of rich brown loam lay in the ditches where they'd fallen from the wheels of vehicles passing in and out of the site.

We turned round at the site entrance and headed back to Rainbow Ridge. The weather looked like it would be fair for the next day, with the sunset creating orange streaks across the sky and filling the landscape with a rich golden glow. If only Jack had been at my side my world would have felt quite perfect.

Marcus's blue car was in the yard next to mine when Nigel and I got home, and the delicious tomato and basil smell of hot fresh-baked pizza wafted through the air to meet me as I entered the kitchen. Marcus stood at the table with a stack of plates while Immi wrestled with a cling-film-covered box of salad.

'I wondered where you were. We made better time on the journey than we thought we would.' She abandoned the box to hug me.

I didn't normally become tearful at the sight of my sister but my emotions seemed to be all over the shop these days.

'Fill us in on everything that's been happening,' she commanded.

Over pizza, salad and a glass of Coke, I told Marcus and Immi all the details of the attack on Jack and the arson attempt. I also told them my suspicions about Jade. They both thought I was right to be wary of her, which disappointed me a bit. I suppose I'd been hoping that they'd tell me I was being overdramatic; I still didn't like the idea of being so suspicious of somebody I'd thought was my friend.

'You need to find her a job tomorrow that will keep her in one place.' Immi waved her pizza slice enthusiastically. 'Then we can keep an eye on her and make sure she doesn't get the opportunity to sabotage anything.'

'That's if she *is* the saboteur. Even if she is involved in some way it may only be as a provider of information.' It was hard to believe we were even having this conversation.

'Yes, but we could see if anybody suspicious stops to speak to her.' Immi refused to be quashed. I think she's been a soap star for so long that she sometimes forgets real life doesn't run to a script.

'It would be nice to have some definite proof. Something tangible that linked this girl to an incident.' Marcus sipped his Coke.

We munched pizza in silence for a moment and contemplated his words.

'I've got something!' I licked my fingers clean and jumped up to rummage in the pocket of my jacket. 'I found these strands of wool caught on the wood when the fence in the paddock was vandalised.' I showed them to Immi and Marcus. 'It's a very unusual shade of wool. Jade has a jumper made of this and she told us that her aunt in Canada knitted it for her. I knew I'd seen it before but I didn't make the connection till now.'

'And you're sure it couldn't have got there by accident?' Marcus asked.

'Tom discovered the damage the morning after it had been done. No one else had been in the field.

And there definitely is a woman involved – Jack says one of the people who attacked him was female, and remember those footprints I found when we thought Marcus was the prowler?' I felt sick as the realisation finally sank in that Jade was the culprit.

Immi, however, had no such qualms and was practically bouncing up and down on her chair with excitement. 'Now we need to set a trap!'

Marcus shot her a look over the rim of his glass.

'What? Don't tell me you weren't thinking the same thing.' She calmed down a little and I decided Marcus was a good influence on her.

'Let me think about it and I'll have something worked out by tomorrow,' he said.

Since I could hardly go to the police with only a bit of wool and my suspicions, I decided to put my trust in Marcus and believe that he could come up with a workable solution to my dilemma.

'So what's happening with you and Jack?' Immi asked while we were washing up and Marcus was safely upstairs taking a shower.

'Nothing.' I tried to look as if it didn't bother me.

'Haven't you called him?' Her tea towel stilled as she tried to read my expression.

'He hasn't called me.' I dumped a soapy plate on to the draining rack.

Immi rolled her eyes. 'You two are impossible.'

She had a point. I was supposed to be trying to learn to be more trusting, to invest something of myself in a relationship, and yet every time it came to the crunch I held back. I should have called Jack after the incident with the firework.

'Just call him, Clo.' Immi put down the tea towel and gave me a hug. 'He is one of the good guys, you know.'

She disappeared upstairs to find Marcus while I finished putting away the clean crockery. I picked up my mobile and wandered into the lounge.

Dave sidled along his perch and proceeded to rub his head on the bars of the cage. 'Topless is extra!' he cackled.

I opened my phone, pulled up Jack's number from the menu, then closed it again. I had no idea what to say. I carried on staring at my mobile as if it would suddenly reveal the solution to my dilemma.

'Give us a kiss!' Dave pinged his beak on the cage, making a metallic ringing sound in a bid to attract my attention.

'Behave.'

I was still distracted about what I should do.

But I knew what I wanted to do. I wanted to hear Jack's voice rumble in my ear and hear him tease me with one of his corny lines. I really wanted him to be next to me on the sofa holding me. If I closed my eyes I could still recall the faint masculine scent of his skin and feel the regular dull thuds of his heartbeat from when I had placed my cheek against his chest.

My heart felt as if someone had torn it from its place and captured it in a vice, only to slowly squeeze it into a million tiny fragments. It was too much. It was time I stopped being stubborn and stupid. Time I reached out to tell him how I felt – time I put my heart back on the line. I flicked my mobile open again and sent Jack a text.

I was wrong, I miss u, I'm sorry, call me.

I don't know what I expected. Part of me hoped Jack would read my message and rush straight over to kiss and make up. Instead – nothing. I stayed up and played Spider Solitaire on the computer, checking my mobile every few minutes in case I'd missed hearing a text or a call, but nothing, *nada*, zip. Eventually I gave up and went to bed for a feeling-sorry-for-myself sniffle with Clive the cat for company.

My eyes were bleary and puffy from crying and lack of sleep when I hauled myself out of bed the next morning, ready for the open day. It was still dark when I disturbed Nigel from his slumber by tiptoeing into the kitchen to retrieve my wellies. The view outside the window promised fair weather. The dark blue sky looked clear and the dawn chorus of birdsong was in full cry.

I made another futile check on my mobile, even though I knew Jack wasn't likely to send me a text at o'dark thirty on a Saturday morning. The stallholders and entertainment people would start arriving in the next few hours so I tugged on my jacket and whizzed outside to get my morning routine under way.

Tom arrived at the same time as the man with the miniature land train and the people with the carousel. By the time Marcus and Immi put in an appearance at nine o'clock Susie and Val had been hard at work for over an hour directing people to their pitches, sorting out generators and generally ensuring everyone was happy. Immi moved into full soap-star mode as she signed autographs and posed for pictures with all the stall-holders before the big opening, generally charming everyone in sight.

Jade was noticeable by her absence. I began to hope that she wouldn't show up at all, then I wouldn't have to worry about what she might be doing. I wondered if Marcus had come up with a plan like he'd promised. I didn't want to have a confrontation with Jade over my suspicions, at least not today, when there was so much going on. A big scene with accusations flying around wouldn't be good for publicity and it would sour the whole event. The chicken-livered ostrich in me kind of hoped the problem of Jade would go away on its own without my actually having to do anything.

Marty arrived looking resplendent in an emerald-green satin suit and her usual accessories of sky-high footwear and a cigarette, ignoring the no-smoking signs. She marshalled the press (mostly local, but some national) around the entrance as Immi posed for pictures with one of the guinea pigs in her hand. Margaret and Doreen were installed in the shed, preparing to admit the public who were already queuing at the gate.

Margaret had brought a Thermos of coffee and Doreen had a hip flask full of whisky.

The gates opened and the public started to roll in. Immi had booked a stilt-walker and a juggler to greet the children and they both seemed to be going down well. Once I was sure that Doreen and Margaret were okay with the tickets I headed for the barn, where there were going to be hourly petting sessions when the toddlers could stroke the rabbits or hold a guinea pig like the one Immi had posed with. I passed Susie's craft stall en route, with its display of hand-made cards, signed photos of Immi and some souvenir pens and keyrings we'd had made with pictures of animals on them.

Immi had ordered a load of bright red polo shirts with *Rainbow Ridge* and an outline of a rabbit sitting under a rainbow embroidered on them, especially for today. She had teamed hers with skinny jeans and heels. Susie still resembled a bag lady in hers as she'd complained of feeling cold and had immediately put a cabbage-green fleece on over the top. Val's was a bit snug around the bust and Tom looked like Santa Claus minus the beard. I felt a bit of a twit as I allowed small groups of children inside the pens and helped them to gently stroke the animals. I'd spent so long fading into the background I wasn't used to people noticing me.

By the time I'd finished the first session and stuck my head out of the barn to see how things were going, the paths were crowded with people. The TV crew had turned up and were filming Immi and the general public with the animals. I sneaked past them and down to the paddock where all the stalls and rides were to see how Susie was faring. I checked my mobile on the way – still nothing. I had to face it: whatever had been between me and Jack was obviously over.

'Clodagh, I've been looking for you.' Marcus appeared at my side and placed his hand on my arm.

'What's the matter?' Something in the sober expression on his face told me it was serious.

'Come with me a minute.'

I followed him through the throngs of people to a quieter spot on the edge of the field next to the hawthorn hedge.

'What is it?' I looked around the fields but I couldn't see anything amiss. Everyone appeared to be having a good time, Immi was sober and, as far as I could tell, nothing terrible had happened.

'I think I saw Jade.' He showed me an impromptu picture he'd snapped on his mobile. 'Is that her? I've only seen her a couple of times but her hair seems different.'

I studied the snap. It was definitely Jade, but the pink streaks had gone from her fringe. 'She's here?'

'Yes, but she's avoided the areas where the other volunteers are and she vanished near the barn. We need to find her. There doesn't seem to be any doubt that she's up to mischief.'

I felt sick. 'Do the others know?'

'Only Immi and Tom. I'll come with you.'

We started back together through the crowds towards the barn and the paths that led to the animal paddocks.

Ahead of us a group had gathered and I had to stand on tiptoe to see what was going on.

'Donkey!' a little girl a few steps away suddenly shouted.

I wriggled forward with Marcus close behind me. Miko and Pasquale were out of their paddock in the middle of a crowd. Mr Sheen sauntered along behind them chewing happily on what looked like an ice cream that he'd probably stolen from a passer-by.

'The animals are loose!' Marcus stared at me in horror.

Rosie, the Vietnamese pot-bellied pig, made a dash past my ankles. I stooped and grabbed her round the middle and she squealed in protest.

'Grab the goat!' I managed to coax Rosie into her field and locked the gate. Then it hit me – Jade had keys to all the paddocks. She could have let the animals free.

Marcus and Mr Sheen were nose to nose. If it came down to a battle of wills I feared Mr Sheen would win. The only thing my goat ever responded to was food. Luckily I had an apple in my pocket and managed to bribe him back through the crowd and into his pen.

The sound of cackling and hisses further along the path, followed by screams from some of the children, told me that the geese were also on the loose.

'Can you manage the donkeys?' I shouted to Marcus, though I didn't have very high hopes that he could manage any of the animals – they were all pretty troublesome in their own individual ways. There were people everywhere and I heard more screams as the geese scattered into the crowd.

'Tell me how to move them.' Marcus eyed Miko as if he was an alien.

'Just pat their necks and call their names and they'll follow you.'

I left him to it, hoping for the best while I forged my way through the crowd to get to the geese. The ducks and chickens wouldn't be too much of a problem, since they could be rounded up later. The geese, however, could scurry forward with their wings up, hissing, which was very frightening for people who weren't used to animals. They would peck at anyone who got in their way and I had visions of being sued by parents of traumatised toddlers.

There was chaos all around me as people tried to get out of the way of the free-roaming animals. Others were trying to pat and pet them. Screams and squeals were coming from the crowd nearest to the poultry field and it became harder for me to force my way through. People kept blocking my way or stopping me to tell me the geese were loose and asking me what I intended to do about it.

Immi and the TV crew were corralled against the fence by one of the more aggressive geese, who flapped and hissed at them every time they tried to move.

'Clodagh!' Immi spotted my red shirt.

'Don't worry, I'll soon have them back in their field.' I chivvied the goose along as people scattered out of our path.

The TV crew continued to film the chaos as I tracked down each stray bird and tucked it into its rightful pen. I mentally vowed to kill Jade if I found her. She'd obviously used her key to go from field to field releasing the animals, knowing it would cause mayhem. She was probably counting on its seeming as if the pens weren't properly secure, spoiling everyone's fun and bringing shame on the sanctuary.

I locked the gate and left Immi to talk to the film crew while I went to see how Marcus had fared with the donkeys. To my relief they were both back in their paddock.

'Thanks.' I locked the gate. 'Do you think she's gone?'

'No, she's still here. Jack's following her.'

Did Marcus say *Jack*? No, I must have misheard him . . .

'She headed off behind the barn, near where Jack got attacked.' We hurried along together.

'What do you think she plans to do?' I was out of breath from chasing animals and trying to keep pace with Marcus.

'We'll find out in a minute.' He had his mobile in his hand and texted as he went.

The crowds were thinner by the barn. We went through a small gate marked 'Staff only' into the area behind the building. The path led to a small shed where Tom stored old cans of paint and wood preserver. It was out of the public domain and away from the animals, and it was also surrounded by overgrown buddleia bushes. The door of the shed stood open and the hairs on the back of my neck began to prickle in alarm. I knew Tom always kept it locked. He was very careful about making certain everything was secure.

Marcus moved to step in front of me but I placed my hand on his arm to stop him. I didn't want anyone else getting injured on my account. My sister would never forgive me if Marcus got beaten up. After all, we didn't know if Jade was alone or if her violent accomplice from the other night was with her.

'Jade! I know you're in there.' Anger burned deep inside me. How dare she try to sabotage the open day? I was hurt enough that for so many months she'd pretended to be my friend, laughing and joking with me, while all the time she'd been feeding information back to George Lovett.

Jade emerged from the store with a defiant look on her face. 'Clodagh.'

'I think you'd better give me the sanctuary keys.'

Her face flushed and for a moment I thought she would refuse. 'Here. I was going to give them back anyway.' She pulled the keys from her pocket and threw them on to the grass at my feet.

'What are you doing back here?' Marcus asked, beating me to it.

Jade's eyes flickered and I suspected she would have liked to bolt, but we were blocking her escape route. There was a narrow overgrown rabbit path running behind the shed that she could squeeze through if she was very determined.

'Nothing.' She edged back and I thought she was about to run.

'I think I know what she was doing.' Jack stepped out from behind the buddleia. We had her cornered.

I wasn't sure who was most surprised by Jack's sudden appearance – me or Jade. I flicked a quick sideways glance at Marcus but it seemed he'd known Jack was there. I guess that must have been what the frenetic texting had been about. Somehow simply seeing Jack again, in the flesh, made my heart skip a beat.

'Smarty-pants Jack Thatcher. You think you know all the answers.' Jade was quick to recover her wits and sneer at Jack.

'Not all of them, but I can make an educated guess at quite a few,' he responded.

My heart raced at the look of steely determination in his eyes, set in a face that was still bruised from the beating he'd received.

'And I think I might know a few more,' Marcus added.

Jade scowled. 'What about you, Clodagh? Cat got your tongue?'

For the first time I realised that Jade hated me. The girl I'd thought was my friend, whom I'd confided in, joked with and wished I could have employed not so long ago, actually hated me.

'I have some ideas of my own.' I wouldn't cry in front of her even though her betrayal cut me to the quick.

She gave a careless shrug of her shoulders. 'Not that it matters.'

'I think the police might think it matters when they follow up on the information we've given them,' Marcus said.

'You can't pin anything on me.' Jade smirked. 'I don't think they'll be able to do much because the animal pens were left open and a few geese got out.'

'Maybe not, but that was just a diversion, wasn't it? So you could sneak up here and finish what you started the other night when you and your friend jumped on me.' Jack's voice was icy.

A shiver ran down my spine. I was used to Jack's hot flashes of temper, the sort that blew up and out and vanished. This cold anger was something more dangerous. It rattled Jade's couldn't-care-lessness.

'You can't prove anything.' Her eyes were fixed on Jack.

'The evidence in the shed can prove you were the one who set the fires that destroyed the feed store and the entrance building.' Marcus took a step closer.

'You're bluffing.' Jade snapped her gaze forward again to look at Marcus as the colour leached from her face.

'We have CCTV footage of you wiping your fingerprints off the petrol cans,' Jack said.

'I don't believe you.'

Jack made a sudden move and pulled Jade's large

canvas bag from her shoulder. 'Shall we take a look in here, too?'

'Give me that!' She tried to snatch it back from him but he tipped the contents on to the grass.

Wire-cutters, firecrackers, gloves and matches spilled out along with more usual handbag-type things.

'Planning another firework party?' Marcus asked.

'Why, Jade?' I stared at the fireworks. She'd been the one who'd almost burned down my house. She could have killed me and my animals. I couldn't get my head round it.

'Money,' Jack answered first. 'Isn't that right, Jade?'

She edged towards the path but Jack moved nearer.

'I don't know what you mean.' Her gaze flicked from Marcus to Jack and then back to me.

I felt sick.

'The money you were getting from George Lovett to report on Clodagh's finances so he could plan a strategy for buying her out.' Jack's tone was hard.

'The money he paid you and your boyfriend to try to scare Clodagh into selling by ruining her business and frightening her out of her home.' Marcus sounded equally steely.

'I thought you were my friend.' I shook my head in an attempt to clear some of the emotions that were crowding my mind.

'Why would I want to be your friend?' Jade tipped her chin up defiantly. 'You and mad Susie, what a pair of losers. Then your stupid piss-artist sister comes along and messes everything up.'

Marcus moved forward and I saw his hands ball into fists.

'You attacked Jack and were prepared to burn down my house.' I tried to reconcile the pale-faced angry woman in front of me with the girl I'd thought I'd known.

'He could have messed things up. I tried to put you off him. Susie listened and believed me and I hoped she'd do my job for me.' Jade was scornful.

So she'd been the one dripping poison into Susie's ear about Jack and getting her to pass it on to me. All to prevent me from possibly selling to Jack.

'Why George Lovett?' I had to know why she'd become involved in the first place. Money couldn't be the only reason.

'Uncle George, isn't he, Jade? Your mother's brother?' Marcus asked.

'I've had enough. I'm going. You can't keep me here.' She stepped forward.

Marcus stood aside to reveal a policeman who'd come along the path behind us without my realising. I'd been too involved with the scene in front of me.

'I think this gentleman would like to have a few words with you first,' Marcus said. He turned to the policeman. 'The video evidence is at your disposal, officer.'

'We took the liberty of hiding a camera and recording equipment in the shed,' Jack explained.

Jade broke into a torrent of abuse as the policeman read her rights and placed a set of handcuffs on her wrists.

I sank down on to a nearby concrete garden roller that

Tom used to keep the lawns tidy when we had mole attacks. Marcus accompanied the police officer and the still-protesting Jade as they left. Jack perched beside me on the edge of the roller.

'Are you okay?' he asked in a low tone.

I could feel the warmth of his thigh pressing against mine as we sat squashed together outside the shed.

'I'm not sure. I still feel confused about everything that just happened.'

We sat in silence for a moment. The noise of the crowds only a few short feet away seemed to have faded to a distant buzz and I focused on a stray daisy near my foot.

'I suppose I feel pretty stupid.' I concentrated hard on the daisy with its cheerful yellow centre and white petals blushing down to delicate pink at the edges.

'You shouldn't. You've never struck me as stupid, ever,' Jack said. 'I'm sorry I didn't reply to your text.'

I stooped to pick the daisy, twirling it between my fingers. 'Doesn't matter.'

In a way it really didn't. Not any more. He had turned up just when I'd needed him most.

'You must have thought I didn't want to see you.'

'There goes that ego of yours again.' I tried to make a joke. I didn't want to think about the last few horrible days when I'd thought Jack had gone out of my life. When I'd taken that final step and told him by text how much he meant to me and he hadn't replied.

'I wanted to call you all week. I kept thinking about you, wondering how you were. I must have had your number on screen a dozen times or more,' he said.

'I wanted to call you, too, but when you didn't text me back . . .' I couldn't bring myself to look at him. Instead I carried on mangling the daisy stem.

'I couldn't contact you. It might have blown everything. I kept telling myself that it was only for a few more days.'

'I don't understand.' It had felt like a lifetime to me and from the look in Jack's eyes I knew it had been the same for him.

'Marcus contacted me and told me what he'd learned about Jade. We decided to try to trap her into confessing.' Jack shifted a little on the roller.

'Did Immi know?' I suspected she didn't. Immi wasn't good at keeping secrets and she'd wanted to go in all guns blazing to try to catch Jade out. I looked at Jack.

He shook his head. 'No. We talked about telling you and Immi but decided not to. I was worried.'

'Oh.' I pulled a petal from the daisy and let it flutter down on to the grass. I couldn't entirely blame him for deciding not to tell me. Clearly, I was a crap judge of character, having misread first Jonathan and now Jade. Maybe it was people whose names began with J. Perhaps I should look more closely at Jack.

'Are you mad at me?'

I could feel him looking at me.

'Yes and no.' I pulled some more petals from the flower.

'I was scared Jade would guess you were on to her. One of the things I love about you is that you're so honest. I knew you were finding it hard to believe what she was really like.' He shifted his position again and sighed. 'I was worried she might do something to hurt you. I'm pretty sure it was Jade who hit me over the head with the cutters that night and it was Jade who burned down the kiosk. I think she proved she has no compunction about injuring people and risking lives when she pushed a firework through your letter box. She didn't know you weren't home and she knew the animals were in the house.'

I bit my lip and stole another peep at his face. His eyes were serious.

'I care too much about you, Clodagh, to risk anyone hurting you. Yes, I wanted to catch her out, but more than anything I wanted to keep you safe.'

My pulse took off again, thudding in my veins like an express train. 'I'm sorry we argued.'

The corner of Jack's mouth lifted in a faint smile, revealing the dimple in his cheek. 'Life would be boring without a few spats. I'm pretty hotheaded myself.'

'And obstinate. You forgot obstinate.' Warmth flooded through my body, washing away the hollow empty ache I'd had ever since Jack had walked out on me.

'Okay, obstinate – the same as you.' He took my hands in his and the daisy fell to the ground. My skin tingled at his touch and set my spirits soaring.

'Can we try to argue a bit less, though? It's very wearing and I'm trying really hard with this trusting business.' I'd phrased it very clumsily but I hoped he understood what I meant.

'I've been working on the trust part myself.' His lips

brushed mine. 'I trusted you with my heart a long time ago, Clodagh.'

My breath caught in my throat as I read his feelings in his eyes. 'And I think I trusted you with mine and never realised.'

'I love you, Clo.'

Bubbles of happiness fizzed about inside me like champagne trapped in a bottle just before the cork pops.

'I love you, too.' It was true, I did. It had been coming on for a long time. From the moment we'd first met at the mayor's ball my feelings had been growing stronger with each meeting. It had been why I'd been hurting so badly without him, why my heart had ached when I'd doubted his intentions. I'd been so wrong, so many times, about him. Jack had been there for me at every crisis. He was everything that Jonathan hadn't been and more. The wonder wasn't that I loved him, but that he loved me.

He wrapped his arms around me and I gave myself up to his kiss. Immi had been right: Jack was one of the good guys. Maybe Jade had done me a favour – maybe I'd finally learned to trust my animal instincts.

little
black
dress

Pick up a *little black dress* – it's a girl thing.

978 0 7553 3959 4

TANGLED UP IN YOU
Rachel Gibson
PB £4.99

Sex, lies and tequila slammers

When Maddie Dupree arrives at Hennessy's bar looking for the truth about her past she doesn't want to be distracted by head-turning, heart-stopping owner Mick Hennessy. Especially as he doesn't know why she's really in town . . .

SPIRIT WILLING, FLESH WEAK
Julie Cohen
PB £4.99

Welcome to the world of Julie Cohen, one of the freshest, funniest voices in romantic fiction!

When fake psychic Rosie meets a gorgeous investigative journalist, she thinks she can trust him not to blow her cover – but is she right?

978 0 7553 3481 0

Pick up a *little black dress* – it's a girl thing.

978 0 7553 3533 6

ACCIDENTALLY ENGAGED
Mary Carter
PB £4.99

Clair Ivars' flair for reading tarot cards deserts her when predicting her own future, and somehow she finds herself accidentally engaged to a stranger. What else have the cards forgotten to mention?

Mary Carter's crazily romantic novel will ensure you'll never dare doubt a fortune-teller again . . .

I TAKE THIS MAN
Valerie Frankel
PB £4.99

When Penny Bracket is jilted at the altar by Bram Shiraz, her mother decides to help out by locking him up in the attic. And Penny has some serious questions for her fugitive groom . . .

'Glib and funny, Frankel's always wickedly entertaining' *People* magazine

978 0 7553 3675 3

Pick up a *little black dress* – it's a girl thing.

978 0 7553 4191 7

THE UNFORTUNATE MISS FORTUNES
Jennifer Crusie, Eileen Dreyer, Anne Stuart
PB £4.99

Ever wanted a charmed life?

Three is supposed to be lucky but the Fortune sisters – Dee, Lizzie and Mare – are about to have the worst weekend of their lives. Unless they can figure out how the hell to work their magic powers . . . and their hearts.

CONFESSIONS OF AN AIR HOSTESS
Marisa Mackle
PB £4.99

Air hostess Annie's life takes a serious nosedive after her boyfriend dumps her but with a plane full of passengers to look after she'll just have to keep on smiling. And you never know, the departure of Mr Wrong could mean the arrival of Mr Right . . .

We hope you relax and enjoy your trip

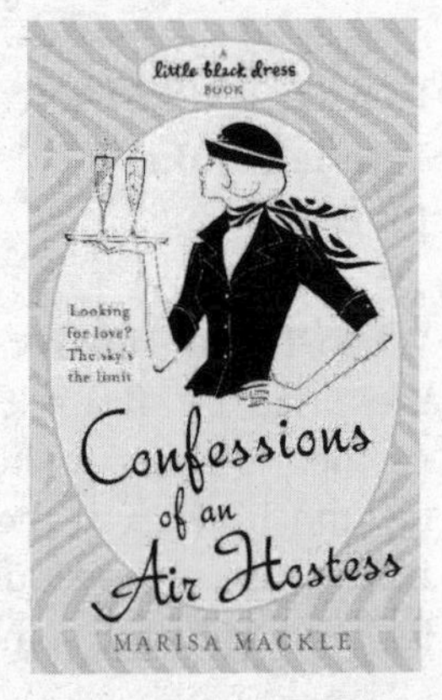

978 0 7553 3989 1